WALKER PRIDE
BOOK 1
THE WALKER FAMILY SERIES

BY

BERNADETTE MARIE

This is a fictional work. The names, characters, incidents, places, and locations are solely the concepts and products of the author's imagination or are used to create a fictitious story and should not be construed as real.

5 PRINCE PUBLISHING AND BOOKS, LLC
PO Box 16507
Denver, CO 80216
www.5PrinceBooks.com

ISBN-10: 1631121170 ISBN 13: 978-1-63112-117-3
WALKER PRIDE
Bernadette Marie
Copyright Bernadette Marie, 2015
Published by 5 Prince Publishing

Front Cover designed by Bernadette Soehner
Photo by: Vasily Pindyurin
Author Photo: David Kappell, 2009

First Edition/First Printing June 2015 Printed U.S.A.

5 PRINCE PUBLISHING AND BOOKS, LLC.

Stan,
There is great pride in being your wife
and the mother of your children.
I love you, forever and a day.

Acknowledgements:

To my Fab 5 who forever inspire me with all of the amazing things they do and the men they are becoming…I love you.

To my man who has more faith in me than I do in myself…I love you.

To my mom, dad, and sister who keep me grounded in who I am…I love you.

To Connie, Clare, and June who grin and nod when I need them to and then get the work done that I neglect… THANK YOU!

To my Street Team, my readers, and my fellow authors who bring me back to the computer every day to do what I love because they share their support with me…Thank you!

Dear Reader,

This is an exceptionally exciting journey! A new series and a new family to fall in love with.

When it was time to build this family, the Walkers, I reached out to my readers and they helped me build this amazing family and they voted to settle them in Georgia. I am blessed to have these special people reach out to me and become my friends.

Eric Walker was an instant attraction to me. I knew from the moment we decided on him that he was going to be a man with some deep seeded feelings. I hope that in creating Susan, a woman with a good head on her shoulders, I was able to make him loveable in the way I felt him.

This family will be particularly fun because not all of them are likable—yet. They all have some demons and some secrets, but the fun will be when we get to sort that all out.

Welcome to the Walker Family. Enjoy your stay!

Happy Reading!
Bernadette Marie

Other books by Bernadette Marie

The Keller Family Series

The Executive's Decision
A Second Chance
Opposite Attraction
Center Stage
Lost and Found
Love Songs
Home Run
The Acceptance
The Merger
The Escape Clause

Aspen Creek Series

First Kiss
Unexpected Admirer
On Thin Ice
Indomitable Spirit

The Matchmaker Series

Matchmakers
Encore
Finding Hope

The Three Mrs. Monroes

Amelia
Penelope
Vivian

The Walker Family Series

Walker Pride

Single Titles

Cart Before the Horse
Candy Kisses

WALKER PRIDE

Chapter One

Fog rolled in over the ground, giving the acreage around the house an eerie feel.

Eric Walker pulled up the collar of his jacket and let out a sigh. It was appropriate for the day to be gloomy, he thought. When you laid someone in the ground, it was fitting for it to rain or be down right cold, as it was today.

He walked down the old steps of the house to his truck, which waited for him like a good horse. Always ready for an adventure. He'd have taken his horse, but his stepmother would frown on it. Not that he'd have cared, but for his father's sake he chose not to.

As he climbed into the old Ford, its red paint faded and its fender bent in, he kicked the mud off his boots before he swung his feet inside.

Some things were sacred like the inside of a man's truck. Though the outside had seen many days in the fields, the inside was an oasis of new interior, which pleased Eric.

The engine would be the next upgrade, he thought as he gave her some gas as he turned the key. There was some hesitation, but a moment later she roared to life, ready to take him anywhere.

Eric avoided the main house as much as he could.

He hadn't been very old when his mother died, but while she lived in the big house, she had added her touches. Rooms were decorated feminine and they just felt homey.

Of course, he would think that. His mother had done the work herself and had taken great pride in it. But when she passed away and a year later his father remarried. Glenda changed everything.

He'd been ten when the last room received its final coat of new paint and he'd held that grudge since.

As the road to the house tossed him back and forth he adjusted the dial on his radio. It was the kind of day for wallowing in misery with Hank.

His mother loved Patsy Cline. He could still hear her singing as she painted his childhood bedroom.

It was foolish for a man of forty to think so far back and get so worked up, but funerals did that to him.

It had been his grandfather, George Walker, they'd laid to rest in the family cemetery and that was what made him start thinking about his mother.

Her headstone was a mere few feet from his grandfather's. CONSTANCE WALKER. The letters had seemed so big for such a small woman.

Eric could have done with walking away after the old man was lowered into the ground yesterday, but now he had to trek to the house to hear the will.

He couldn't have cared less about who got what. His grandfather had always promised him the house on the edge of the property, where he'd lived since he was eighteen. There was no reason to assume he'd go back on his word.

Eric wondered about some of his cousins though. Would greed set in?

His own brothers were much like him. They were grateful for what they had. They worked hard and made honest livings. Everett Walker hadn't raised his boys to be anything less than honest men. That alone gave Eric some pride.

He loved his brothers. He was eight when Dane had been born and there had been a lot of honest animosity, but that had come from a boy who missed his own mother.

Glenda, though she changed the house's décor, was the best replacement for his mother Eric could wish for. She never treated Eric as though he were someone else's child. She raised him as her own, with respect to his own mother.

Eric kicked up the heat in the truck as he crossed over the little bridge that connected the two original pieces of land over the small creek, which divided it.

All of his cousins had been at the funeral. Well, everyone but Bethany. It was completely possible his uncle Byron had forgotten to tell her that their grandfather had died at all. Or, she was so busy with her life in L.A. it was just too much to pack up to say goodbye to a grandfather she really didn't know.

Eric's uncle was a piece of work himself, he thought as he slowed to check the cattle grazing in the field to his right.

Byron Walker had five children, just as his father did. Only he'd been married and divorced twice and he'd never even married Bethany's mother.

His father and uncle were complete opposites. Everett Walker, his father, was a family man. He was committed to each member of his family and to his wife. He saved money, nearly to a fault, Eric thought, and he worked harder than any other man Eric had ever known.

His uncle Byron, on the other hand, loved to live life as if it were a party. He'd nearly gone bankrupt three times.

It was well known he was not a faithful husband, which could have been why he'd been married and divorced. And his children were just people who had passed through his life.

Eric got along with his cousins, but they had never had a chance to become close. They came for visits when they were growing up and Todd had worked on the land for years, but he kept to himself.

It only made the drive to the house that much worse by thinking about everyone being in one room—together.

There were at least a dozen vehicles parked in the loop out front of the main house, each one as different as its owner.

Eric parked the furthest away. If he were able, he'd be the first one out. He stepped out of the truck onto the soft ground. Rain had softened the ground and he was sure his stepmother was already fit to be tied with the shoes coming into the house.

His father wouldn't tolerate her asking everyone to kick them off at the door. Eric could lay down bets that the carpet cleaner van would be parked there by tomorrow morning.

Not wanting to make a grand entrance, as the last one to arrive, he walked around to the back of the house and pulled open the back door.

The woman standing in his mother's kitchen jumped and placed her hands on her chest.

"You startled me," she gasped and let out a breath.

Eric looked her over. He'd seen her before, but he couldn't put a place to it.

The woman kept working. There were assorted trays on the counter and island. Obviously she was a caterer, and that was where he realized he knew her. She'd catered the reception after the funeral.

Eric toed off his boots. It was the least he could do for his stepmother, even if he hated the idea.

"So what's going on in here?" he asked.

"Mrs. Walker wanted to have a small sandwich service while the attorneys were here."

Eric nodded. "Platters of meats and breads. She hired you to do it?"

The woman shrugged, perhaps brushing off the insult he'd landed on her. "It's what I do. Yesterday's buffet was okay wasn't it?"

"Yes, it was fine."

She grinned as she continued to work. "Fine. This is why I need a sit-down restaurant so I can create items that are more than fine."

"I didn't mean…"

She raised her eyes to meet his. "I know. This is what I have to do to pay for culinary school. Someday it will be much more than sandwich trays and buffets."

"You want to own a restaurant, huh?" he asked as he reached over to the tray and took a black olive and popped it into his mouth.

Her eyes followed him and her lips tightened. "Yes. This isn't forever."

The unmistakable clicking of his stepmother's shoes pierced his ears. He could hear the mumbling of his entire family, close and extended, down the hall. There was no doubt she was coming looking for him.

"Eric, I thought I heard that old truck of yours. The entire family is waiting for you."

He gave the woman rolling ham into rolls a glance and she was smirking, her back toward his stepmother.

"I'll follow you down," he said as his stepmother turned and walked away. He leaned in toward the woman. "No fair laughing as she scolded me."

The woman laughed then leaned in closer. "She scares me a little."

"Yeah, she's scared the hell out of me since I was eight." That warranted a laugh. "I guess I'd better go. I can think of a million things I'd rather be doing."

He picked up a ham roll and took a bite as she narrowed her eyes at him.

"She's going to probably count each of those to make sure she's paying the right amount."

"If she short pays you I'm good for it. If she doesn't tip you enough either, let me know. I'm good for that too."

"Something tells me you're trouble."

He bit off another bite. "I've been known to be that too."

She moved the tray of meat out of his reach. "I'll be sure to be in touch if I need to collect."

Eric held out his hand to her, but before she took it, she wiped her own on her apron. "Eric Walker."

"Susan Hayes."

"Eric!" His stepmother's voice echoed down the hall.

"I'm forty years old. You think she'd realize I don't play by her rules anymore."

"Do you play by anyone's rules?"

"Just my own."

She took back her hand and reached for a bag of rolls. "Like I said something tells me you're trouble."

Eric shot her a grin as he stole a roll from the bag. Perhaps after putting up with his entire family he would actually stick around and watch the caterer work. He hadn't had anyone pique his interest in a long time. It might be worth mingling with his family just to let her interest him a little more.

Chapter Two

Eric was still finishing the roll he'd stolen from Susan's catering tray when he walked into his father's home office. When his entire family was in one small room, he realized just how big a family it was.

His father and uncle sat in the chairs that faced the desk. His grandfather's attorney sat behind the desk.

Tension was thick in the air as all eyes diverted to him. Without a word, he only gave the glaring crowd a nod and leaned up against the doorjamb next to his brother.

The lawyer opened the sealed envelope and Eric watched as his stepmother's hand came to his father's shoulder. She was worried she'd lose her home. Truth was, he was a little worried he'd lose his as well.

As the lawyer began with formalities, stating that when his grandfather penned the will he was of sound mind. Eric wondered how sound minded one would have to be to sit down and document who gets what when you kick the bucket.

Bethany caught his eye in the other corner of the room. At least someone told her the old man had died. He gave her a smile when she looked his way and she diverted her attention back to biting her nails—a bad habit she'd always had.

Eric thought it was odd that both of his uncle's ex-wives were there. He could be absolutely sure his grandfather hadn't left them anything. He'd never liked either woman his uncle had married. Nor had he liked Bethany's mother either. Uncle Bryce had never had luck with the women.

That thought stuck with him. He was forty and he hadn't had much luck either. Perhaps he'd better not judge too heavily.

The lawyer continued on with the formalities, noting that his father was to be the executor of the estate. That hadn't been a surprise to anyone in the room. Everett Walker was much more responsible then his brother Byron—even in his sixties.

"The homestead will need to be divided," the lawyer continued and that had a few more heads rise. "Within a year of my passing the North pasture and house will become the property of Elias Morgan."

"What?"

Eric realized he and his father had spoken at the same time.

The lawyer raised his hand to quiet them both. "It was settled in a bout of bad luck years ago. The Morgan family will regain rights to the property which I purchased from them nearly fifty years ago."

Eric stepped further into the room. "It just goes back to them? He bought the property. I've seen the bill of sale and the deed. Why would he just give it back?"

He noticed his father's fist tighten on his lap as he shrugged his wife's hand off his shoulder and turned toward his brother.

"Byron, I have the strangest feeling this has something to do with you."

His uncle's chin darted out. "You would."

"Don't you…" His father stopped as his stepmother placed a hand on his shoulder again. He took a breath. "Why is it that a piece of very good property, legally purchased fifty years ago, now goes back to the original owner in a 'bout of bad luck?'"

Eric watched as his uncle wiped his brow. "I might have lost it in a poker game."

His father came out of his chair and Eric moved in quickly before Dane grabbed hold of his arm.

"Let him explain," Dane said through gritted teeth.

"Everyone suffers a bit of bad luck," Jake, Byron's eldest son, said in defense of his father.

"Bad luck?" Eric shrugged off his brother's grip. "That piece of land belonged to our grandfather, not your father. Who has the right to do something like that?"

"Eric," his father's voice broke through as he stood. "My father would pay off any debt of his children. I can't imagine what we'll find out in the next year."

Byron pushed to his feet and his daughter Audrey moved in next to him. She was anything but fierce, so Eric could only imagine that she'd stepped in hoping no one would yell any further.

"I've made my share of mistakes," Byron said and both of his ex-wives gave a grunt in reply. "I lost the land."

"You lost my home," Eric argued.

"Spoiled, aren't you?" Byron said, his eyes narrowed on Eric.

"Spoiled? How can you even…"

"Stop!" His stepmother moved in between them. "Byron, you know as well as everyone in this room that Eric has selflessly worked that land since he was old enough to do so. Taking it away from him is taking away his livelihood."

Byron's eyes diverted to the ground. "It wasn't my intention."

Eric's father stepped in. "What did you look to gain?"

"Does it matter? This was years ago."

"It matters to Eric for sure," his father argued. "And it'll matter to the income of this property. If we lose that acreage…"

"We lose everything," Byron said softly under his breath.

"At least you know that," his father scrubbed his hand over his face.

Russell, Eric's youngest brother, stepped forward. "The Morgan family has just acquired the fifteen-hundred acres to the East of their property."

Eric looked over at his brother. "When?"

"Last month. That'll double their size."

"And if they get our land back they will triple," Eric let his head fall back and his eyes close. If the Morgans monopolized the area he could guarantee there would be nothing left for the Walkers. He was also certain that the Morgans would do anything to see that happen as well.

The strife between the Walkers and the Morgans had been brewing as long as Eric had lived. Of course, that might have started over him as well. After all, his mother was Constance Morgan before she became a Walker—and that had been frowned upon.

"Should I continue reading?" The lawyer looked at the men who had seemed to huddle in front of the desk.

"Are we going to lose more?" Eric asked through gritted teeth.

Susan finished the display of meats and breads. Though she hadn't heard what was specifically said down the hall, she knew voices were rising.

She brushed her hands over her apron and thought of the new recipe she wanted to try soon. If she could have her menu perfected before the day she opened her first restaurant—well that would be a dream come true, but she knew better than to dream.

Here she was, thirty-five years old, going to trade school and preparing sandwich trays in other people's kitchens. This didn't seem to be the success she'd been hoping to have.

Susan rearranged the trays on the counter to keep her mind calm and off of the voices down the hall.

She thought of her ideal business location. Perhaps she'd have that restaurant if it hadn't been for that bastard she'd spent so many years with. He'd left her with nothing—except that dream.

Well, if for no other reason, she'd make sure she was the biggest success Georgia had ever seen in the business. She had some very steep competition there, but she could do it.

The voices down the hall began to rise again. Susan wrung her hands together as she heard footsteps coming toward her. It was time to put on her smile and serve this family that yesterday was very cordial—today, however, she didn't know what to expect.

The young woman that walked into the kitchen looked very pale and out of place. Her hair was long, red, and a mess of wild curls.

She hadn't been at the funeral. Susan would have remembered this beautiful woman.

"Can I make you a plate?" Susan asked with that plastered smile in place.

"Oh, I…perhaps I should leave. I don't think I belong…"

"Bethany," the name carried from down the hall and a moment later Eric walked through the door.

Susan felt her breath catch when she saw him walk into the room with determination in those dark eyes. He had to be well over six feet tall. From the scruff on his cheeks, the hair that was slightly too long, and the worn jeans he wore—every inch of him screamed masculine.

He towered over the redhead who was shorter than Susan's five foot four. She'd be very disappointed if she turned out to be his wife—or beautiful lover.

"You don't have to leave," he said in a low growl.

"I don't belong here. He might be my father, but this isn't my family," she said and wiped a tear from her cheek.

Susan reached for a napkin and handed it to her before taking a giant step back.

Eric shifted a look her way and then back to Bethany. "You are part of this family. Don't ever think otherwise."

"No one in there respects me."

Eric chuckled. "You and I are the lone bastards, aren't we?"

Finally, Bethany smiled. "I suppose we are." She wiped her cheek again. "I didn't come here thinking that something would be left for me. I'm not a gold digger. I have a career."

"And you're very good at it."

That brought a smile to her lips and at that moment Susan knew who this woman was. Now it was time to keep her professionalism intact. Though, she wasn't sure how she was going to do that. She was standing in the kitchen with Bethany Waterbury!

Eric leaned his hip against the island as if to shoulder Susan out of the conversation. "Why did you come?"

"He was my grandfather."

"You didn't make the funeral."

Bethany's eyes narrowed. "I wasn't told about the funeral. In fact, I hadn't heard he'd passed until yesterday. I flew right out."

Eric nodded. "I wondered."

"To be honest, I thought that if I showed my father some compassion, he'd offer some in return."

"I heard your mother passed before Christmas. I'm truly sorry."

Now Susan saw the actress emerge. Bethany's eyes had brightened and her shoulders pushed back. But she could see through her. This was just a costume as she stood up to her cousin.

"Thank you. No one from here sent a card."

Eric winced. "Right. Byron didn't mention it until after the New Year."

"Like I said before, I'm not part of this family." Susan watched as Bethany's eyes moistened again. "In that room I have two sisters and two brothers arguing over what should come to them. Not one of them said hello to me."

Susan felt as though she might cry now. What kind of family doesn't even accept one of their own?

"I should go," Bethany said as she wiped her eyes one last time with the napkin. "Though I don't know where I'll go. I came out here thinking he'd accept me, at least for a little bit. I'm between jobs and houses."

Eric shoved his hands in his pockets and his eyes deepened in color.

"You came out here looking to stay?"

Bethany shrugged. "I should have been welcome, right?"

"Yes. But did he know that's what you were doing?"

"Even he hasn't but given me a glance. I think he forgot who I was."

Susan didn't mean to gasp out loud, but she had. "I'm sorry." She walked toward them. "You need a place to live?"

"Yes," Bethany answered slowly—perhaps carefully.

"I'm in need of a roommate," Susan said realizing that living with an unemployed, but terrific, actress might be too much adventure for her. But she needed to find a roommate.

"I don't currently have a job," Bethany said flatly.

"I have six more catering jobs in the next eight days. I could use some help."

Bethany fisted her hands on her hips. "You don't know me. I might be a lousy waitress."

"Don't let her fool you," Eric chimed in. "She's an actress. She's a fantastic waitress."

Susan noted the sarcasm and turned her shoulder to him as he'd done when he'd been talking to Bethany. "I'm Susan Hayes," she said holding her hand out to Bethany.

"Bethany Waterbury."

"I know. I've seen some of your films. You were really great in *The Boyfriend Tomb*."

Bethany raised her brows. "You like horror movies?"

"Totally addicted to them. Can't stop watching them. Can't go into anyone's bathroom without checking behind the shower curtain."

That warranted a laugh from each of them. "Eric, what do you think? Can I trust her?"

Eric gave her a lookover and shrugged. "I'm sure she's not as shady as some of the people you know in L.A."

"True enough," Bethany said. "I'd like to see where you live and perhaps take you up on the offer."

"Wonderful. I could certainly use the help and the rent." She could now hear the others coming toward her. "I have to get to work now."

Bethany looked over her shoulder as her sisters walked through the door with their mother. "I think I'll slip out. Can I go up to your place, Eric?"

He too looked around the room that was filling. "Yeah. I won't be far behind you."

Chapter Three

Eric stood in the corner of the kitchen while his family mingled about. They'd separated themselves enough, he thought. Byron's daughters and their mother Cassandra sat huddled together on the sofa with Naomi, Byron's second wife. Her sons stood nearby with Byron basically in a corner chatting.

Eric's parents sat with the lawyer at the table and he could hear talk of golf games and sunny destinations.

His brothers sat at the end of the same table and focused on the plate of food Susan had made for them.

Did they all realize they were just a bunch of people who didn't even want to be in the same room?

"Here. I made you a plate too," Susan handed him a plate filled with everything she'd had displayed. "You're paying for it. You'd better eat it."

"Thanks." He took the plate and lingered a glance at her. Her hair was tied up in a tight bun on the top of her head, which probably made her look older than she was. Her fingernails were bare, which was a food thing. But she had a set of crystal blue eyes that were just a little too dreamy, he thought.

"I made a plate for Bethany too," she said snapping him from his stare. "You can take it to her later."

"Mighty kind of you."

"I take care of people. It's what I do."

Eric nodded. "My stepmother does that." He looked toward Glenda who kept her hand on his father's arm as if it were a silent alarm should he say the wrong thing. "She nearly meddles in people's lives just to help take care of them." She'd done it to him since he was eight. That hadn't been so bad, he thought now in hindsight.

"Still washes your laundry, huh?"

"Never ask her to," he said and Susan laughed. He liked her laugh. In fact, he liked being in the kitchen with her and not sitting among his family. "I suppose that's the benefit of living close to home."

"How close?"

Eric pointed out the window. "You see that road right there?"

Susan followed his gesture with her eyes. "The one that forks. You either come to this house or go on."

"If you go on, you end up at my house. Another six miles down the road."

She chuckled as she put her hands in the pockets of her apron. "So you're twenty-six miles out on that nasty bumpy road?"

"The more bumps, the less visitors."

A hum came from her as if that didn't surprise her.

He set the plate she'd handed him on the counter. "Are you sure about Bethany living with you?" He rounded back to the conversation about Bethany. "She's not that savvy when it comes to money."

Susan began arranging the trays again, now only half full with food. "She seems like a nice person."

"She is. At least what I know of her."

"You don't know her too well, do you?"

Eric shook his head. "I'm lucky to know any of them, really. Byron kept his families separate. Or more accurately, they were kept separate from him."

Susan scooted closer to him. "So the two women on the couch?"

"Those are his ex-wives. Why they're here, I have no idea."

"They seem to get along."

"They should. They were best friends."

"Ouch. Love triangle?"

Eric shrugged. "I don't know. I suppose. Dirty laundry," he said then chuckled. "Not mine—my stepmom cleans that."

She laughed again and this time it caught Glenda's attention and she stood from the table and moved toward them.

He noticed Susan stiffen.

"You picked a good caterer," Eric was sure to say quickly to ward off any stress.

"Eric, darling, that's why I hired her. I'll have to pay her extra for the nice desserts and the tense room she's having to work in."

"Oh, Mrs. Walker, I've been in more stressful situations and the desserts were in the bid."

Glenda smiled. "I should tip you then just for keeping Eric in line."

Susan looked back at him. "I told him he was trouble."

"She did," he said in agreement.

Glenda gave them a nod. "I think everyone is finished here. So anytime you'd like to clean up you're welcome to. Eric will help you load your car, it's out back, correct?"

"Yes, ma'am."

"Wonderful. I will write you a check. Excuse me," she said as she walked out of the room and toward the office.

"I guess my job is done," she said somberly.

"What do you do with what's left?"

"I leave it for the hostess if they want it."

"And if they don't?"

She puckered her lips as if keeping in a smile. "Then I don't have to buy groceries for a few days."

"That a girl."

Susan had packed away everything in order to offer the leftovers to Mrs. Walker, but she'd refused them. That never was a bad thing for Susan. Often it was the only meals she had for a few days if business was slow. Luckily it hadn't been slow for the past month.

Mrs. Walker had been very generous too with a tip, which she said had been well deserved.

Perhaps that would turn into a referral. Both of Mr. Walker's ex-wives had taken her business card.

Susan carried the first box to her small car parked out back of the Walker's house.

"How do you get all of this in here?" Eric asked lifting the hatchback.

"Clever packing."

"Subaru? I don't see you as a Subaru kind of girl."

She set the first box into the back and they both walked back into the kitchen. "What do you see me driving?"

"Cargo van?"

She laughed. It was easy to laugh around him, but she assumed that was part of his charm.

"Someday maybe. The Subaru has been with me since college."

"They last forever."

"Thank God." She picked up another box and so did Eric. They headed back to her car. "Would it make more sense if I told you I used to live in Colorado?"

"I suppose. Let me guess, you had a mountain bike attached to the top of this thing."

"And here I thought you'd been locked up on this ranch. You have seen a few things, huh?"

He shoved the box into the car. "Oh, I've been around."

And that was her warning that he was still trouble.

They carried out the last of her boxes and closed up the car.

"Thank you for your help."

"You're welcome, but remember I was forced to do it."

"Eh, something tells me you're gentleman enough to have done it without your mother asking."

He gave her a wink. "You'll never know."

Susan reached into her pocket and pulled out a business card. "Here, will you give this to Bethany for me? I'm seriously looking for a roommate."

Eric took the card and looked it over. "Susan Q. Hayes? What does the Q stand for?"

She grinned as she opened the door to her car. "I think I'll keep that to myself. Don't forget to give her the card and her plate of food is in on the counter still."

Eric looked toward the house. "You did that on purpose. You're making me go back in there."

"It didn't seem like a hostile atmosphere. I mean you all were in some kind of disagreement and yet you all sat together and had lunch."

Eric shrugged. "That's what families do, right?"

"Not many." Susan slid into her car. "It was nice to meet you."

"I'm sure we'll meet again," he said and walked back into the house with her card in his hand.

"Leave your boots at the door," his stepmother was quick to say as he walked into the kitchen.

He did as she'd requested.

"Is she single?" Glenda moved in toward him. "She's very pretty, Eric."

"Is that why you hired her for a second day?"

"No. I didn't want to cook for your uncle and his women. I was hoping this would be quicker, but they seem to be hanging around." She was whispering now.

"I'm thinking once they're gone we won't see any of them for a long time."

"I don't think that's the case."

Eric wasn't sure what that meant, but as soon as Dane walked toward them Glenda stood tall. "Did you get enough to eat?"

"Ma, of course I did. That lady filled my plate and you added more."

"You'll always be my growing boy," she said wiping a crumb from his cheek.

"All the more reason for me not to move to Ohio for a job. How will you take care of me?"

The line between Glenda's brows deepened. "You have to do what's best, Dane. You worked hard for that position."

He nodded. "I know. I just would like to be closer."

Glenda moved in and kissed him on the cheek. "Go for a while. See what it brings. You never know what fate has in store for you in Ohio."

Both men winced at the word when she said it and then walked away. Glenda Walker was a huge believer in fate and none of the rest of them were. Of course, it had worked out for her. As fate would have it a very distracted Everett Walker backed into her car some thirty-three years ago and now she had a husband, a family, and a very nice home.

Fate—to Eric—was a nasty little word.

Dane leaned his hip on the counter. "Aren't mothers supposed to beg you to not move away?"

Eric had to laugh. "Especially when you still live in their house you mean?"

His brother winced. "Moved back in. Don't forget I've been an adult."

"She's right though. Who else has had a chance to move to Ohio for bigger and better things?" He had to laugh. It sounded ridiculous.

Dane wasn't laughing though. In fact, Dane was always just a bit too serious. "I'm worried about Dad. I don't think this is the time to make life changing decisions."

"Dad is fine."

"And Uncle Byron has put everyone at ease by gambling away half of the ranch." His sarcastic tone was noted.

Eric ran his tongue over his teeth and bit back the oath that could have ripped through. Instead, he took the calm approach. "There is too much Walker pride to let the Morgans get their hands on what grandpa purchased fair and square."

"Isn't that hard for you to choose sides? You're half Morgan too."

Eric shook his head. "The day they disowned my mother was the day I became *not* a Morgan. You don't throw away your family because they fall in love with someone."

"Dad was a threat to them."

"He shouldn't have been. Georgia has enough land for everyone."

Dane let out a breath and pushed himself from the counter. "Bethany hiding at your place?"

"How'd you know that?"

Dane shrugged. "She was here all of an hour and I don't think anyone but you talked to her."

"She's feeling left out."

"I'm feeling pretty lucky at this moment to be part of *this* side of the family." He gave Eric a slap on the shoulder and headed out of the kitchen.

Eric figured he'd spent enough time around everyone already. Two days in a row was unusual for him. He liked his privacy too much to want to be this social. Add the tension in the air over his uncle losing his house to the Morgans— now he felt like he needed a stiff drink.

He looked down at the card in his hand. The Q still had him extremely curious.

If Bethany did move in with Susan, maybe he'd finally get to know what the Q was for.

Perhaps it was time to head home and relinquish the card to Bethany. They could share that stiff drink as the bastards of the family. Then, they could discuss their new friend, Susan Q. Hayes.

Chapter Four

Bethany didn't even stir when Eric pushed open the sticky front door to his house. She'd fallen asleep on the couch and pulled an afghan up over her shoulders.

Eric toed off his boots by the door and hung up his coat. He carried the plate to the kitchen, set it on the table and opened the fridge for a beer. Usually, he'd wait till the sun was down to have a beer, but today he'd look past the fact it was only two in the afternoon.

"I didn't hear you come in," Bethany said from the other room.

She sat up on the couch and Eric watched her from the kitchen.

"I don't know how you didn't hear me. Between my old truck and that sticky door, I wasn't exactly quiet," he said shutting the door to the fridge.

She rolled her head from side to side. "L.A. is noisy. I suppose I've learned to ignore the noise."

Eric picked up the plate he'd brought in from Susan and carried it out to her. "Here. Your future roommate sent you a plate of food."

She chuckled as she took it. "She seemed nice, huh?"

"I knew her for all of an hour," he said with a shrug as he sat down in the chair across from her. "But, yeah. She seemed nice. I mean, she didn't run when everyone started yelling at each other down the hall."

Bethany laughed as she sat back with her plate on her lap.

"I suppose I could just ask you to let me live here."

Eric stopped drinking mid pull from his beer then swallowed down the amber liquid.

"You want to live—here?"

She set the plate on the coffee table in front of her. "No. Not after that reaction."

Now he'd burned her too.

"I just live alone. I always have. I suppose…"

"Eric, stop. I don't belong on the ranch and I shouldn't have said that."

"Like hell you don't belong here. You belong here as much as I do." He set his beer on the table next to him and leaned in, his arms on his knees. "I'm a tad touchy right now. I don't even know how long I'll get to live here."

"My father was wrong to do that. He had no right."

"Damn straight he had no right." Eric let out a breath then sat back in his chair, picking up his beer.

Bethany picked up her plate and eased back on the couch, tucking her sock-clad feet under her. "Glenda knows how to get a hold of Susan, right?"

That was when he remembered the card in his pocket. He pulled it out and looked at it again. "What kind of girl's name starts with a Q?"

Bethany was mid bite of her sandwich when she looked up at him and just stared. She chewed and swallowed. "I have no idea. Do you have a woman looking for a second date and you forgot her name?"

"Funny." He tossed the card toward her. "Susan wanted me to give that to you."

She picked up the card and studied it. "Susan Q. Hayes?"

"See what I mean about the Q?"

She laughed and tucked the card into her shoe on the floor in front of the couch. "I'll call her." She looked up at him, her eyes dark as if the world of worries clouded them. "Can I stay here tonight, though? I just don't want to be alone."

Eric nodded. "Of course you can."

He finished his beer and watched as she devoured the food on her plate.

"Where's all your stuff?" he asked as he stood to throw his bottle into the recycle can his stepmother insisted he keep.

Eric turned when there wasn't an answer and watched as she wiped tears from her cheek.

"I don't have anything."

"Nothing? Who has nothing?"

She raised her head and looked across the room at him. And even then he could see the sadness in her eyes.

"Me."

He felt as though he needed another beer to get through this story. He pulled open the fridge and pulled out his last two beers and carried one over to her.

"Something tells me this isn't strong enough."

She smiled as she took it from him.

Eric sat back down in his chair across from her and waited until she was ready to talk.

"When mom died she had nothing. I mean nothing." She pulled from her beer. "She'd worked all her life to have a modeling career and an acting career, but she was never very successful."

"I thought Violet Waterbury was a big Hollywood name."

She let out a snort. "Not in Hollywood. There were only four of us at her funeral."

"Oh, Bethany, I'm so sorry."

She wiped at her eyes again, and then drank her beer. There was a lot of pain in that small body, he thought as he watched her.

"Anyway, it took everything I had to set her affairs in order. I'd been living off a friend for a few weeks and had thought about coming out here. Then when I heard about grandpa, I thought it would be the right time. I thought perhaps he'd be more willing to let me in."

He bit down on the inside of his cheek before he said, "You're welcome here as long as you need."

She burst into a laugh that had him staring at her. "Oh, you would die. I already saw your reaction when I asked to stay. There's no way I'll stay longer than tonight. In fact," she bent and retrieved the card. "I'm going to call her right now."

"I'm going to go check on things. I'll be out for a while," he said thankful for a job to be done. "I don't have much in the way of food, but maybe we can go into town and get something later."

"That sounds nice."

Eric slipped on his boots, plucked his hat off the peg and rested it low on his brow. He swung on his coat before he hurried out the door not wanting to eavesdrop on any part of her conversation.

He liked his business to be his own, and he was sure others were the same. Well, most people were the same. His stepmother loved to meddle into his affairs and those of others. Christ, hadn't she already asked him if Susan was single?

And wasn't that thought weighing just a little too heavily on his mind?

He looked at the sky, which had cleared. Perhaps he'd walk toward the barn and saddle up Whiskey River for a ride. The mind-numbing task of saddling up a horse and letting him take him through the fields sounded like a better time than getting into his truck and wallowing in Hank's music.

It would have been easier to drive over to the barn and it would have kept his boots dryer. The point wasn't to make everything easy, he thought. The point was to do his work he'd neglected that morning and to keep away from the house as long as he could.

Bethany could make her phone call. She could finish that nap. She could wallow in her father's neglect if she wanted to.

Eric just wasn't sure how much conversation they could have if he stuck around much longer. If he calculated it right, he'd only ever been around Bethany about a dozen times in her twenty-four years. That wasn't much to build a good family relationship on.

However, they had always seemed to have a flow. Again, it was probably the fact they were the lone bastards.

Eric opened the door to the barn and walked toward Whiskey River's stall. The horse welcomed him with a hearty neigh and a grand nod of his head.

"Oh, you're glad to see me are you?" He patted the horse's nose. "Yeah, I'm glad to see you too. I've had a lousy couple of days."

Whiskey River nudged him with his nose as if he understood. Perhaps he did. They seemed to have a better relationship than Eric had with anyone else.

Once he'd saddled the horse, they headed out. The ground was soft and a breeze nipped at Eric's skin through his coat. The cattle grazed the field between his house and his parents' house. He could see that there were still a few cars there. Glenda had hoped they'd all leave, but that hadn't seemed to be the case.

He rode up through the pasture to the highest point of the property where he could oversee everything. The main house. His house. The original Walker land and the land his grandfather had purchased. He could even see the Morgans' land.

The main house on the Morgan land was far enough away it was but a small dot on the horizon, but it was there.

There was a tightening in his chest when he thought about his mother growing up on that land and being buried on Walker land. They'd pushed her away when she'd fallen in love with his father. Could pride be so disgusting?

The people who lived in that house—that house which sat only miles away from his own—were family. His blood. They didn't even know him.

In that house lived a grandfather he didn't know. He had cousins he'd never met and yet they could see each other's houses. It was gut wrenching.

Eric wondered how many times had they crossed paths and never known?

It hadn't been anything he'd thought of until his grandfather died. They had never been a threat or much of a second thought.

He nudged Whiskey River off the point and back toward the furthest fence. There was always the need to check the fence and make sure everything was in order.

By the time he had ridden back to the barn, rubbed down the horse and fed him, he'd been gone nearly two hours.

Bethany's car was still parked outside his house, but now so was his brother's truck. He clucked his tongue. What did Dane need?

Eric was hungry and worn out. All he wanted was dinner and a good night's sleep. But he had to admit to himself, he still wondered what the Q meant.

Had Susan and Bethany worked something out to meet? Was Susan Q. single, as Glenda had asked? If she wasn't, she wouldn't need a roommate.

What kind of restaurant did she want to have?

Why did she live in Colorado with the Subaru?

Indeed, these were more promising questions he'd like to get answered, which would also distract him from having to worry about where he was going to live in the next year.

He kicked the mud from his boots as he walked up the front steps. When he opened the door he could hear his brother's voice echoing through the small house.

"Biggest sum-bitch I've ever seen!"

Bethany laughed and so did Dane. Eric didn't have to ask. This was a hunting story from when Dane was fifteen. He'd heard it a million times and to him it was no longer a knee slapper.

Eric pulled off his boots and set them on the mat by the door.

"What are you doing here?"

"Being friendly," he said. "I have a set of cousins I never get to see. I'm thinking I'm done not knowing them. So, I came to visit."

Bethany smiled up at him from the couch. "He's a hoot. Are all your brothers this funny?"

Eric looked at Dane. "No, he's our comedian."

"And the good looking one, he forgot to add," Dane said.

"She's related. You don't have to impress her with your bit about being good looking," Eric said as he hung up his hat and coat.

"Eric," Bethany stood. "I talked to Susan and she invited me over to check out her place. I don't know my way around that well, so will you drive me there? I'll even spring for that dinner we talked about."

"Dinner?" Dane's brows lifted. "I want to tag along."

"Of course you do. You're like a puppy."

"Am not. Besides you'll miss me when I move away."

"I'll remember that," Eric said on a snort. "Let me wash up."

As he walked to the bathroom he smiled. It looked like he was headed into town to see Susan's place. The thought of looking into those blue eyes again quickened his heart rate.

The last thing he needed in his life right now was the complications of a woman. But he sure could use the distraction of one.

And he was going to find out what that damn letter meant. Then there was the benefit from it all. He could pawn off Bethany too.

No matter what, Eric liked his privacy. One night with her on the couch was going to get to him. He'd offered more, and he'd have given it, but it looked as though Susan was going to earn his loyalty just by getting his family out of his way.

She was becoming a more attractive distraction by the minute.

Chapter Five

The moment Susan hung up the phone panic had struck her in the chest. She had just invited a perfect stranger to live with her. What had she been thinking?

This woman was familiar in name and face only. Susan had seen at least five movies with her in them. And didn't she get killed off in every single one? Yes!

Perhaps this was a huge mistake. Not only had she offered her a place to live, but she'd offered her work too. There wasn't enough money in her catering company to make herself money, and now she was giving it away.

Oh, her brain wasn't in order and this wasn't her style.

What had made her become so trusting of the world? That wasn't her style either.

It was then she thought of those dark eyes, that strong chin, and the body of that tall cowboy that had walked into the kitchen earlier that day. How he'd escaped her notice the day before, she had no idea. But Eric Walker had been filling her mind from the moment she laid eyes on him.

He was a distraction she couldn't afford. She'd spent the last ten years being distracted by a handsome face and this was her time to rebuild her life. There was no need for her to get worked up over a set of chocolate eyes that had her knees going weak.

The thought crossed her mind that if Bethany lived with her Susan would be forced to be around Eric more. A moment later she nearly laughed aloud. Hadn't Eric himself told her that he hardly knew Bethany? It didn't seem as if he'd be hanging around to make sure her transition was smooth.

Or would he?

It really didn't matter. Bethany had a house to tidy up, dishes to clean, and a presentation to develop for a catering job that could lead to a weekly corporate luncheon. The last thing she needed to worry about was Bethany and her cousin Eric.

There was a huge chance Bethany was going to walk into the little townhouse and shake her head. But it was Susan's home and it would remain just that until Susan made her mark on the city of Macon, Georgia. Then she'd take Atlanta by storm.

Susan had been so busy tidying up she hadn't heard anyone pull up out front. She'd jumped when the doorbell had rung.

She hurried down the steps to the front door and pulled it open.

The glorious redhead stood on the porch with a smile that lit up her face, but it was the man behind her that commanded Susan's attention. He towered over Bethany and his smile wasn't bright at all.

"Hi. I didn't hear you pull up," she said.

Bethany laughed easily. "Really? Eric's truck is a beast."

"It's a good truck."

"He's sentimental over her. Can we come in?"

Susan nodded, but it took her a moment longer to command her body to step back and let them into her space.

Bethany instantly let out an, "Ah! This is wonderful."

Susan smiled graciously. "Thank you."

Eric said nothing. His eyes scanned the walls as if he were looking for spider webs or cracks in the plaster.

It was stupid to care what he thought of her house. What mattered was Bethany liking it. And if she didn't like it, then there was nothing lost and tomorrow would be another day in Susan's life.

"C'mon, I'll show you around." She started through the living room but noticed Eric stood at the door. "Are you coming?"

"No need for me to walk around. I'll wait here."

Susan nodded and walked back toward the kitchen with Bethany.

Eric shoved his idle hands into his front pockets. He should have let Bethany come on her own. Just being in Susan's personal space was making him itchy. The neighborhood wasn't upper class, but it wasn't sketchy either. The outside of the townhouse was in need of some repairs, but she seemed to have made the inside something special.

Each room, that he could see, was boldly painted. The living room was yellow and the dining room blue. He looked up the steps, which no doubt led to her bedroom. The walls were red; black and white photos lined the wall almost like an art gallery.

The photos weren't of faces. There were people and places—things. A collection of sewing items. A girl on a swing with her hair blowing as she reached the sky. An old tractor. A wilted rose.

But the one that caught his attention was a pair of tennis shoes. It was very simple, but it was captivating.

"Eric, you shouldn't walk around people's houses without them," Bethany said and he realized he'd walked all the way up the stairs looking at the art.

"Sorry. I got caught up in the photos."

Bethany looked at them and her eyes grew wide. "Oh, these are lovely. Did you do them?"

Susan looked up at him as if to judge his appreciation, or lack of it, toward her artwork.

"It's a hobby of mine. I took some classes when I lived in Colorado."

Bethany continued her appreciation of the photos as she climbed the steps, but Susan hadn't released her stare from him. And he hadn't let his gaze wander—not yet.

"This is brilliant," Bethany's tone rose and each of them broke their stare and focused on the photo in front of her. "Who is this?"

"That would be my grandmother, my mother, and me," she said in an uneven tone.

Eric stepped down to stand behind his cousin. There were three sets of hands holding one another. Each set grew older. And each set had a wedding ring adorning the ring finger.

Eric felt the pang of jealousy hit him in the chest. Well, wasn't that stupid? He'd known the woman all of a few hours. What the hell did he care if she was or had been married?

Bethany caught his attention as she wiped at her eyes.

"Are you crying?" he asked and she turned toward him shooting him an angry look.

"It's beautiful. It moved me."

He looked back toward Susan now, but her eyes never met his.

"I'll let you two finish your tour," he said stepping past Bethany on the steps.

"I have more photos in my room." She lifted her eyes to his. "Would you like to see them?"

No. No, he most certainly didn't want to see her bedroom.

Eric swallowed hard. Okay, that wasn't what she'd said. When he didn't give an answer, she walked past him and Bethany followed.

He rubbed the back of his neck as he stared at the photo of the hands. It was a moving photo.

Oh, hell. What would it kill him to look at the rest of her art?

Susan walked through the door of her bedroom with Bethany in tow still oohing over her photos. Eric, however, didn't seem to be right behind them. All the better.

"These are ones I took of the Flatirons in Boulder," Susan said explaining the rock formations in the pictures. "And these are near Red Rocks Amphitheater."

"Was that where you lived?"

His voice carried through the room and had rattled right into her bones.

She looked up at him leaning so casually against the doorjamb.

"Yes."

"That's a nice area."

Why did he look so sexy with that scowl standing there watching her?

"It's beautiful."

"So what made you decide to be a caterer? Obviously you're an amazing photographer."

That was an uncomfortable question, and it shouldn't have been. But it didn't need an answer—really.

"It's just a hobby to decorate my walls." She let out a slow breath. "Let's go down the hall to the other room."

Susan noticed that Eric hadn't moved from his position as she neared the door. She slid past him, fully aware that his eyes were on her as she did so.

"This is the bigger room. It has an adjoined bathroom and a small deck off the back."

"Oh, awesome!" Bethany said as she walked into the room. "Why didn't you keep this one for yourself? This is beautiful. Oh, look at the view!" she said, pulling the blind up on the window.

The city showcased itself just above the treetops in the distance.

"Quite a change from L.A.," Eric's voice again carried through the room and had Bethany turning toward him.

"That would be the point of change." She walked toward the closet and pulled open the doors. "Look at the room! Really, why didn't you keep this room?"

Susan shrugged. "Easier to rent if the person is getting something for their money."

"How much money?" he asked.

Susan straightened her shoulders. "We can discuss numbers. Bethany and I."

He gave her a slow nod. "You're kindly telling me to butt out."

"Unless you're paying her rent."

"Business woman."

"To the core," she retorted as she watched him and wondered what it was he was digging for.

"I love it," Bethany chimed in. "If we can work something out I'd love to live here. Does the bed come with the room? I don't have anything but a suitcase."

Susan chuckled. "Yes. It comes with the room."

"Good." She looked back at Eric. "You're off the hook, cuz. If we can work this out, you won't have me on your couch at all."

"You're going to negotiate this now? Dane and I are hungry."

"Dane?" Susan asked.

"My brother. He's in the truck."

"Oh, I didn't mean to keep you."

Bethany shook her head. "They're men. They think with their stomachs. Don't pay any mind to them."

Susan thought that might be hard to do. The man seemed to be consuming her mind this afternoon.

"Why don't you come with us? To dinner." Bethany offered. "I'll bet Dane would find you fascinating."

"Oh, I don't…"

"Yes. You're coming," Bethany grabbed her hand and pulled her through the door past Eric once again. She was sure she heard a grunt from him as they passed.

Suddenly, she did want to go—especially if it was annoying him.

Chapter Six

Susan had quickly gathered her jacket and her purse as Bethany drug her from the house.

"Tell me where you're going and I'll meet you there," she said as she noticed Eric getting into his truck. "There isn't room for three of you in that truck let alone four of us."

The man who had been waiting in the truck stepped out. She recognized him from the funeral and the reception at the house. He wasn't near as tall as Eric, but they had similar features. He too was handsome, but with a more forlorn look.

"Susan, this is Dane," Bethany said as he stepped out of the truck.

"Nice to meet you."

"Likewise," she said with a gracious smile. "So where are we going?"

"The Rookery," Eric said flatly.

"On Cherry?"

He gave her a nod. "I'll meet you there."

"Dane, go with her. I can't tell her how to get there. I don't even know where I'm at," Bethany added as she climbed into the truck.

Did he wince? Susan was sure that was what he'd done. How was this going to be a fun night?

Bethany shut the door to Eric's truck and they pulled away from the curb.

"He's short tempered, isn't he?" she asked as she walked toward her car in the driveway.

"He likes his space. He hasn't had much of that the past few days. Now he's in town going out for dinner. Not much his style."

As she opened the door to the car and eased in behind the wheel, she decided that Dane wasn't as dull as he'd appeared to be. This was a man with a lot on his mind.

"He's just a hermit, huh?"

Dane shrugged. "He's the protector, I suppose. You know, the one who makes sure everyone gets where they're supposed to."

"But at his own cost."

"Maybe. He's lived on the ranch his whole life. Lost his mom at eight. My mom loves him as her own, but it's always different. And now…" He turned his head toward her as she pulled onto the street. "Maybe he doesn't want anyone outside the family to know what's going on."

"I'm not put out. I was just the caterer."

Dane nodded. "I'll bet you pick up a lot of information just hanging out in the kitchen."

She grinned. "I always thought it would be interesting to be a mail carrier or even a trash collector. Can you even imagine what they know?"

"Society's silent observers?"

"Exactly," she said on a laugh and Dane relaxed into the seat.

Perhaps he wouldn't be as dull as she thought he might be.

Eric drove without a word, but he could feel Bethany's eyes on him.

Finally, he shifted a glance her way. "What?"

"I'm just trying to figure you out. You're a mystery to me."

"Likewise."

Tossing her mane of curls behind her shoulder, she looked out the window. "I used to dream about you. Did I ever tell you that?"

"That sounds a bit incestuous."

"No, no," she laughed as she turned back toward him. "I used to dream that you were my brother. In fact, when I was much younger, I would tell my friends that I had a brother who lived in Georgia."

"Why would you do that?" he asked as he turned down Cherry Street.

"The few times I'd been around you…I mattered."

Eric shifted in his seat. He wasn't one for deep, family talks and it looked as though this was where she was going.

"Of course you matter."

"Not to my father." Her voice softened. "My brothers and sisters don't know me very well. I'm sure there are a lot of harsh feelings there. But you were always nice to me."

"I'm old enough to be your father. I wasn't going to be mean to you."

She was still smiling. "Let's just say I appreciate it. I hope that now that I'm here the others will learn to accept me."

He wanted to assure her that they would, but he didn't. He wasn't sure if it would be a lie or not.

Eric pulled into the parking lot and was surprised to find Dane and Susan standing by her car waiting.

"Did you fly here?" he quipped as he opened his door and climbed from the truck.

"You must have taken the long way. She knew a short cut." Dane chuckled.

"I'm a city girl," Susan said with a shrug. "I learn my way around fairly quickly. And…I've been here for nine months. This isn't my first meal here."

Eric nodded as they walked toward the building. "You still drink unsweetened tea, don't you?"

She laughed easily and touched his arm. "I don't eat meat either. Truly not a Southern girl."

"You have a pair of Birkenstocks in your closet?"

She nudged him now and his blood grew hot in his veins with her flirtatious laugh.

"I own two pairs and socks to go with them."

Bethany spun around to look at her as she walked backward across the parking lot. "You don't seriously wear that in public do you?"

"In the comfort of my own home."

"Whew, I thought you were going to need a fashion intervention," she said as she turned around and walked through the door, which Dane held open for her.

"I still might," she joked, as she too walked through the door.

Dane shook his head as he and Eric walked in. "These two are going to get along just fine aren't they?"

Eric nodded. They were a couple of Western misfits in a town of Southern gossip. Lord knew what people were already thinking.

Eric watched Susan nibble at a salad and drink a glass of water as if the meal didn't matter to her. She engaged in conversation, laughed a lot, and her eyes always sparkled. Dane eased around her and he wasn't usually that laid back.

Bethany certainly wouldn't be as talkative or excitable if Susan wasn't with them, he was sure of that.

He was on his second beer, his burger long eaten, listening to Susan talk about a catering job at the library—and he was enthralled. There was a dimple at the corner of her mouth on the right side. She had a tiny little beauty mark on the edge of her left eye. Her ears were pierced four times, but she only wore one set of delicate silver hoops.

Eric wasn't a man to touch others. A fine woman who was willing, that was another story. But he wasn't a hugger or a person toucher, but she was.

She'd touched his arm in the parking lot and his head had nearly blown off from his blood pressure spiking. In the course of her nibbling on her salad, she'd touched Bethany's shoulder and Dane's arm. It was safer to sit across from her and just observe.

"Why Georgia? Why Macon? Why not Atlanta?"

Bethany was perched with her elbows on the table, absolutely enthralled with the conversation she was having with her new roommate.

Susan shrugged. "Atlanta is too expensive. And I needed a total change of scenery."

Her voice dropped when she said it. There was more to moving across the country than a change of scenery and he found himself needing to know why.

The conversation shifted quickly to Bethany and her move.

"When my mom died there was nothing left for me," she said. "I'm not sure what is here for me…"

"Your family," Eric finally spoke.

"You and Dane are the only two who have even acknowledged me. And your mother," she said as if it were an afterthought.

Dane nodded. "Of course she did. You can count on her to get the rest of them to come around."

Susan leaned in over the table. "How often did you see your dad?"

Bethany pushed a French fry around with another. "I've been here maybe ten times. I've heard my father was infatuated with my mother, but you would have thought he'd have made more effort if that was the case."

Eric set his beer on the table. "There is little effort given when it comes to your father. Sorry," he added in case he'd hurt any feelings.

"I caught that today at your parents' house. No one expects too much from him."

"You pave a path for yourself. His has been paved with mistakes the entire family has had to pay for."

"Including you."

Eric winced when she mentioned it and he looked toward Susan, who had stopped mid drink to watch his reaction.

He wasn't good conversation or company. "I'm going to find our waitress and settle the check."

"Oh," Susan said setting her drink down. "Here I need to give you money."

"For what? Your garden and your water? I got it."

"I wasn't looking for a free dinner."

"You owe me one," he said and walked away from the table.

Bethany chuckled as she pushed her plate away. "He just asked you out on a date."

"He did not," Susan argued.

Dane nodded. "In his very horrible way…he did."

"Trust me, the last thing I need is a man who is that short tempered. I have a lot on my plate right now and it sounds like he does too."

She watched as Eric returned to the table and simply looked down at them all as if they knew that was their queue to stand.

Bethany and Dane both pushed back from the table and stood. Obviously he had control over his family. Even the members he didn't seem to know too well.

When she looked up at him, she swore she saw panic in his eyes. What had they hit on over dinner? Something more had happened while she was fixing up trays of food for his family this afternoon.

The curious nature that had gotten her into more trouble as a child, and even as an adult, buzzed inside of her. Suddenly she wondered how he would feel if she showed up at his place tomorrow with lunch.

Chapter Seven

There was peace...finally.

Eric kicked his feet up on the coffee table and rested his aching head against the back of his chair.

Dinner had been longer and a whole lot more involved than he'd anticipated when he'd offered to feed Bethany.

But the payoff was that she wasn't sleeping on his couch.

Actually it didn't help to think about where she was sleeping because then his mind only wandered to Susan.

His stepmother randomly hires some woman to serve sandwiches at his grandfather's funeral and now his head is filled with images of her face.

He dropped his feet to the floor. There were pressing issues in his life right now. The fact that his uncle had lost Eric's home in a poker match with one of Eric's unknown relatives should be foremost on his mind.

So why wasn't that the pressing thought in his head?

How come all he could think about was that dimple, that beauty mark, those blue eyes, and that photo of her hands?

He looked at his watch. It was nearly eleven and his body was exhausted. Tomorrow he'd need to fix that gate in the south pasture before he moved the herd over next week. That was going to take the better part of his day, so he had no time to sit around and think about anything, but getting some sleep.

Eric stood, turned off the lamp, and walked to his bedroom. Susan's bed had been made, he thought as he looked at his unkempt room. It had smelled of her—lilacs.

He scrubbed his hands over his face.

It had been a mistake to go with Bethany into that house. How come he hadn't stayed in the truck with Dane?

Because he hadn't wanted to, he realized as he undressed and fell onto the bed. He'd wanted to see where she lived—how she lived.

It was an intimate peek into a stranger's life.

Tucking his hands under his head, he wondered if it was so bad to want to know more about someone you just met. Maybe if he pried a little into her life, he could forget the mess brewing in his own.

Eric woke the next morning to the sound of vehicles outside his house and voices. It took a moment to fully come to grips with what he was hearing. He'd certainly been in a much better place in his dreams—dreaming about Susan.

Trying to reach the commotion, he nearly fell out of bed. Realizing he had not one stich of clothing on, he found his jeans and pulled on a T-shirt as he ran through the house and out the front door in his bare feet.

There were six pickup trucks parked just beyond his front porch. His father, his brothers Dane and Gerald, and his father's lawyer stood in a line facing three other men.

"What in the hell is going on here?" He called out from the porch.

"Trespassing is what's going on," his father yelled back.

"My land. Remember?" An older man in a black button up shirt said equally as loud, but he never turned his head toward Eric. Though he wore sunglasses, his stare was aimed at Eric's father.

"My father bought this land fair and square. I have the bill of sale. I have the deed," his father argued.

"And I have the declaration that your brother gave it to me in a poker game. Equally as fair and square."

Eric stood nearly frozen on the porch. At that moment, he knew who the man was standing there arguing with his father.

He'd lived on that land for forty years and never had he actually been this close to Elias Morgan—his grandfather.

It hardly seemed possible that he'd never met the man and had only seen him when he was younger once when they were in town. What did it say about a man who had never even sought out his own grandson?

"You stole my family," Elias said walking closer to Eric's father. "You don't get to keep everything."

He turned his head toward Eric, but said nothing to him. Then he turned back toward Eric's father.

"Everett, I'll have what's mine. All of it. You can't keep her. And you can't keep my land."

Elias and the men he'd come with walked back to the two trucks they'd driven in and sped off, kicking up mud in their wake.

Eric watched his father stand still and no one spoke for a long moment.

"What did he mean, you can't keep her?" Eric asked nearing the edge of the porch, his feet now frozen against the wooden planks.

"Go make some coffee. I'm going to call Ben and Russell. I think we need to make a plan," his father said, pulling his phone from his pocket.

"Dad, what did he mean? You can't keep her?"

When his father looked toward him, Eric's heart nearly burst. There were tears in his father's eyes.

"He wants to move your mother."

Eric felt dizzy.

No one would disrupt his mother's resting place. They'd have to kill him first.

Perhaps it was time for him to meet Elias face to face.

But as his father began walking toward the house, the phone to his ear calling Eric's brother Ben, he realized he'd have to do that later—and no one could know.

Right now the men needed coffee. And he'd find something they could put in it to kick it up a notch.

~*~

Susan sat at her desk in the corner of the living room. Her computer was a vivid display of colorful spreadsheets and lists.

She'd meet with the head of the library at eleven. Then she had plans to take lunch to Eric. If that went well then she'd go to Costco on her way home and pick up the items for tomorrow's job.

If the drop by at Eric's didn't go well—she didn't want to think about that. She had a curiosity about the man and it just needed to be satisfied.

She could just ask Bethany, who still hadn't climbed out of bed and it was nearly ten o'clock, but what fun would that be? There was a story behind the little lines on Eric Walker's face and Susan wanted to find out what it was.

When the front door opened, she nearly fell back in her chair.

"Oh, did I scare you?" Bethany walked toward her. Her long red curls were pulled back in a ponytail and her iPhone was strapped to her arm.

"Did you go running?"

Bethany nodded, still catching her breath.

"I thought you were sleeping."

"Heavens no. I've been running for nearly two hours."

"Why?"

Bethany laughed. "You can't even get looked at for movie roles if you don't keep up your body. I keep healthy. Some of those girls are just skinny because they don't eat and they live on coffee."

"You look great."

She smiled. "Thanks. I need to get a shower. What are you doing today?"

How much did she want to tell her? "I have a meeting in an hour, then some shopping to do. I have a corporate event to cater tomorrow. Are you free to help and learn the ropes?"

"Free as a bird."

Bethany gave her a brilliant smile and then ran up the stairs. Susan wasn't sure after two hours of running how you'd have enough energy to even get up the stairs let alone run them.

She turned back to her spreadsheet. There were enough jobs planned for the next month to get a little money into savings. Tuition for summer semester was going to be a little tight if she was paying Bethany to help. But in the long run, it would all be worth it.

She'd paid her dues married to a man who hated every idea she'd ever had. Now she was forging her own life, doing what she wanted to do. That restaurant she'd build wasn't too far down the path, she thought. Every day the reality of it grew closer and closer.

Susan looked at her watch again. She needed to head out for her meeting.

Turning off her computer, she gathered her paperwork and headed to the kitchen. On the counter was her cooler with everything she'd need for lunch at Eric's—china, silverware, and glasses. Of course, a lovely chicken salad she was trying out. She'd pack herself a nice tossed salad. It would be up to Eric's reaction whether she used the chicken salad for future events.

The china and silverware were probably overkill, but she was looking to make an impression. She wanted to know about him and she'd caught his stare last night. Did he even know? He'd watched her all night long. Certainly there must be some kind of interest. And what about that "date" he asked her out on?

He would be her brief distraction. She just wanted to know who he was, nothing more.

The meeting at the library hadn't quite gone the way she'd planned. They wanted more food and a cheaper price. Susan just wasn't sure she could make that work. This might be the very first job she had to turn down.

She promised them she'd go over the numbers, but there was little she could think of to cut costs and offer more.

The cooler in the seat next to her reminded her of the lunch she'd planned, though when she'd planned it she was more optimistic. He had no idea what she'd planned. If she didn't show up what would it matter? No one would be the wiser. It would be her own secret.

But by the time she'd talked herself out of going to Eric's, she'd already turned down the dirt road that would bounce her about for the next twenty-six miles. *The more bumps, the less visitors*, replayed in her ears. She wasn't going to be welcome when she got there. She was setting herself up for disappointment.

One thing she enjoyed was risk-taking, though. It wouldn't be like her to turn that car around. She'd settled for too many years. She was in the need for some adventure. The entire move to Georgia, going to school, and starting a catering company was her kind of adventure. Why not spice it up with a man that wouldn't leave her mind? Again, she just needed to satisfy her curiosity.

After nearly a half hour of being tossed from side to side, Susan saw the fork in the road that led to the main house—his parents' house. This time she would veer right and spend another six miles of bouncing to deliver an unexpected lunch.

Soon she saw the small house in a clearing of trees. A barn out back dwarfed the house.

A porch encircled the small house and gave it a warm feel. She could imagine sitting there on a warm summer night looking out over the fields that rolled out like a carpet.

Susan laughed. That was the most ridiculous thought ever. Eric was her distraction and the cousin to her roommate. There would be no dreaming of front porch sitting.

When she made the last turn to the house, she noticed that there were three more pickups in front of the house and none of them were Eric's.

Had she just spent an hour driving out to his place only to find he wasn't there?

But just beyond the house, by the barn, she saw the battered pickup he'd driven.

She followed the road to the barn and parked next to his truck. Waiting for a moment to see if he'd come out, she finally opened the door and stepped out.

The air was chilled and she'd wished she'd brought a heavier jacket. Though she hadn't thought she'd be anywhere other than in his house.

She watched through the open door for a moment and saw a man walk to a stall. There was no reason to assume it wasn't him.

The enormous barn was filled with horses. Tack lined the walls and hay was stored in stacks at the other end.

She wasn't sure she'd ever get used to the smell of animals, she'd never been around them. Though the smell of fresh hay did delight her a little.

Susan could hear his voice now. He spoke in a low, nearly hushed tone.

"What are you doing here?"

When she looked up, she saw his head looking out over the gate of one of the stalls.

"Hi." She hadn't answered his question and his furrowed brow begged for a different answer. "I came out to look for you."

"You found me. What do you need? I thought Glenda paid you."

Suddenly the kink in her neck and the tightness in her back, from the near hour on that dirt road, made themselves present.

"She did pay me. That's not why I came out."

"Why then?"

Once again she remembered that bumpy roads kept visitors out. This must have been why.

There was no reason not to be straightforward with him. She'd promised herself it didn't matter what he said.

"I brought you lunch."

Eric nodded slowly. "Leftovers?"

Susan shoved her hands into the pockets of her jacket. "No. I actually created a meal for you. I was trying to be nice. I can see that I've interrupted you and I'll just take my lunch and head back to town."

She turned to walk away, but she heard him walking toward her so she slowed.

"Wait," he called after her and she stopped. "I'm sorry. I've had a crappy morning and I'm not very good company."

She wasn't sure he'd ever be that.

Susan turned to face him. "I can just leave the cooler and get it some other time."

"You didn't come this far just to bring me lunch."

"No. I didn't have a very fine morning myself, so this was supposed to be my highlight. I was wrong."

Eric lifted his hat from his head and ran his hand over his hair before replacing it low over his eyes. "I'm afraid with me you'll always be disappointed if you're looking for good company. I've never been known for that."

"Then let's just consider this payback for last night's dinner. We can dismiss it as that."

Susan turned and walked back toward her car with him in tow.

"Do you want to go back to your house and eat?"

He looked past her toward the house. "Looks like my family is making themselves at home today." He shook his head. "I don't want to go back there. Besides, I'd guess you only brought enough for two. There are at least four other men sitting in my house eating my food. Let them suffer with what's there."

She laughed. "Where do you want to eat?"

"Bales of hay make for great tables."

Eric took the cooler from her as she pulled it from her car. Their hands had brushed and it sent that same jolt through him as it had when she'd so innocently touched his arm the day before.

He hadn't expected to see her, but he couldn't help but feel a little more at ease with her there. Perhaps it was just a distraction from what was going on—and hadn't he wanted that?

Perhaps she'd have been a welcome distraction if all he had to think about was losing his home. But now that it included losing his mother all over again—that was different.

"Are you okay?" Susan asked and he realized he'd walked in front of her without a word. "If this is a bad time…"

"I'm just a little distracted today." He set the cooler on a bale of hay. "Let me get a blanket."

He went into the small room off to the side which he used for an office and gathered two blankets from the chair in the corner. She'd opened the cooler before he'd returned.

"You even brought plates?"

"I must have known something was going to come up."
She smiled at him and that dimple on the corner of her
mouth winked at him. Damn!

"It's not very warm in here."

She rested her hand on his as he began to unfold one of
the blankets. "It'll be fine. It's just a quick lunch."

Why was it that every time this woman touched him his
temperature rose at least ten degrees? And why was it that
she made him forget about the crap going on around him for
that instant?

There was an attraction. Okay, he could admit that the
woman made things stir in him that no one had in a very long
time, but this wasn't the right time for this. But his body
certainly didn't care. Why at a moment like this did thoughts
race through his head that certainly weren't appropriate—
especially with a woman he'd only met the day before.

Eric spread the blankets out over the hay and Susan set
out what was probably the most elegant lunch he'd ever seen.

China, silverware, and stemmed glassware. This was the
kind of set up a guy put out when he was going to propose,
not just have a quick lunch.

"I knew it was the middle of the day, so I brought a
sparkling cider to go in the glasses."

There was no holding back the smile that had pushed
through to Eric's lips. "You thought of everything."

"If I had I'd have a table and chairs. But this is much
cooler."

"Why did you do all this?"

She looked at the elegant—unique—table she'd just set
then shifted those deep blue eyes up toward him. "I just
thought you'd enjoy it. I owed you a meal. And," she took a
deep breath, "I wanted to get to know you better."

"I'm not a great deal of fun."

"I'm not so sure about that. Something tells me there's a lot to you. Maybe I'm interested in finding out who you are."

Eric pursed his lips. "Why? What do you gain by knowing me?"

"So far I've netted a few catering jobs, a roommate, and dinner. If we stop talking I'll have had a lunch date and a nice drive before I have to head back and get to work."

He smiled again. She was something.

"I'm thinking I've made out better," he said as they both sat down on the blanket covered hay bale. "I've eaten nicely for a few days and was inspired by your art."

"Inspired?"

"Inspired to ask you why the picture of your hands, with your mother's and grandmother's, had a wedding ring."

Her eyes quickly lost their sparkle. "You were thinking too hard about the art. Focus on the fact that you ate well for a few days."

"I think this is the fanciest chicken salad I've ever seen," he said as she spooned a serving onto his plate.

"This is nothing."

"Maybe you could show me something else someday."

She nodded without looking up at him, but he could see the dimple that came about when she was happy.

"So," he picked up his fork. "The picture."

Susan picked up the container with her salad and her fork with a loud sigh. "Did that photo keep you up last night?"

"Yes."

"Liar."

He'd let her think that, but in fact it had.

"I was married for ten years. There you go. I'm a recently divorced woman who fled her home state to make something new of herself. Story over."

"Nah, there's more."

Susan stabbed a piece of chicken and bit it noisily off her fork. "Why is your house full of relatives and you're in the barn hiding?"

"Because that's a hell of a lot more fun to me. Besides they're not just visiting. We had drama. I don't do drama, so yes, I'm hiding."

"Someone contesting the will?"

"Why'd you leave Colorado?"

Her lashes fluttered when she was humored. Her eyes grew deeper blue when she was flirting. "It looks like perhaps we've been on each other's minds. I have my own set of questions and you have yours."

"Looks that way."

"This could take a long time to sift through."

"I don't have dinner plans."

Her eyes flew open wide and then she smiled. "I have to prepare for a job tomorrow. I don't have time to cook dinner."

"What time is your job tomorrow?"

"Four until six."

"So you have time for breakfast?"

The smile faded. "You want me to stay the night, here?"

Eric wanted to laugh. Was it fair to think she was as cute when she was irritated as she was when she was flirting?

"That wasn't really what I was thinking, but I'll let you decide that." He saw the color rise to her cheeks. "I was thinking you could come out here for breakfast. I'll cook."

"You cook?"

"Breakfast."

"You're bribing me with breakfast to tell you why I left Colorado?"

Eric shrugged. "You're bribing me with lunch just to get me alone at my house."

Again, he'd managed to shock her with his words, but he figured she was on to him. The shock quickly eased back and a smile—perhaps a little seductive—formed on her lips.

"Do most women chase you?"

"Most women can't handle me. I'm a man with a lot of pride. That seems to get in the way of things."

"If I want something I get it," she said as she took a grape from her salad and popped it into her mouth with her fingers.

"You want me?"

"Didn't say I did. But you seem to think that I've come to get you alone in your house."

Eric nodded as he took a bite of his salad. "Is it fair to say we're just two adults who find the other interesting?"

"That's all I would say."

"No hidden agenda?"

"None."

"Have breakfast with me?"

"How could I refuse?"

It was settled. He'd see her again. Now, if only he could focus until she arrived the next morning. And damn it, there better not be any relatives in his house by tomorrow morning.

Chapter Eight

There was a grin that permeated Susan's lips as she walked through Costco with her clipboard and her list. People must have noticed it too, because they'd smile back when she looked at them.

It was fun to be happy—finally. Who would have thought it would be a man that made her happy again. Her work had been holding that position for a while now—since the last man in her life had made her so miserable.

She couldn't say she wasn't interested in him. She was. And it was more than just his story. She sincerely wanted to get to know him.

Susan giggled when she thought it might be nice to wake up at his place and have breakfast. A woman next to her shifted a glance toward her, obviously having heard her. She simply smiled and moved on.

Her thoughts of Eric and his mesmerizing dark eyes were cut short when her phone rang. Quickly she pulled it from her pocket and looked down at the display. She didn't recognize the number, which meant she'd answer in a very professional manner. It could be a new client.

"Susan Hayes Catering. This is Susan."

"I was given your number by an acquaintance and would like to talk to you about catering an event," the man said on the other end of the phone.

"Wonderful. I love referrals. What kind of event are you having?" she asked as she pulled out of the way of other shoppers and turned over her list to make notes.

"It's a formal dinner party actually. There will be about fifteen of us."

"Formal dinner. Will you need the dining room set as well?"

"No. That'll be taken care of. We will just need the catering and service."

"I can do that. I usually meet with my clients and go over the menu and the schedule. Would that work for you?"

"I'd like to give you the name and phone number of my assistant. She will be finalizing the plans."

"Okay. What is her name?"

The man hesitated for a moment. "Lydia Morgan."

"Wonderful. I look forward to hearing from her." Susan clicked her pen closed and began to ask, "Who referred…" But the phone went dead.

She let out a long breath as she looked down at the screen. Most men who wanted to cater an event had a woman doing the background work. This call shouldn't surprise her. But she couldn't help but hope that the event wasn't as uncomfortable as the phone call had been.

~*~

The afternoon had been filled with beer. Ben and Russell had stayed all day. They'd helped fix that section of fence that Eric needed fixed, and it was worth paying them with beer. But now none of them were going anywhere.

"He's a son-of-a-bitch!" Russell slurred as he opened another bottle. "And I'm talking about Uncle Byron."

Ben chuckled as he set his bottle down on the coffee table and it wobbled. "I wonder what else we will lose before he's done."

Eric let out a long burp as he stretched his weary legs. "We're not going to lose anything. Morgan can't have what he wants. We own it and there has to be some legal thing that means we keep it. And I'll be damned if he moves my mother. Over my dead body will he move her."

His voice had risen and he realized, as his head swam, just how loud he was.

"Bethany came home hoping he'd accept her too. I hate to see him screw her over. She doesn't deserve that," he said as he slowly stood and tried to steady himself. "How in the hell are we even related to that asshole?"

He wasn't as steady as he thought he was he realized when he kicked the leg of the coffee table.

Russell laughed and quickly tried to hide it behind a cough.

"Screw you," Eric shouted.

"Get over yourself," Russell retorted. "Enjoy your buzz and relax."

Ben took a long pull from his beer, finishing it off. "He can't relax. Have you ever known him to relax? He thinks he has to take care of everyone and everything all the damn time."

"I'm the oldest. I'm supposed to."

Ben stood, wobbled, then with his hands fisted on his hips, he managed to be still "Why don't you let everyone help you for once? Let us help fight for your house. Let us help you with the land. Let us, I don't know, set fire to the Morgan's."

Eric stood and stared at his brother. He'd always felt alone among his large family. He'd do anything for his brothers, but even sober, he couldn't remember a time he'd depended on them.

He never made it to the kitchen for another beer. He fell back into his seat and just stared at his brothers who simply stared back.

"He wants to move my mother," he said flatly.

Ben sat back down on the couch. "I know. That's not going to happen."

"I lost her once. I can't lose her again."

Russell nodded. "It won't happen. He's messing with you, Eric. He wants to wear you down."

Ben leaned back and rested his hands behind his head. "I haven't drunk this much in a very long time."

Russell slapped Ben on the arm. "How wasted is this? There aren't even any women around."

Women, Eric thought. Woman—he thought more clearly. "You have to get the hell out of my house." He stood then quickly sat back down.

"I ain't driving anywhere," Russell argued.

"No. I have a woman coming."

That sent both of his brothers into hysterics and only seemed to piss him off.

"You have a woman?" Russell nearly choked on his laughter. "I have never seen you with a woman."

"Yes, you have," Ben argued. "That one with the funky eyes."

"Oh yeah. What did you see in her?"

Eric felt his sobriety begin to surface. "She's coming here in the morning. I'm making breakfast."

"You don't cook," Ben reminded him.

"I told her I could cook breakfast."

"Toaster waffles?" Ben asked and that again sent him and Russell into another bout of laughter.

"C'mon, get out." Eric managed to stand.

"No way," Russell leaned back on the couch. "I'm not moving from this space. You wouldn't make me leave if you really cared."

Eric grit his teeth. "I'm going to bed. You'd better be gone by the time the sun comes up."

"Can't we get a few blankets?"

"You know your way around. You can either both sleep out here or use the guest room."

"I get the bed," Ben quickly claimed.

"No skin off my nose. I have the fire out here." Russell kicked his feet up on the couch and rested his head on the arm.

"Glad I could accommodate you guys. Now remember to get out before she gets here."

Russell closed his eyes. "Sure, bro. We'll be gone if she shows up."

Eric shook his head. Brothers were a pain in the ass, he thought as he walked to his bedroom and shut the door behind him. He wouldn't trade them for anything.

Russell and Ben were still sleeping when Eric headed out to feed the horses before the sun. This would be a unique sunrise. He hadn't looked forward to seeing the sun for a very long time.

For the past month, each sunrise brought the uncertainty of his grandfather's health. A few days ago the rain moved in just as his grandfather passed. But today felt different. Perhaps the sun would actually shine today.

Eric zipped up his coat as he walked down the front steps of the house. He pulled the collar of his coat up toward his ears and straightened his hat. The slightest sliver of sunshine was peeking over the horizon. As soon as he was finished with the horses he'd be kicking those brothers of his out of the house. Eric wanted this promise of a perfect morning to be just that—perfect.

It was just a bit too cold to want to walk to the barn. And if the old truck was too loud this morning, maybe it'd wake his brothers up without him having to punch them in the arm. The memory of doing just that when they were younger had him chuckling to himself as he pulled open the door to the truck and slid in to the cold environment.

A moment later he turned the key and the engine protested before rumbling, loudly, to life. Yep, that had to have awakened one of them.

Eric shifted the truck into drive and headed out toward the barn, but as he crested the small hill toward the barn, he noticed there was a car parked outside.

It wasn't just any car. It was a Subaru. Her Subaru.

Susan shivered in the cold morning air with her camera poised and ready to capture the perfect sunrise over the horizon. But her attention shifted when she heard the rumbling of Eric's old pickup truck coming toward her.

She turned her camera to the truck and began shooting as he approached and the bright lights of the headlights grew closer.

When he stopped, she finally lowered her camera. It was still dark enough she couldn't see his face, until he opened the door and the dome light highlighted his scowl.

She'd like to think he was unfriendly and that was just how he looked, but she knew it wasn't the truth.

Susan stood from where she'd been crouching and walked toward him. Her heart pounded in her chest like a bass drum in a parade.

"What are you doing?" His voice was gruff. She wrote it off as his first words of the day.

"I wanted to get a picture of the sunrise. I figured breakfast usually comes after sunup. Why not be here to capture it?"

His shoulders eased and he took another step toward her. "Sunrises are prettier in color."

That brought a smile to her face. He'd noted all her work was in black and white. "I take color photos too."

Eric was right in front of her now, towering over her and that scowl had faded away. She swallowed hard against the fear that crept into her. She hadn't been this close to a man in a year. There was certainly something between them and she wondered if he felt it too.

"Let me see your camera," he reached out his hand.

Susan didn't hand it right over. What did he want with it? At least there wasn't any film him could just rip out of it.

She took a breath of hesitation and blew it out before she handed him the camera.

Skillfully, he turned it to look at the shots she'd already taken. There were only a few. Pictures of the barn and the silhouette of the horizon where the thin hint of yellow had begun to promise a new day. The last pictures were of him driving closer to her.

Eric then turned the camera up and pointed it at her. He looked through the eyepiece and then clicked the picture, then another.

"What are you doing?" Her voice stammered.

"Taking your picture."

"Why?" She began to reach for the camera, but he took a step back.

"Because you're beautiful."

Susan stopped. Her lips parted and she blinked as she heard the click of the shutter again and again.

A moment later he lowered the camera. "Do you often go speechless?"

"Hardly ever," she admitted.

"That's what I thought." He offered her back the camera and then walked past her toward the barn.

Was that it? He was just going to tell her she was beautiful then walk away?

The sky was turning color, but the urge to follow Eric into the barn was greater than that of staying outside to capture the perfect picture.

Quickly she followed him inside. She hung her camera around her neck as he began to talk to the horses as if he'd just walked into an office building of co-workers.

This was a moment she couldn't help but raise her camera for.

The dimly lit barn gave that particular horse, which Eric talked to most, a glow. Eric had walked to him first and rubbed his nose and spoke softly to him.

They both turned their heads toward her as she lowered the camera.

"He wants to know what you're going to do with those pictures."

Susan moistened her lips. "I don't know. I just take pictures of things that move me."

Eric looked at the horse. "Did you hear that, Whisky River? We move her."

The horse gave a neigh as though he understood and agreed with him.

Eric stepped back from the stall and moved toward her. His hat rode low over his brow and he resembled an angry cowboy as he walked toward her. She pushed back her shoulders and lifted her chin.

"I had a crappy day yesterday," he said.

"I'm sorry. I shouldn't have come out…"

"Your coming out here was the best part." He lifted his cold hand to her cheek. "You came back."

"You invited me."

"Didn't mean you'd come."

"I'm here." Her breath carried on the cold air in the barn and her teeth chattered, but that was probably from nerves she decided.

"We agreed there was an attraction—an interest between us."

"Yes." Was he a businessman too? Was he going to go over all the points of this?

"It's killing me to find out just how much interest there is."

Eric stepped in closer, forcing her to step back and soon she was pushed up against a wall of hay bales. The hammering beat of her heart leapt into her throat as those dark eyes of his gazed down at her.

"I'm not scaring you, am I?"

"Are you trying to?"

His lips curled into a grin that toyed with her. "Not really."

"Then no."

The hand, which had been caressing her face, now lifted and braced against the hay bale behind her. His other hand came to her waist.

"I'm interested, Susan," he said as he lowered his cold lips to hers.

Suddenly the cold wasn't a factor as his mouth warmed against hers. She parted her lips to feel the warmth of the kiss as he pressed his tongue against hers.

She gasped for air, but it only managed to deepen the kiss. Her camera pushed against her as he moved in closer. Her head swam in wonder of this magnificent kiss from nearly a stranger—whom she hoped to share a few more of these kisses.

Eric's hand on her hip moved to her lower back and pushed her even closer to him. There was heat between them. More than just pressed together body heat. It was an electric surge that pulsed through both of them.

Did his head sway as hers did? Did he feel the zap of the kiss clear down into his boots, because she sure could.

She raised her hands to his chest and then wrapped them around his neck. A moan escaped his throat at he deepened the kiss even further.

"Whoa!" A voice came from the doorway and Susan pulled back, but Eric didn't. "Didn't mean to interrupt."

"Go away, Russ," Eric said keeping his eyes on Susan.

"Right. Just wanted you to know we were headed out."

"Good."

"Okay, we'll see you later."

Susan never had seen the man that spoke. She was trapped beneath Eric, his eyes opening slowly and focusing on her.

"Do you need to see them? Go talk to them. Tell them…"

"Tell them what? He knows what I'm doing here. He saw."

"Yes, but…"

"I wasn't done yet," he said as he lowered his head and took his time kissing her until her blood had fully warmed and now nearly boiled in her veins.

Chapter Nine

Eric thought he'd kill his brother later, but for now he was going to keep kissing Susan, until their legs didn't hold them any longer.

It had taken a moment for her to relax again, but when she had, the magic was back.

Her arms were around his neck, her thumbs making small circles on the base of his head. What was it about this woman that he just couldn't get enough of?

He didn't know her, not really. But when their mouths and bodies came together there was a sizzle that had him pressing his body even closer, until the camera between them pressed deep into his chest.

Eric pulled back, breathless.

Susan sucked in air beneath him. "I didn't expect that," she said and that made him smile.

"I hadn't wanted you to."

Her blue eyes were dark now as they gazed up at him. "This just complicated things, didn't it?"

"I don't think so. We didn't have anything to complicate. I think this just made breakfast more interesting."

She laughed as she relaxed her shoulders against the hay bales. "I'm not a woman who falls into bed with men."

"I invited you for breakfast. I think I told you, you could decide on the spending the night. Maybe someday we'll get to that."

"Right." She pushed herself up and stood solidly on her feet before him. "I could go start breakfast."

Eric shook his head. "I'm cooking breakfast. Though I didn't consider it would be this early."

"Can I help you in here?"

"You know about horses?"

"Not a damn thing."

Now he laughed. "Why don't you go back to the house and make coffee? I'll be in shortly. The door is unlocked."

Susan nodded. "I like you," she said as he turned to walk back to Whiskey River.

For a long moment, he studied her still standing where he'd kissed her breathless.

"I like you too. I don't waste kisses on women I don't like."

She nodded. "I just thought I should mention that."

Eric gave her a tip of his hat and went about getting the horses fed.

I like you. Did she have to sound so juvenile, Susan thought to herself as she headed toward his house.

It seemed important at the time, though. He needed to know she didn't just go about having breakfast with men and kissing them. Why it was so important, she wasn't sure. But it was.

Maybe because he needed to know she wasn't easy or a home wrecker. She was a trusting person and that sometimes screwed her over.

She let out a breath as she slid in behind the wheel of her car. The last thing she needed was to bring parts of her old relationship into this new one. Or whatever it was. How did you have a relationship with someone you just met?

As she cleared the turn to his house, she saw that there were still two pickup trucks outside. They were the same trucks that had been there when she'd arrived earlier that morning.

He'd told her to go to the house and start the coffee. He wouldn't have told her to do that if there were people there. The man, Russ he'd called him, said they were heading out. They must have done that.

She'd let herself in and make that coffee.

Susan parked the car and climbed out into the cold. Walking up the steps to the unlocked front door, she pushed it open and then stood frozen in place looking at the two men looking at her.

"I'm sorry. Eric told me to come over and start the coffee."

The man on the couch laughed. "He promised you breakfast and is making you start the coffee?"

"Well…I…we…I should…"

The man seated in the chair stood and walked toward her. "Come in. I'm Russell Walker," he said as he held his hand out toward her. "Eric's brother." He turned toward the other man. "This is Ben. Eric's other brother."

"It's nice to officially meet you both. I'm Susan," she stuttered out. "I'll just head out. Let Eric know…"

"C'mon in. I already made coffee and I just want to bust my brother's chops a bit."

"Oh, I don't know if I want to be here for that."

Russell smiled at her and she noticed he had the same smile as Eric. "Stay. He's forty years old and I've never seen him kiss a woman like that. Don't get me wrong, he's had women around, but the PDA isn't his style."

She nodded. "It wasn't really a *public* display."

"I know. Makes it even sweeter on my part."

He started for the kitchen as Susan took off her coat and hung it on the hook.

"I enjoyed your food," Ben said standing from his seat.

"Oh, thank you. Those were very simple menus."

"I'm a bachelor. Cereal is a good meal."

"I'm in culinary school now. I'd like to open my own place some day."

Ben's eyes opened wide. "That's adventurous. What kind of place?"

"I haven't really decided exactly. I'm a vegetarian, so I'd certainly incorporate that."

Russell walked from the kitchen with two mugs in his hands. He handed her one. "Vegetarian? So no bacon or ham with your eggs? Do you eat eggs?"

She laughed. "I'm not vegan. I just don't eat meat. It's not a health thing really. It was with my ex-husband. For me, it's more of a gross factor."

That made Russell laugh. "You don't eat meat and you're dating a man who lives on a cattle ranch?"

That did sound a bit ironic. Then the rest of his sentence hit her. "I don't think we're dating."

"You kiss men like that a lot? Because I haven't been kissed like that in a long time."

She could feel the heat rise in her cheeks. "I don't do that. I haven't kissed a man since I've been divorced. I don't just do that."

Ben chuckled as he stood and headed toward the kitchen. "You said that."

She heard Eric's truck and only a moment later he pushed open the front door.

"I told you two to be gone when she got here. You said you were leaving."

Russell laughed and sipped his coffee. "Oh, we were until I saw you. Then I thought it would be more fun to watch you squirm."

Eric hung up his coat. "I'm not squirming."

Ben laughed from the other room. "Oh, yes you are. But we'll get out of your hair. He just wanted to see your reaction coming through the door."

"You're not twelve," Eric retorted.

Russell shifted a look to Susan. "I take it back. I have seen him kiss someone like that. I was twelve." He grinned.

When Susan looked at Eric, she wasn't so sure he wasn't going to pounce on the younger Walker. His eyes were dark. His cheeks filled with color. When he grew angry, there was a crease that formed deep into his forehead.

"I think you've both outstayed your welcome. Get out."

Russell set his coffee mug on the end table next to the couch. "He's really a cranky old man. He's always been a cranky old man," he told her with a grin. "He has four brothers, you know. None of us are quite that cranky."

"You're going to be dead brothers if you both don't get your ass out of my house in the next…"

Ben moved from the kitchen swiftly and yanked Russell along. "We're gone. It was nice to formally meet you, Susan. We'll see you around," he said as he shoved his brother out of the house, then backtracked to pull their coats off the hook by the door before leaving.

Susan watched Eric process his irritation with his brothers. She wasn't sure, anymore, that it was anger. She'd seen her own sister get irritated in such a manner more than once. It was endearing to see someone else do the same.

"I see you have coffee already," he said, his voice strained.

"I do."

"Sorry about that. I'd swear to you they are usually more mature than that, but then I might be lying to you."

"I enjoyed them. Don't be too mad at them."

His eyes settled on her. "Nothing rattles you."

"I wouldn't say that. That kiss in the barn rattled me."

"It surprised you."

"It did."

He stepped to her and she could smell hay and cold on his clothes. "I don't like people in my business. They hung around longer than I'd wanted them to."

She'd known him to be a bit snippy, and she'd agree with Russell, perhaps a little cranky, but now he sounded mean.

"So maybe I should just drink my coffee and go. We could count this as breakfast."

Susan could see his eyes cloud with what she thought might be confusion—then clarity.

"I didn't mean I wanted you to leave."

"I don't mean to be in your business."

The irritation was back and he let out a groan. "Listen, things are unsettled this week. I'm not going to get into it, but with my grandfather dying and funerals and wills…I'm just tired of family in my way."

Susan turned and set her mug on the end table next to where Russell had discarded his. "I think we should do this some other time. Considering all you've been through this week the last thing you need is a stranger getting involved."

"You're not a stranger—not anymore."

"Hired help of your step-mother. Roommate to your cousin. We will certainly cross paths."

His eyes narrowed as he tucked his hands into the back pockets of his jeans. "*Will?* I invited you out here because I wanted to be with you. You're not a stranger because I've seen inside your soul."

"How did you do that?"

He took a step toward her. "I saw your photos." His eyes darkened. "I saw where you sleep."

Susan swallowed hard and crossed her arms over her chest as if it would give her a protective barrier. "So what are we doing?"

He stepped closer still until he was toe to toe with her. She dropped her arms and found she had pushed herself against the back of the couch. Something told her this was a situation that called for the utmost care. With one move, she could be a victim to a man she didn't know—alone in his house. Or she could find out she liked him even more than she'd meant to.

"I want to get to know you," he said as he slid his hand up her arm. "The timing of it is just off."

Susan sucked in a breath, trying not to lose herself in his touch. "I was always told if you wait for the right moment it'll never come."

His hand moved over her shoulder and up into her hair. "The moment I met you, you struck me as a very smart woman."

The last man who looked at her like Eric was looking at her had told her she was the stupidest mistake he'd ever made. It was quite a contrast to this man telling her how smart he thought she was and he didn't really know her at all.

Susan lifted her hands to his chest. She could feel his heart pound beneath her fingertips. When she lifted her eyes to meet his they were dreamy—lost—staring back into hers.

It was foolish to think that this man was going to be around for longer than a month. He was only warding off the week he'd had. She was his distraction.

Then he moved his head, lowered it to hers, and covered her mouth with his. Susan closed her eyes and inhaled his kiss.

Maybe he was equally her distraction too.

Chapter Ten

The table was full of different plates. After Susan had mentioned that she was a vegetarian at dinner, Eric had done some thinking. It had warranted a stop at the store, which wasn't convenient, but necessary.

Before he'd made bacon and sausage for himself, he made sure she wouldn't be offended. Then he made hash browns, cinnamon rolls, toast, and eggs. He'd offered pancakes, but she'd only laughed.

Now she sat back in her chair and looked at the plates in front of her. "I don't know when I've ever eaten that much for breakfast."

"Most important meal of the day."

"Couldn't agree more, but usually it's a bowl of cereal or a green smoothie."

Eric shook his head. "I don't get that. Why drink your vegetables? Hell, why eat them at all?"

She leaned in on her elbows and smiled at him. That did something to his heart that he wasn't quite ready for and he certainly wasn't going to let her in on it.

"You don't eat vegetables?"

"Not if I can avoid it."

"I'll bet if I cooked them for you it wouldn't be a problem."

"Sounds like you just offered to cook me another meal."

She smiled and that feeling in his chest spread throughout his body, but he sat still.

"It looks like I did." Susan picked up her fork, pushed around the leftover hash browns on her plate before looking back up at him. "Your brothers made a comment about us dating."

"I'll punch them both if you want me to."

A laugh surfaced that sent a tingling sensation up his spine. He might have reacted to that, but she hadn't let on.

"No. I like them."

"You said you like me."

"Your like is bigger."

He couldn't help but purse his lips to that statement to keep it from becoming vulgar and inappropriate.

Susan dropped the fork. "I haven't dated anyone in the year that I've been divorced. I haven't wanted to. I wanted to find me first."

They were treading into a territory that said danger to him. He hadn't thought there would be any deep conversations during breakfast. He'd just wanted to get to know her better. Then he decided this was how that worked.

"Did you do that?"

She sat back and tapped her fingers on the table. "I think I did." She smiled when she said it. "I'm doing exactly what I want to do. I'm on my own time frame. I work harder than I ever thought I would and I love every moment of it."

He could see it. There was passion in her eyes. He couldn't help but wonder what else she did with such passion.

"Just so you know, I don't date."

By the flash in her eyes he knew that wasn't what she was looking for him to say. He wasn't even sure it was what he meant to say.

"Oh."

"I mean, I haven't wanted to."

When her shoulders dropped, he realized there was a reason he didn't date. He wasn't very good at this.

"Let me try that again. I haven't met a woman in a very long time that was interesting enough to make me want to spend time with her. You are interesting enough."

That made the dimple wink at him and he knew he'd managed to dig himself out of the hole he'd dug.

"I'm going to take that as a compliment."

"Good. That's how it was meant."

She looked at her watch. "I have to get back and get some prep work done."

"I need to get to work too," he said, standing and gathering up plates.

Susan stood and picked up the mugs.

"I can get that. You don't have to clean up."

She shook her head. "Not acceptable between two people who are dating."

Eric set the plates on the counter and let her words sink in. So this was where all that talk about dating was coming from. That's what he got for finding a woman interesting and kissing her as he had.

Was that so bad, he wondered? Why did the thought of being involved with someone rock him? It shouldn't. He was the one who kissed her. Hell, he'd walked Bethany into her house because he'd wanted to. He'd gotten lost in her art and wanted to see her bedroom. He did this. All she had done was put together a nice meal service for his family at a time of need.

She set the mugs next to the plates he'd laid on the counter. Her body was close enough to him that he could feel the heat of her—smell her.

Oh, hell. He'd gotten himself into this and he either needed to get out of it or embrace it.

Shifting a glance to her he noticed how delicate the skin was on her neck. It would be a damn shame to not press his lips to that pulse point just once.

The thought alone nearly had him light headed.

When she looked up at him and her eyelashes batted a moment before she licked her lips, he was gone.

Eric swiftly pulled her to him and took possession of her mouth as if his life depended on it.

There had been that moment when Susan thought Eric was going to ask her to leave and not come back. Now here she was, again, pressed to him with his mouth doing glorious things with hers.

She'd quickly wrapped her arms around his neck just to hold on for dear life because when the man touched her, her knees went weak.

The kiss in the barn had been mind blowing, but now, this one with his fingers tangled in her hair and his other hand pressing into the small of her back—this one topped the charts of all kisses she'd ever been part of.

He turned her so her back was against the counter and his kiss trailed from her mouth to her jaw and then down her neck. Her pulse quickened under his lips and she knew for certain she wasn't standing by her own will. She was merely leaning up against him, holding on for dear life.

What glorious things could this man do if he could kiss like this?

The moment she heard her phone ring in the other room she winced. Nothing could be as important as Eric holding her—kissing her.

He let out a groan and buried his face in her neck.

"Do you need to get that?"

She held her breath for a moment to gather her thoughts. "It might be my client."

He nodded and stepped back as she hurried out of the kitchen. A moment later his phone rang and she heard him curse as he answered.

"What?" Eric snapped out the word.

"Pardon me?"

Glenda's voice pierced his ear through the phone.

"I'm sorry."

"You should be." His stepmother was very specific about manners even at forty. "I'm sorry to have obviously bothered you, but that pipe under the sink is leaking again."

Eric pinched the bridge of his nose. "Where is Dane?"

Glenda laughed. "I love my son, but I've never known him to be handy, have you?"

Eric had to laugh at that. "No." He looked out the window and saw Susan writing in a notebook. Her call was work related and she'd probably have to tend to whatever it was. "I'll be there shortly. Can you shut off the water?"

"I did that. I don't want your father tinkering with this. If he does it'll be worse."

"Yes, it will. I'll be there soon."

He said his goodbyes and disconnected the call. Then he stood and watched Susan conduct business.

He couldn't hear her, but he knew she was being very professional. There was a certain look to her when she was listening intently. Then when she talked there was something that lit in her face. She truly loved what she did and that showed.

It wasn't good to want to be with her every moment. There was work to be done for both of them and their schedules were never going to meld. What was he thinking by starting something with her?

He was thinking she was attractive, smart, and he wanted to know her more. It wasn't fair to pull her into his life when it was about to be turned upside down, but watching her, he couldn't think of anything else.

Really, he couldn't remember a time when he was more attracted to a woman than he was with Susan. Every other woman could wait until his day was done to have his attention, but he knew when she drove away he'd be thinking of her.

What if she didn't want that? What if her schooling and her business plan was what she wanted and he was in her way?

Well, he could always find out how she felt about that. After all, he was related to her roommate. That was going to come in handy, he thought.

Eric watched her put away her notebook and shut the car door. When she walked through the front door, she carried the cold air on her. Her cheeks were red as well as her nose.

"This is nothing compared to Colorado weather, but I'm frozen after that," she said.

"You're cute with your nose all red."

That made her laugh. "I don't see you as the kind of man who tells people they're cute."

"Can't say I've ever said it to a person with two legs before. I usually save that for creatures with at least four legs."

She smiled.

That smile had a way of easing him—melting him. How could that be? He'd only known her for three days and yet he could simply stare at her and feel happy.

"I have to go back to town now. I have a lot of work to do and you probably do to."

Eric nodded. "I do."

"Thank you for breakfast."

"My pleasure."

There was a long, awkward silence between them as if neither of them knew if they should move or not. This was why he didn't do relationships. How was anyone supposed to know who was supposed to make what move? He'd already kissed her, wasn't it her turn to move toward him?

He waited.

Finally, she did so. She crossed the room to him and kissed him on the cheek. "Are you in town often?"

"Hardly ever," he said, then realized it was probably not the answer she was looking for. "Maybe once a week."

Susan nodded slowly. "Drop by if you're around. I have that job tonight. Class tomorrow. I just got a proposal that could lead to…well, anyway, it looks like word is getting around and I'll be busy. I could come out some morning if you're open for visitors."

"Sure. Call me and I'll make sure I'm around."

Her lips tightened. That wasn't what he was supposed to say was it? How was he supposed to know what to do?

Susan smiled, but it was forced. "I'll see you later," she said and turned and walked out of the house.

He watched her again from the window. She walked to her car, opened the door, and sat for a moment with her hands gripping the wheel before starting the engine. She looked frustrated. Was that him or the job she'd picked up?

There was a reason he was single at forty.

Eric hurried out the front door and to the car just as she put it into reverse. The car jolted as she noticed him and she put it in park before she rolled down the window.

"Did I forget something?"

"No I did. Get out."

She stared at him for a moment before unbuckling her seatbelt and opening the door. When she stepped out of the car he gathered her in his arms.

"I suck at this. Plain and simple. I'm forty years old and I don't know how to date."

Finally, the smile that formed on her lips was as genuine as the sparkle in her eyes. She lifted her arms around his neck. "It's been a very long time for me too. So what do we do?"

"I don't have any idea. But how about I come into town tomorrow and have breakfast at your place?"

"I think that sounds wonderful."

"I'm going to screw this all up. I'm going to tell you straight off. When you're done messing with me, you just tell me. I won't be offended."

Susan rose on her toes and nipped his lips with a kiss. "I think this will be a fun adventure."

Chapter Eleven

The drive back to town didn't even bother Susan as she was tossed back and forth in her seat on the dirt road. She'd caught sight of her stupid grin in the mirror a time or two, but she couldn't stop.

Oh, she hadn't moved to Georgia to meet a man, but she had. She'd met him at his grandfather's funeral. How morbid was that? Honestly, she couldn't even say she liked him that much when she'd met him. She'd thought he was rude picking food off the trays. But now—she sighed—now she couldn't wait to see him again.

There was a fluttering in her chest and a nervous energy that pulsed through her as she merged onto the highway from the dirt road she'd been driving. It humored her that he could live so far away and yet at the end of that road there was a big city sprawling before them.

He was going to come to her in the morning and have breakfast—breakfast in her kitchen on her plates.

What should she make? She could make a wonderful spinach frittata. She'd ask Bethany first. Maybe she'd have some insight into what he liked to eat.

Of course a few hours later when she posed that question to Bethany she was met with laughter.

"Are you kidding? How do I know what he likes? I don't know the man at all, really."

Susan hadn't really considered that.

"I guess I make it and we find out."

Bethany stood at the kitchen table wrapping plastic silverware in paper napkins and then dropping them into the plastic bucket that would hold them. "Why are you asking? Are you planning on making him another meal?"

Susan bit down on her lip as she chopped tomatoes, lifted them on the side of her knife, and deposited them into the bowl.

"I invited him over for breakfast."

Bethany continued her job without laughing or appearing too surprised. "What do you have going with Eric?"

"Eric and I have a thing. I mean neither of us know what's going on. We're both terribly awkward about it, but," she sighed, "when he kisses me I can't even think."

"You're kissing him?"

"It happened this morning."

"You were with him this morning?"

Susan nodded. "He made me breakfast."

"You were gone awfully early."

Susan grinned. "I was taking photos."

"Right."

"No, really. I was."

Bethany dropped the last roll of silverware into the tub and then closed it with a lid. "And just how early did you leave for breakfast? Last night?"

Susan could feel the heat rise in her cheeks. They were adults. It was fair of her to think that. "I left early this morning to catch the sunrise. My intent wasn't to do more than be early enough for the sunrise. But he went out to the barn to feed the horses, and well..." She sighed as she thought of it. "One thing led to another."

Bethany walked across the kitchen and stood next to her, leaning a hip on the counter.

"I can't believe you're dating my cousin."

Susan let out a snort. "You and his brothers are very free with that word."

"You're not dating?"

"We're exploring the possibilities."

Bethany took a grape tomato from the wash pile and popped it into her mouth much like Eric had. "Did you know him before the funeral?"

"No."

"You're a very trusting person, aren't you?"

Susan shrugged. "Oh, I don't know about that."

"I do. I've known you three days and I live with you. He's known you four days and you're dating him."

Susan couldn't help but burst into laughter. It sounded ridiculous. "Perhaps I'm desperate for company."

"I think if that were the case you'd never have moved to Georgia."

Her smile disappeared then. "Right."

"I just treaded on something."

"Nothing. Can you get that asparagus out of the refrigerator in the garage? We need to get it washed and cut."

Bethany puckered her lips, but her grin was still there as she walked out of the kitchen.

Susan let out a long breath and gathered her thoughts. The morning had slipped away from her and Eric and they hadn't discussed her reasons for leaving Colorado. Perhaps it was time to face the reasons she had left before she dove into a new relationship.

Suddenly tears stung her eyes. She batted them away as quickly as possible.

Susan wasn't quite ready to face it all, she realized.

~*~

Eric wiggled under the sink to try and ease the sharp pain running up his back. Seriously, would it be too much to have his stepmother look into having a plumber fix this pipe? He'd fixed it three times. Obviously it needed a professional.

But he knew what would happen. If she said she was going to hire a plumber, his father would strap on a tool belt and then a week later Eric would have to fix twice as much pipe and drywall.

This was how it went and had for nearly twenty years. Perhaps Eric should look at it as a blessing. He was needed.

"She got you fixing stuff again?" Dane's voice came from beyond the hole that Eric had tucked himself into.

"You live in this house. You should do this."

He could hear his brother cackle. "Right. I develop software. Have you seen my fingernails? Bitten off but no dirt under them."

Eric let out a groan. "Real work would do you good."

"My work is real. Without me, people couldn't run their businesses. I'm helping mankind."

Eric turned the wrench and batted his eyes from the water that dripped down onto his face. "Where is Dad?"

"Last I heard he was in town with the lawyers. They're trying to find some loophole in Byron's poker game."

"Good. That'll keep him busy for awhile. I don't want him walking in and trying to help me."

Eric continued to work on the pipe, very aware that his brother had never moved. After at least fifteen minutes of him standing only a few feet away, Eric slid out from under the cabinet and looked up at Dane.

"You're just going to sit and watch me do this?"

Dane shrugged. "It's entertaining. Besides, I wanted to ask you about Susan."

Eric ran his tongue over his teeth. "What about her?"

"Russ says it's hot and heavy between the two of you. I told him he was full of crap. But he's persistent."

"What would it matter either way?"

That had Dane fighting off a grin. "You weren't very nice to her the other night. And now you're making out in the barn? Or so says Russ."

Eric shook his head and climbed back under the cabinet. "If you don't have any other purpose in being here why don't you find something else to do? Go program some software."

But Dane didn't leave. Eric slid out from under the sink, again, and looked up at his very serious brother.

"Why is this bothering you?"

Dane tucked his hands into the front pockets of his pants. "I like her."

"I like her too."

"You're not real cool with the ladies."

"Says the man living in his parents' house at thirty-two."

Dane narrowed his stare on him. "If you're not serious about her I want a chance. If this is another one of your love 'em and leave 'em things…"

"It's not."

The answer seemed to surprise them both. Eric hadn't even thought about it when he said it. The words just flew from his mouth. That had merit then, didn't it?

There was no reason to even ask Dane why he was being the way he was. Eric had a reputation and certainly if Susan learned about it she just might find he wasn't someone she wanted to get involved with.

He'd never touched a woman and hurt her. He'd never been outwardly cruel to them either—insensitive, yes.

The back of his neck grew damp from perspiration. Why should this matter so much?

"You drug out your relationship with Angelica for six years. Not once did you tell her you loved her," Dane reminded him.

"I guess it was because I didn't love her."

"She bought a wedding dress."

"She was stupid to do that. I never proposed."

Dane swiped his hand across his forehead. "That's what I'm saying. You use these women for your own purpose. If you're in town you look them up. You hide in your house as if you're some old man hiding from the world."

"So what? I have a lot of work to do here."

"And it's always more important than the women in your life."

"What's your point?"

"I think if you're just going to discard Susan then let me have a chance with her."

Eric pushed to his feet. Wiping his hands on his jeans he faced his brother. "I'm not going to mess this up. Just step back."

Dane held his hands up in surrender. "Fine. Don't break her heart. Something tells me she's not one to put up with your crap."

If they were younger, Eric would consider punching his brother for questioning him as a considerate man. But there were facts that Eric couldn't deny. He'd stomped on a few too many hearts and he wasn't known for being any kind of Casanova.

"Give me a chance." He pulled a rag from his back pocket and wiped his hands. "I have to go dig for a part in the garage. Don't let him touch this if he comes back."

Dane ran his hands over his hair. "He'll be quite a while. He's also making sure that they can't move your mother."

Eric felt any spark of life in him fizzle out as he looked at his brother. "They'll only move her over my dead body."

"Don't say that. I wouldn't hold them against that."

He looked at his watch. "Have Glenda call a plumber," he said as he started out of the kitchen.

"Where are you going? You can't leave this."

"I'm going to talk to Elias Morgan."

Dane hurried after him and grabbed his arm, stopping him. "Are you crazy?"

"He's my grandfather. He should listen to my side of things."

"He's a bastard. He's never been any part of your family. What makes you think he'll listen to what you have to say?"

"Because I know Smith and Wesson."

"Eric…"

"I'm not going to shoot anyone. I just need them to know they disowned her then, they can't claim her now."

"Dad is taking care of that. You have to trust him."

Eric squeezed his eyes closed. He didn't want to trust him. He wanted to break some arms. But that wasn't going to solve anything.

"Fine. I'm going to drive into town and buy the parts I need. Don't let him touch this if I don't get back in time." The look Dane gave him was the same one Glenda would have given him too if she didn't trust him. "I'm not going to the Morgan's. I'll trust the system for now. But when it fails I'm going to go knocking on their door."

Chapter Twelve

Two hours before a job was crunch time. Items were cooking and final touches were being added. This was Susan's shining moment. This was where organizational skills were a must.

Bethany had followed her every direction and that had helped to get everything ready for the book club dinner she was catering. It would be thirty people and would give her enough insight into Bethany's people skills.

She hadn't asked again about Eric or questioned about that emotion she'd tripped on with Susan. She'd simply worked steadily alongside her.

"We can start to load up the car," Susan said as she checked on the chicken breasts in the oven.

"Do you have a special van or something parked elsewhere? How do you get this all in that car of yours?"

"Trust me. It fits."

Bethany gave her a chuckle as she began to stack the boxes with dry items.

They both stopped and looked at each other when the doorbell rang.

Bethany gave her a shrug. "You're one of the only people I know in town and the only one that knows I'm here. It must be for you."

"Will you see who it is? And if it's not a Girl Scout with Thin Mints then I'm not buying anything."

"Oh, those are my favorite too." Bethany squealed. "Let's hope it's a Girl Scout."

Susan continued to pack up the dinner but stopped when she heard the familiar voice. She turned her head to see Eric walking through the door with Bethany.

"I told you it was for you."

There was something about the way he looked at her that sent a shiver down her spine. He didn't smile. He didn't even look very happy. But there was something in the way his eyes fell on her that said seeing her was exactly what he'd needed.

"I didn't expect you."

Eric nodded. "I'm not one to just drop by. But I had to come into town for some plumbing items."

There was more to that, she was sure.

"Well, you're just in time to help us load up."

Bethany picked up one of the sealed tubs. "She thinks it'll all fit in that car of hers. I think she's wrong."

Now he smiled. "She's not wrong. I've seen her do it."

And right there they'd had a moment. A moment he'd reflected on that was theirs. It was simple, but it was there and it gave her heart a little jump.

"Just set it in the back. I'll get the chicken out and we can organize it all."

Bethany gave her a nod and headed out to the car.

Because there wasn't any time to mess around, Susan kept working.

She grabbed the potholders and pulled the chicken out of the oven, setting it on the stove while she maneuvered the roll of foil.

"How long is this function tonight?" he asked still standing in the doorway.

"I'm scheduled for three hours."

He rocked back on his heels. "Is Bethany helping or is she in your way?"

Susan shrugged. "So far she's a help. We'll see how she handles people."

"I know her father. Give her some leniency."

That was a slight cause for alarm, Susan thought. Though Bethany's father had been kind to her the few minutes she'd ever been around him.

"I'm sorry I can't be a little more social," she said as she draped the foil over the pan holding the chicken.

"You're busy. I just…" He stopped and wiped the back of his hand over his brow. "I just wanted to say hi."

That alone turned her to mush. She was sure he wasn't the kind of man to just drop in and say hi.

She hesitated for a moment, turned, and walked toward him. "I'm glad that you did." She wanted to pull him in, kiss him softly, but she kept her hands to her side. "You're still coming in the morning, right?"

He nodded. "Looking forward to it."

"Good." It was killing her to not move in, so she did. Worst-case scenario, he'd step away. Wrapping her arms around his neck, she eased when his hands came to her waist. "It's going to be a long night."

"Tell me about it," he said before dipping his head and kissing her softly.

"C'mon, you two." Bethany sighed behind them. "Seriously just thought you were going to flirt with each other. Didn't know it would end up like this." She passed by them. "By the way, Eric, your flirting is horrible."

He gazed down into Susan's eyes and she could see that wrapped in her arms there was a peacefulness that washed over him.

"I must have done okay," he said keeping his eyes locked on hers. "I'll see you in the morning." He kissed her gently one last time before walking out of the house.

Bethany laughed behind her as she watched him walk away. "You know that getting involved with anyone will ruin your plans."

"What do you mean?" Susan went back to the stove and carefully placed the chicken in a carrying tote.

"You'll get all involved and forget about what needs to be done. I don't know my cousin well, but I know for a fact that he rarely comes to town. He's not the kind of man to just stop by and say hi to someone. Once his routine is threatened, he'll stop coming. Keep focused on what you're doing. You have plans."

Bethany picked up another tote and headed out of the house.

Susan let out a long breath. She didn't want to think that way, but there was some merit in what Bethany said. She'd come this far. She couldn't let her feelings for a man get in her way for success. That had already been done and she didn't want to go back there.

But she didn't want to let it go yet either. He was surging feelings through her she hadn't felt in a very long time. It was nice to be touched, gazed at, kissed.

Susan picked up the tote and headed out the door. It would be in the back of her mind. She'd promise herself to not get worked up about the what-ifs. She'd just make the best of what was.

Right now, she was going to focus on the job at hand and hopefully there would be a few referrals coming her way when it was done.

~*~

Eric cranked up AC/DC in his truck. Some days called for Hank and some days called for something a little heavier. There had been no real need for him to make that trip to town. It was an hour round trip, not to mention buying a part he was sure he had somewhere just to drop in and kiss Susan one more time.

They were going on less than a week of knowing each other and he couldn't get enough. This was maddening. He was stressed and she was going to pay for it.

He noticed his father's car when he drove up to the house. He'd hoped to have the sink fixed before his father arrived. That's what he got for stopping in town—for indulging in that distraction.

When Eric walked through the back door of the house he wasn't surprised to see his father looking at the work he'd done before he left.

"I suppose this is going to need to be redone someday," his father said running his hand over his silver, thinning hair.

"If you start that she'll want a kitchen remodel."

His father smiled, though his eyes remained weary. "Yeah."

He stepped back to let Eric in with the part he carried in his hands.

"I'll leave you to this. Why don't you come see me in my office before you go."

Eric gave him a nod and watched him walk away. He didn't like how his father sounded. Suddenly he wasn't too optimistic about his father's meetings.

An hour later Eric walked into his father's office, tapping on the doorjamb first.

"Come in. Shut the door," he said.

Eric pulled the French doors closed then turned to see his father wiping his fingers over his obviously tired eyes.

"Everything okay?" he asked as he took a seat in front of the desk.

"Could be better," his father said on a heavy breath. "My brother has a gambling problem."

"Obviously."

"In the last six months he's racked up over a hundred thousand in debts."

"I don't see where that's our problem."

His father's eyes lifted and locked on his. "He's my brother."

Eric felt his words as if they'd been punched into his gut. He'd never turn away his brothers in a time of need. Gambling was an addiction—a disease. He needed help and Eric knew that meant his father was going to do everything he could to help.

"Elias didn't win the property exactly. He paid off Byron's debt of nearly a million dollars."

That had Eric out of his chair and pacing. "A million dollars?"

"He knew he'd inherit half of the property. He used it as leverage to save his life."

"What about our lives? What about our livelihood? Do you know what will happen to the cattle if we lose that acreage?"

His father nodded. "I know."

"You're willing to go through with this, aren't you?"

There was pain in his father's eyes and it hurt to see it. "There is little we can do now, except try and reason with Elias Morgan."

"Fine. I'll march over and have a word with him. I'm his family. He should listen to the grandson he never bothered to get to know." His voice had risen until he was nearly yelling at his father. He hadn't noticed until his stepmother opened the door and walked in.

Eric raked his hands through his hair and sat back down as Glenda stood behind his father and rubbed his shoulders.

"It's not sounding like things went well today," she said before she kissed the top of his father's head.

His father patted her hand and Eric could see a connection between them that he wasn't sure he'd ever noticed before. There was unconditional love which was almost so thick in the air he was sure he too could feel it envelope him. Maybe they'd always been that way and he'd been too hurt and angry to ever see it.

When his father took his stepmother's hand and kissed it, he let out a breath. "No matter what happens, everything will be okay. No one will suffer," he said.

Eric let out a groan and the intimacy of the moment was lost. "No one? What about Byron? He walks away? Look a the pain he's causing you."

His father lifted his eyes and narrowed them to make a point. "No one suffers."

Eric wasn't sure about that. There should be some retribution for what he was doing to the family. And Eric couldn't help but feel a bit jaded. He had a lot to lose. That house had been his home for twenty years. He'd built that barn with his own two hands. The horses he boarded were his business and if they lost the land, he'd lose that too.

Someone needed to suffer and if it wasn't his uncle then maybe it should be his grandfather. His breath came quicker now and so did the anger that rose through him and squeezed at his chest. This wasn't over. They weren't just going to hand over the property and walk away.

Eric stood to excuse himself, but his exit was stalled when his stepmother moved in front of him. "I hear you've been spending time with Susan."

He winced. Somebody had a big mouth. "Yeah, we've hung out a few times."

A smile formed on her mouth and her eyes went soft. "Is that what you're calling it?"

Now he was beginning to understand who told her about them. Russ just might get a punch in the gut he decided.

"We're just enjoying each other's company and getting to know each other. That's all. We're not serious."

She touched his arm, much as Susan had that first day he'd met her. "I like her, Eric. She's a very nice girl. Why don't you invite her over on Sunday for dinner? And also invite Bethany. I'd like to get to know her too."

Eric nodded then gave his father a wave as he left the house. He wasn't sure if he had one emotion left that hadn't been touched on today. Every muscle in his body was drained and as he passed the clock in the kitchen, he realized it was dinnertime.

He'd settle in and make himself a steak. Yeah, that's what he was going to do.

As he passed by the basket of fruit on the counter, he snagged an apple. Whisky River would enjoy a little snack and Eric could use the time to sort out his feelings. Whisky River was a good listener.

Chapter Thirteen

The job had run smoothly. Bethany's serving skills and people skills were also a success. In fact, Susan figured that the three referrals she received were because of Bethany alone. She'd entertained that book club and Susan was sure not once had they talked about books.

The thought made her laugh as she loaded the dishwasher with the utensils used from the job.

There had been one connection made tonight that had her second-guessing one of her next jobs. She'd met Lydia Morgan, the granddaughter of the man who had called her a few days ago. They spoke briefly and set up a phone appointment for the next day. The woman had been very quiet—reserved. Susan wasn't sure she was too comfortable to be around, but then again she had a quality that drew Susan to her.

She wished she knew what that was. What was so familiar about that woman that made Susan want to work with her?

As she closed the door on the dishwasher and started it, she looked at the clock over the microwave. It was 10:30 already and she was exhausted. Maybe a nice soak in the big—she stopped thinking. The big tub was in Bethany's bedroom now and she'd gone straight to bed. Maybe she should have kept that room.

Susan rolled her shoulder back and moved her head from side to side to work out the kinks. Perhaps she'd better get to sleep too. After all, she had a guest coming for breakfast.

When she thought of him, her body heated. It was silly to get so worked up over someone she'd just met, but she couldn't help herself. It had been a long time since someone made her feel giddy inside. Eric did that to her.

It was a high of sorts, which she knew then meant there would be a crash too. Something made her want to chance it.

The next morning Susan rose early enough to catch a few photos of the sunrise, which was filled with the brightest of colors. She managed to not fall over in the warrior pose while doing yoga, which was a first. In anticipation of the wonderful morning, Susan's pot of coffee was especially comforting.

Her cooking skills, on the other hand, seemed to be a little off. As she cracked the eggs for the frittata, she had to scoop out at least four shells. The spinach had frozen in the refrigerator, so only half of it was useful. Then it burnt.

Bethany walked through the front door fresh from her run and coughed as she walked into the kitchen. Susan stood next to the oven fanning the towel against the smoke.

"That doesn't look appetizing."

"I can't believe I burnt it. I never burn things. This is horrible. What do I do now?"

Bethany gave her a chuckle as she moved to the window to open it. "I'm sure he'd be happy with cereal. He's not a picky guy. I don't think anyway."

"I don't mind cereal," his voice came from behind her and she spun to see him standing in the doorway. "Front door was open. I assume to vent the smoke."

Bethany winced. "I did that. I saw the smoke and hurried in."

Susan closed the door to the oven and threw the towel on the counter. "I don't have cereal."

Eric smiled at her, one of those endearing grins that had her insides twisting. "C'mon, I'll take you out. It's a nice morning. We can walk down the street to the waffle place. That's vegetarian, right?"

There was ease around him, but she wasn't sure he was like that with many people.

"I'll take you up on it, but I'm going to cook for you. This was rare."

"I'm sure it was."

Bethany cleared her throat. "Well, I'll just go get a shower."

As she passed by Eric, he reached for her and she stopped. "Glenda wants you to come out for Sunday dinner."

"Me?" Her eyes opened wide. "I'm sure your family doesn't want me around."

"She asked for you to come. She'd like to get to know you. There are no hard feelings toward you."

Bethany puckered her lips. "Just toward my father?"

"It seems the feelings aren't that hard there either. My family seems to be a lot more forgiving than I am."

"I wouldn't be. He doesn't deserve the loyalty," she said sharply and Eric couldn't agree with her more. "I'll be there, if you'll be there."

He nodded. "I'll be there." He shifted his gaze to Susan. "She invited you too."

Susan felt the blood draining from her head. "Me? Why would she want me there?"

"She likes you. She wants to get to know you." He shrugged. "It seems as though Russell has a big mouth."

The blood was back and it quickly rushed to her cheeks. "Oh."

Bethany laughed and pushed past her cousin. Eric walked into the kitchen fully with his hand behind his back.

"I brought you something. It was supposed to be just for the hospitality, but now it seems like a pick-me-up."

She felt the edges of disappointment slip away. "What did you bring?"

When he pulled his hand around he gripped a small bundle of tulips. "They don't look so well," he said looking down at the limp flowers.

"It's a little early for tulips," she said reaching out for the flowers.

"That would explain the price of them. I have a few that come up in the spring. Maybe when that happens, I'll bring you more of them."

The pitter-patter of her heart was overwhelming. Didn't waiting for spring mean he was planning on her still being around? Was that what he wanted? Was it what she wanted?

Susan moved in closer to him. "I think they are lovely."

"Purple made me think of you."

"One of my favorite colors."

Eric raised his hand to her cheek and lingered it there. Susan pulled in a quick breath and looked up into his eyes. At that moment she knew she'd miss him if they went their separate ways. There was something about this man whom she met in his parents' kitchen that made her giddy to be around him. Even her ex-husband had never made her feel as she did when she was around Eric.

Perhaps that should be a warning she thought as she diverted her gaze to the flowers and then back to him. No. She wouldn't talk herself out of this. Whatever was happening between them could be real. At that moment she knew that was what she wanted. She wanted the love of a man. Oh, they were far from exchanging the words. In fact, she wasn't sure she felt love—lust perhaps, but there was something to grow on. That was for sure.

"What are you thinking?" he asked as his thumb brushed over her cheek.

Susan swallowed hard. "About how I feel when I'm around you."

When he smiled, there was a small dimple in his cheek. "And? How do you feel?"

"Alive," she said as she was very aware of the blood pumping through her veins at a quickened pace. "You make me feel things I haven't felt in a long time. Perhaps it's too early in our relationship—if this is indeed a relationship—to say something like that. But that's how I feel."

"Alive?"

"Yes."

His smiled widened as he stepped in, closing the small gap between them. "I think that echoes what I feel. I don't know that I could have found eloquent words to cover it as you did, but yeah, that's what I'm feeling."

Okay, that was a moment to never forget, she decided. Eric Walker didn't seem like the kind of man to have soft, gentle moments such as this one. However, he'd shared it with her. That was worth something.

Eric raised his other hand to her other cheek. "I have a lot going on in my life right now. Everything is unsure and it's consuming me."

She nodded, feeling the drop in sensation from the good to the bad. This was where he let her down gently. Where he told her that he has feelings for her, but it's not the right time. Susan pushed her shoulders back and braced for his words.

He dropped his head and placed a gentle kiss against her lips, his eyes locked on hers. "I'm very glad that you're here to distract me from the negative. I'd rather focus on what could be than on what has happened around me."

Perhaps it was wrong, but she needed to know what it all meant. "I'm just a distraction?"

His eyes opened wider. "No. That's not how I meant that."

She felt the wash of relief move through her.

Eric slid his hands down from her face and over her shoulders. "I'm not good at this. I never have been. But, there is something about you that makes me just want to forget about everything else and only focus on you. No one has ever made me feel like that. My home, my family, my business have always been the most important things in my life. But since I met you, that scale seems to have shifted." He let out a little chuckle. "I'm not one for deep, romantic conversations either. Looks like you bring out an entirely different side to me."

"It's been a long time since I was at the beginning of a relationship. Is that what we're building here? A commitment to each other?"

His hands slid down her arms and to her waist. "I'd like to try that."

She felt her hands begin to shake and a fear take over that quaked her at her core. "I want that. But as you can tell by my track record, I'm not very good at it."

Eric shook his head. "A ten year marriage is nothing to sneeze at. I don't see that as your failure."

Tears now stung her eyes and this wasn't a moment to cry. This was a moment to celebrate. "You don't?"

"Are you willing to completely stop loving because it didn't work out once? That's like saying you're willing to stop living because your marriage ended. But here you are. You're building something new for yourself—by yourself."

Pride in what she'd done over the past year filled in the hole that doubt had created. This was it.

Standing before her, Eric was validating everything she was doing. There hadn't been a morning in the past few years where she hadn't awakened feeling as though she'd lost track of who she was and where she was going. But now, just with his few simple words, she realized she had become who she'd sought out to be. She was independent. She was successful.

And now with Eric standing before her with his hands on her hips and limp tulips in her hand, she knew she'd moved on from the failure she thought she was.

If she was to ever fall in love again, he was the man worth falling in love with. There was simply no more doubt. Though doubt still resided in her. Saying she'd love him was something she'd need to evaluate much further. After all, she'd only met him, but it just felt so right.

Susan raised her arms around his neck and plunged them both into a kiss that had them clinging to each other as if every breath after that depended on that moment. The friction between them heated her throughout. Every moment his lips pressed to hers was another moment that she tumbled into a bliss she never thought she'd have again.

When they parted breathless, Eric pressed his forehead to hers. "We'd better go get breakfast. My mind is spinning in directions I hadn't planned on going yet and I still have a full day ahead of me."

Susan laughed a deep throaty laugh. "Me too. I have a very important meeting today and class tonight. But…" She looked up into his eyes. "If your mind is spinning where mine is, I think that's something we'd better think about."

The dimple in his cheek was back. "Thank God you're not some prude. I'm a man after all. Being a full fledged gentleman might kill me."

Susan cupped his cheek in her hand. "I don't want that to be on my conscience."

Chapter Fourteen

Breakfast had been simple at a diner she'd been to once or twice. Eric was the kind of man who enjoyed his breakfast meats and had them all on one plate. She preferred a lighter fare.

He was also a man, she quickly realized, who didn't like being in public. There was a comfort with him in his house or hers, but when faced with scrutinizing eyes he seemed to become quiet and reserved.

It didn't take a genius to realize that a man who lived away from town liked it that way. She'd seen him yesterday morning moving in to take care of his horses. There was peace with him. Over breakfast, however, he'd looked as if he were the cattle being sent to slaughter.

As soon as he could, he paid the check and they left the diner. He didn't mention that anything was wrong and Susan didn't ask, but she studied him. The closer they got to her house, the softer his tense shoulders became. And when he kissed her goodbye with her back pressed against the front door, she knew there wasn't anything wrong with that man that twisted her insides. But there was a story there, she decided as she watched him drive away. Perhaps he'd share it with her in time. After all, he'd seemed to be the one talking relationships. Maybe it was his way of telling her he trusted her with whatever was in his soul.

Susan looked down at her watch. She had her phone meeting with Lydia Morgan in an hour. As she walked toward her desk, her mind switched from the giddy, tingly feeling that new romance offered to the solid-minded businesswoman that had been the core of who she was for so long. After having met Lydia Morgan last night, Susan was sure that this could be a very big account to have. It would be best if she kept her mind about her.

An hour later, with the phone ringing in her hand, Susan took a deep breath and waited for Lydia Morgan to answer. On the fifth ring she finally did.

"Good morning, Ms. Hayes," Lydia's voice was steady and sure on the other end of the line. "Thank you for calling."

Susan, a bit dismayed by not having a simple hello, put a smile on her lips with hopes that it would convey through the phone.

"Ms. Morgan," she coolly offered the salutation. "My pleasure. I have sent you an email with my options and prices on them. Did you receive that?"

"Just now. Thank you. I will show this to my grandfather and let him decide." There was a moment of silence before Lydia spoke again. "Ms. Hayes…"

"Please call me Susan," she said still managing that smile that was supposed to resonate in her voice.

"My grandfather would not approve of that, Ms. Hayes," she began again, "my grandfather asks that our working together be held in the strictest of confidence. He would like your word that you will not mention the job or whom it is for."

Susan's shoulders dropped. This was beginning to sound like a bad Craig's List ad.

"That's not a problem, Ms. Morgan. I understand confidentiality."

"Good. He also asks that you not bring your new server, Ms. Waterbury."

The smile faded quickly. "May I ask why? She's very personable and extremely efficient."

"Yes, I met her last night and I agree. Those are his wishes."

She didn't like this one bit. The Morgans were going to have to spend a hefty amount of money if she wasn't to use her staff member or talk about them using her services.

"Understood. Do you have a date in mind for the event?"

"February sixteenth. Seven p.m. sharp."

Susan bit down on her lip. That was a night she'd have class. She wasn't going to turn the job away yet. There was something intriguing about the secretive way Lydia approached everything. She'd let the money talk for her. If the payday was going to be worth it, she'd miss class and leave Bethany behind. If they argued price, she'd pass on the job.

"I will put that on the calendar. Ms. Morgan, I'd like to follow up with you on Monday and discuss your menu choices and the cost of the event."

"That will be fine."

They set up a time, said their goodbyes, and Susan rested back in her chair.

Lydia Morgan wasn't as old as she'd sounded on the phone. She did come across as a bit dry in her personality, but Susan didn't buy into it. When she thought about it a bit more, she could see a lot of herself in Lydia. When Susan was married, she simply wasn't the person she was now. She watched her words and her mannerisms as if she were afraid to show herself. Her husband had his expectations of how his wife should act and she'd fallen right into the role.

It wasn't fair really to pin it all on Bret, her ex-husband. She'd allowed herself to be what he wanted her to be. She just hadn't realized, until ten years later, that it was killing her inside.

Was that Lydia's story too? Did her grandfather expect her to behave and present herself in such a dormant way?

Susan tapped her pen to her chin. She was going to friend Lydia Morgan.

The smile formed back on her lips, this time honestly.

The mystery intrigued her now. Who was Lydia Morgan under all the manners?

~*~

Eric gripped the steering wheel of his truck tightly as he bounced down the dirt road leading to his house. A bead of sweat trickled down his neck and he wiped it away with the palm of his hand.

What was he doing starting something up with some woman? He had a lot on his plate. Right now wasn't the time to lose focus by mixing in some boyish crush with the thought he might get sex. But he knew it was more than that. If he'd only wanted to be physical with someone, he had options. This was deeper. Susan was different.

Eric rolled his shoulders back and tried to ease the pinch between them. The conversation he'd had with his father yesterday over his uncle's gambling addiction pressed its way into his mind as his house came into view. They all sought to lose if Elias Morgan took over the property. He wondered how his cousins Jake, Todd, Pearl, and Audrey felt about their father's *betrayal*. Poor Bethany was so disconnected to all of it he wondered why she'd even stayed the few days she had. But then he realized she and Susan were kindred souls. They were both looking for something new and they'd found that in the strangest of places—his grandfather's funeral.

Regardless of what happened to his home, this was a turning point for his family. Eric vowed at that moment, to himself, that he'd take care of Bethany. It was obvious her father wasn't going to make her part of the family. A wave of disappointment washed over him when he realized that her brothers and sisters didn't seem to be making advances there either.

He still had a good mind to talk to Elias Morgan, with or without Smith and Wesson. However, he'd give it a few days and let his father and his lawyers continue to work on it a bit. Then he'd move in.

Eric knew he could build a house somewhere else. Georgia was big enough. Hell, if things worked out, he could move in with Susan—though the thought of city life left a vile taste in his mouth. But there were options. The one thing he wasn't going to let happen was the dismantling of his family.

It hadn't gone unnoticed to him that his father was looking worn down and weak. His brothers seemed to be on edge and he'd be damned if they ever moved his mother from the cemetery in which she rested. The Walkers were not going to be torn apart just because Byron was an idiot.

As Eric pulled up to his house, he had a sense of rejuvenation. The Walkers weren't going down without a fight.

Eric stepped out of the truck just as Dane ran around the side of the house from the barn.

"Whisky River," was all he said on a raspy breath from running.

Nothing more needed to be said. Eric ran toward the barn as quickly as he could with a panicked jolt running through his chest.

When they arrived, Whiskey River was lying still, on his side. His breathing was labored.

"What happened to him?" Eric knelt down next to him, brushing his coat with his hand.

"I don't know. I came out here looking for you and I found him this way. He looks really sick."

"No, shit!" Eric ran his hand over the horse's body looking for traces of a bite or a cut. "Get on the phone. Call Dr. Parks. Tell him it's an emergency."

Dane nodded and ran for the office.

Eric sat down next to Whisky River's head and ran his hand down his nose. "C'mon, ole man. Hold on there. We'll get you fixed."

He pressed his head to the horse's and a tear fell from his eye. Nothing had been as precious to him over the years as the horse, which lay next to him, struggling to breathe. How sad was he to have only had a relationship with a horse? But that's what it was. They'd built his business together, he and his trusty horse. He couldn't lose him now.

Eric was aware of the other horses in the barn. There was restlessness among them. Something had set them off, he thought. Was it more than Whiskey River falling sick?

He gave the horse another pat and stood to survey the stalls. Each horse was there, but they neighed and moved between their walls as if they had something to say.

There was a huge responsibility to him to keep the other horses calm and safe. They were his business.

Dane ran out of the office. "He's on his way."

"Check out that mare on the end. Raven Wing. Make sure she's calm."

Dane gave him a nod and ran toward the horse, which reared up on her hind legs just as Dane reached her. Her front hooves caught him on the jaw knocking him back into the wall of the barn.

Eric ran toward the horse, grabbing a rope off the wall as he passed. The horse spun circles in her stall as Eric approached. Her eyes were wild and a moment later she too collapsed onto her side.

"What the hell?" Eric moved in, dropped the rope, and touched the horse. She too labored at her breathing.

The groan behind him reminded him that his brother was hurt. He turned to see Dane on his hands and knees, blood pouring from his chin.

"Christ, you need a doctor."

"You think?" Dane stayed on all fours as if he too couldn't move. "Damn horse. I don't think she broke my jaw, but I'm going to need stitches," he said as he turned to sit on the ground.

Dane pulled his outer shirt off and pressed it to his jaw.

"You're going to have one hell of a black eye too."

"What happened to them? This isn't normal."

Eric continued to pet the mare as she fought to breathe. "I don't know. I don't see any bite marks or cuts."

He pulled his phone from his pocket and called Ben. They needed help and Dane needed a hospital.

Within ten minutes, Ben and Russell had both arrived. Russell, the brother with the queasiest of stomachs, helped Dane to his truck and headed toward the hospital.

Ben moved through the stalls and checked the other horses. "They all seem fine."

"Whiskey River?"

"He's fighting," Ben said as Dr. Parks's truck pulled through the large door to the barn.

Eric moved toward him swiftly. "I have two horses down. No bite marks, no earlier signs of sickness."

Dr. Parks nodded. "Were they together?"

"No. The mare on the end is a boarded horse. Her owner usually works her out every day."

"What symptoms?" he asked as he knelt down next to Whiskey River with his medical bag.

"This is how he was when I got here. Dane found him like this. Raven Wing was agitated and then she completely freaked out. She kicked Dane in the face and then she collapsed."

Dr. Parks looked up at him. "Dane? Is he okay?"

"Russell just took him into town to get stitches. He's going to look nasty for a few weeks."

With a nod, Dr. Parks went about his assessment. Eric stood and looked around the barn. The horses seemed to have settled down. Ben sat with Raven Wing, but the look on his face when he made eye contact with Eric, wasn't promising.

What had gotten to his horses? It was obvious his lack of focus toward his animals and his business had caused this in some way.

Regret buried into his gut. He was responsible for this.

Chapter Fifteen

Eric brushed his hand over the top of his head and slid his hat back on, low over his brow. He, Ben, and Russell had taken turns staying up with the horses all night and he was exhausted.

This was the life he'd chosen—the animals, the land, the responsibility to others to keep their animals safe. He'd failed.

Raven Wing had succumbed around one in the morning. Her owners had been with her at the end, but Eric still had to face them.

Whiskey River hung on and Eric still wasn't sure he'd pull through.

The truck was there to collect the fallen horse. In the corner a young girl, Emily, cried. Her parents stood huddled with Dr. Parks as Eric approached them.

"Eric, I'm glad you're here," Dr. Parks watched him approach with weary eyes.

Mr. and Mrs. Wilson, Raven Wing's owners, shifted their hard glances to him as he joined them.

"Mr. and Mrs. Wilson, I'm so sorry for your loss. We'll get to the bottom of this. I promise you," Eric offered, hoping to give them comfort.

"I think we might have," Dr. Parks said. "I drew blood from both horses last night. They weren't bitten by anything and it wasn't an illness that took down the horses. These horses were poisoned."

Eric felt his heart stop in his chest. "Someone did this to my animals?"

Dr. Parks nodded. "Do you have surveillance here?"

Eric winced. "No. I've never needed it."

"You should have," Mrs. Wilson snapped. "You should know who comes and goes from here. Someone killed our daughter's horse and now she's heartbroken. You can't fix that, Mr. Walker."

Eric turned and looked toward Whiskey River's stall where his brother sat with the horse. He understood their pain. No, he couldn't fix that.

Three hours later Eric had talked to the police. The other horses, which he'd boarded, were relocated and Whiskey River clung to life.

Russell walked up behind him as he watched Dr. Parks evaluate Whiskey River.

"Dad just called," Russell said resting his hand on Eric's shoulder. "There are three cows down in the west field."

Eric closed his eyes and let his shoulders drop.

"Elias has gone too far this time."

"You don't know it's him."

Eric turned toward his brother. Heat seared in his veins. "You're going to stand there and tell me it's not him? We're contesting him getting this land. It's just like him to do something like this. Just like he turned his own flesh and blood away when she chose to love a man he didn't approve of."

"You're making this all about you. Maybe it's not."

He gave Russell a shove. "Get out of my face. I'm going over there and I will knock the first man that tries to stop me on his ass ."

Russell stepped aside as Eric hurried toward his truck.

Dirt kicked up as he sped away from the barn and headed toward the Morgan's house for the very first time in his entire life.

A mere ten miles from his front door, he crested the hill and the grand house came into view.

Son-of-a-bitch he thought as he looked at the house. Someone who could afford such a place needed more space? He needed to destroy the very existence of the Walkers?

The speedometer on the old truck bounced between 75 and 80. Eric simply couldn't get there fast enough.

At the turn, Eric skidded his truck through the arched, iron gateway. Some people were full of themselves. How was it that his mother had come from this family? It was no surprise that she had left.

The circle drive in front of the house was filled with cars. It was no surprise to find his uncle's car there, but to find his father's—that threw him into a state that he couldn't even wrap his head around.

Eric slammed on his brakes and stopped just inches from his uncle's back bumper. He could have cared less about destroying the man's car, but it would have been a shame to put a dent in the truck.

A woman ran from the side of the house. "You could kill someone driving like that. Who do you think you are?"

He had no idea who the woman who stood perhaps just inches over five feet with the short wispy hair was, but she was familiar enough to him. There was a resemblance to his mother in her and that ached in his chest. Whoever she was, he was probably related to her.

"I'm Eric Walker and I'm looking for Elias Morgan, and I'm not leaving until I talk to him."

Her eyes opened wide and she stopped a mere foot from him. The anger seemed to defuse in her eyes—eyes that matched his mother's.

"Eric," she said softly.

"Where is he? I have little patience to sit here and have discussions with total strangers."

Her mouth dropped open. "He's busy right now."

Eric looked around at all the cars. "I see that. You know what, I'll find him my damn self."

He pushed past her. His long legs took him closer to the house as she turned to jog after him. "Eric, wait. You can't go in there. Eric!" She shouted just as a man opened the front door and stepped out.

"What's going on?"

The woman caught up to him. She panted for breath. "He's looking for grandpa," she said and that had Eric tightening his jaw.

So she was a cousin. What a way to meet kin.

"You're not going anywhere," the man said as he moved toward Eric. "Why don't you get back into that piece of crap truck of yours and go home."

Anger boiled inside of Eric, but the words to argue wouldn't surface. He simply couldn't take his eyes off the man in front of him.

They stood eye to eye. All six foot, four inches of them were the same—the same build, the same eyes, and obviously the same fever to be in charge of the situation.

"I'm not leaving until I talk to Elias."

The man's eyes narrowed on him. "You'll have to go through me."

"Are you sure that's what you want?" Eric grit his teeth and fisted his hands at his side.

The man smiled. "Like I said, you're not going in unless you go through me."

The anger that had balled up inside Eric released into his veins. He pushed into the man with all intent to push past him, only to find the man's shoulder forcing itself into his shoulder. A moment later the man's hands were on his chest pushing him back.

"I'm trying to save you from yourself. Go home."

Eric shook his head and charged toward the man. He could hear the woman behind them squeal and beg them to stop, but it was too late.

The man threw the first punch, which landed right in Eric's gut. Forcing himself to not hunch over, he brought his right fist up with an uppercut to the man's jaw, knocking him off balance for only a moment before the man opened a full assault on him.

Eric was only aware that the woman had run inside the house yelling. Both men continued their battery of the other. Eric had been hit in the eye, the cheek, the mouth—but he'd landed just as many punches on the man who looked so similar to him.

"Break it up. Break it up!" He heard his father's voice say and a moment later two sets of arms pried the men apart.

Each of them hunched over to catch their breath.

Eric's cheek and lip stung and his eye was freaking going to swell shut. He spit blood on the ground and felt the wave of nausea roll through him. He was not going to puke. He'd die before he did something cowardly like that in front of relatives he'd never met.

When he could focus, he saw Elias Morgan in the doorway of the house.

"No good will ever come from him being here," he said, his words directly aimed at Eric.

Eric spat more blood on the ground.

"Grandpa, you shouldn't speak like that to people," the soft voice of the woman came from behind Elias. "He's kin."

"Not mine." Elias turned and walked back into the house.

It was incredible how hollow two words could make a man feel, Eric thought.

"What are you doing?" His father moved toward him resting his hand on his shoulder. "What have you gotten into?"

"They poisoned the horses. They poisoned the cattle. He wants the land, Dad. He wants to move mom. They're trying to run us out. I'm not going to stand for that."

His father shook his head. "Go home."

Eric opened his eyes as wide as he could and focused them on his father. "I'm not going to lose everything I've built because some old man has a grudge against you."

"Go home, Eric."

His father's even tone still could stop him at forty. He didn't like how weak it made him feel.

But when his father gave him a nod and that simple look it said that things were under control. Everett Walker had obviously taken care of the matter at hand. It didn't calm Eric. He'd like to have taken a few more shots at the man who was now being comforted by the woman.

Eric pressed the back of his hand to his eye. "I'm not losing my home. They cost me my business today. I'm not giving up on this."

"Go home," his father said softly, but sternly. He then turned to the others. "Lydia and Tyson, tell your grandfather I will be back in the morning. We're not done discussing things."

The woman nodded. Eric's father pressed his hands to Eric's shoulder and turned him toward his truck.

"Go home and get washed up. I'll be there in an hour."

The tone was the same as when he was a child in trouble. There was an angry undertone beneath the calm exterior. Though this time Eric thought it might not be because he'd been fighting with some unknown cousin, but it might be because his own father was equally as angry.

Eric gave him a nod, opened the door to his truck, and climbed in.

His father walked toward his car, but waited for Eric to drive away before he climbed in. Eric could see him follow him out of the gates of the Morgan's estate.

Why was his father taking this in stride? They were killing off animals—their business. They couldn't sit by and watch the Morgans destroy what they'd built—or destroy them.

The shower Eric took actually hurt. His knuckles were bruised and so was his shoulder. His left eye was nearly swollen shut and the gash on his lip was going to have him choosing his food wisely for the next week.

When he'd slipped on a new pair of jeans, he pulled on a worn out T-shirt and headed to the living room to gather his hat. He needed to check on Whiskey River.

His father's presence on his couch should have startled him, but deep down he'd expected him.

"I have to check on Whiskey River," he said moving toward his boots.

"You have a few minutes. Sit," his father demanded without looking up at him.

Eric sucked in a breath and moved to the chair across from his father.

Everett Walker was built just like Eric. He was tall and sturdy, but he could contain his feelings without punching people. Eric seemed to be still learning that.

His father's arms rested on his knees and his fingers were steepled. This meant he was deep in thought.

"I don't want you going over to the Morgan's again, do I make myself clear?"

"I need answers."

"Do I make myself clear?"

Eric bit down. "Yes."

"Elias had nothing to do with the misfortune we've had."

"Misfortune?" The word had Eric shooting up out of his chair. "Horses are dead. Cattle are dead. Misfortune?"

"Sit," his father said calmly and Eric did so. "I've known Elias my whole life. If he says he didn't do something, he didn't. Besides he has legitimate alibis for his whereabouts the past few days."

"So he paid someone. He certainly wouldn't have done that himself." Even Eric knew that.

"Don't go back there," his father said as he rose and Eric followed. "Byron messed up, but I keep my word. No one will suffer. Not Byron, not you, and not Elias Morgan."

"How can you care about him?"

"He's part of you, Eric. That's blood."

His father's words stung as badly as the cut on his lip. "Who were the others? Lydia and Tyson?"

"Your mother had a brother who was killed in combat in Desert Storm. Lydia and Tyson are his children."

"I can't believe I live ten miles from family I've never met."

His father nodded. "Elias was very clear on that matter many years ago. I wonder if he'd reconsider now." He moved toward the door. "You do have your gun nearby don't you?"

"Always," Eric said slowly. "Why?"

"I believe our problems are not Elias Morgan, but that troubles me too. Because I don't know who is behind all of this. Protect yourself," he said as he opened the door and walked out of the house.

Eric watched as his father drove away, then put on his hat and walked out to the barn.

Ben was sitting with Whiskey River now and Dr. Parks hovered over him.

"It won't be long now," Dr. Parks said and Eric felt the heaviness of grief swell in his chest. "He's comfortable though."

Eric moved toward the large animal that lay in his stall on his side. He knelt down next to his nose and gently stroked him.

"I'm sorry buddy," he said as a tear welled in his eye. "I'll avenge this."

Ben looked at him. "You know who did this?"

Eric bit down on his lower lip. "Not yet, but someone will pay for it."

Whisky River nudged Eric's hand with his nose as if to say goodbye and then he was gone.

Chapter Sixteen

Susan dropped her purse and bag into the oversized chair in the living room and then plopped herself into the loveseat. It had been a long day.

She smiled, though, when she thought of breakfast with Eric. That had made the day go by perhaps a little better.

"You're home late," Bethany said as she walked through the doorway with two cups of tea.

Susan was sure she jumped a bit. She was still getting used to another person living in her house.

"Some night's classes just go a little longer."

Bethany handed her a cup of tea. "I did my bedtime yoga and I was still too awake. I thought this would help."

"You do yoga before bedtime?"

Bethany nodded as she took a sip from her cup. "Yes. It's wonderful. I could teach you some if you'd like."

"Maybe someday." Susan sipped from her cup. "Let's see, you run, you do yoga, and you sip tea. Is this all Hollywood stuff?"

The question had flustered Bethany a bit, that was obvious by the tightening of her lips and then the forced smile. "You always have to look your best."

"You're not in Hollywood anymore."

"Can't let go of myself. What if I get a call tomorrow?"

"Will that happen?"

Bethany eased down on the loveseat next to Susan. "It might. I have some contacts."

"Do you want that to happen?" she asked, reading more into Bethany's answer.

"I don't know. Right now what I'd like to do is get to know my family."

"It sounds like you'll get to do that at Sunday dinner."

Bethany nodded. "I'd like to get to know my brothers and sisters though. I'm sure we'll work into that." She sipped her tea again and then looked up with wide eyes. "I did get a call from Dane today. He said he was at the hospital."

"What happened?"

"Got kicked in the face by a scared horse or something. Ten stitches across his jaw."

Susan winced. "That's horrible. Is he okay?"

Bethany shrugged. "I'm sure he is. It was nice he thought to tell me. It made me feel like a part of the family."

"You are a part of it. I suppose in this time of loss everyone is just a bit out of sorts. I know when my grandfather died it took me a while to get over it."

Bethany smiled. "I suppose that's it." She took another sip of her tea. "I think this is working. I'm going to head to bed. See you in the morning," she said as she rose from the loveseat and walked out of the room.

Susan leaned back, tucked her legs up under her, and cradled the cup in her hands. She thought about her grandfather. She missed him still. They'd had many adventures together. He was the first one to ever eat something she baked. She'd baked him a cake in her Holly Hobby oven.

Perhaps that was what Eric was going through. What memories did he have of his grandfather that made him who he was?

Susan let her head fall from side to side stretching out the muscles in her neck. Maybe she would let Bethany show her some of those yoga moves after all. The tea had seemed to calm her and she too was ready for bed.

Kicking her feet out from under her she stood and walked to the kitchen. She rinsed out the cup and set it in the sink. She turned off the lights and as she walked toward the stairs she noticed someone walking up the front steps. The figure looked like a man through the frosted glass.

She glanced at the clock. It was eleven. There was no reason anyone should be at the door that late.

Fear crept into her throat as she contemplated yelling for Bethany.

The person tapped on the door. "Susan. Are you in there?"

She tiptoed closer to the door.

"It's Eric if you can hear me."

She quickly moved to the door and pulled it open.

He was leaning with his hands on either side of the doorjamb. His head was down and his face shadowed by the porch light behind him.

"What are you doing here? I didn't expect you."

He didn't speak but slowly lifted his head.

The moment she saw his face she covered her mouth to stifle the gasp. "Oh, God! What happened to you?"

She reached for his hand and pulled him through the door. Lifting on her tiptoes she pulled off his cowboy hat and studied him in the dim light.

"Did you get kicked by a horse too?" she asked as she reached her hand to his face.

"I wish. How did you know about that?"

"Dane called Bethany today and told her. He was checking in on her."

Eric nodded. "Can I stay for a bit?"

"Yes, yes." She pulled him in further and shut the door behind him. "C'mon, let's get something on that eye."

She hurried to the kitchen and pulled a frozen bag of peas from the freezer. Gathering the dishtowel from the handle of the oven, she wrapped the peas inside the towel. "Sit."

He let out a small chuckle and did as she said. "I have a lot of people telling me what to do today."

Susan moved to him, positioning herself between his long legs, and pressing the bag to his eye. He winced again. "Does it hurt?"

"Only when you touch it."

She should have let him take the bag from her and hold it, but she didn't want to move. Deciding to stand there, very intimately in front of him, she placed her other hand on his shoulder.

He looked up at her with the uncovered eye. "You look beautiful."

That made her laugh. "My hair is in a knot on my head and I have flour on my clothes. I don't know what you're talking about."

Eric lifted his hands to her hips and she sucked in a breath. "Thanks for letting me in. I've had a crappy day and about an hour ago I realized that I didn't want to wallow in it any longer. I wanted to see you."

Susan licked her lips and gazed down into his dark eyes. "What happened to you today?"

Eric raised his hand to the bag and pulled it from his eye. Laying it on the table, he turned back and took her hands in his. "I lost my horse today."

"Oh, Eric." Her voice cracked as she said it. "I'm so sorry."

He nodded. "Lost a mare too and four head of cattle by the time the day was over. My business officially is shut down since I had to move out the rest of the horses. I found out they'd been poisoned."

"That's horrible. Who would do something like that?"

"I have my ideas, but I'm told I'm wrong. Anyway, I met family I didn't know about. Specifically my cousin."

"That's good, right?"

"Sure. I met him when he punched me in the gut, which obviously was the beginning of the fight I got into."

Susan moved in closer to him. "I think you're right. You had a crappy day."

"It started nice though," he said softly.

Susan pulled back and looked down at his swollen eye, and cut lip. "I was thinking that before you arrived."

"You know what would make my lip better?"

"What?" she said breathlessly.

"If you kissed me—softly," he added.

His hands were on her hips again and she steadied herself by placing her hands on his shoulders. "Are you sure about that? I don't want to hurt you."

"At this moment, I think it would hurt more if you didn't kiss me."

Susan gently cupped his face in her hands and tipped her head to press a soft kiss to his lip. "How is that?"

"Feels better already."

She kissed him again, this time lingering a moment longer. When she pulled back, she gazed down into his eyes.

Eric nodded. "Yeah, that's doing the trick," he said smiling. He maneuvered himself so that now she was straddling both of his legs and he eased her down onto his lap so that their chests pressed against the other's and their mouths were exactly even so they could deepen the kiss.

Susan wrapped her arms around his neck and he wrapped his arms around her waist. It was so much more intimate than ever before and she found herself sinking into him, wanting more.

Eric's hands slid up her back and she let the moan that stirred in her ease out.

Cupping her hands over his face she deepened the already heated kiss only to have him jerk away.

"Oh, God! I hurt you. I'm so sorry." Susan pulled her hands back.

"I guess it's sorer than I thought."

"We should really put those peas back on your eye."

Eric groaned. "Is that really where we're going? My day was getting better."

"You're hurt. You should rest."

Eric pressed his forehead to hers. "Sleep in my arms. Let me wake to you beside me and for a few moments in the morning I'll have forgotten what transpired today."

"You want to sleep here?"

The corner of his mouth curled upward. "I do."

Susan nodded. If she wanted to take hold of her life, right now was the moment. She'd known him nearly a week and now she was contemplating him sleeping in her bed. Oh, who was she kidding? There was no contemplation of sleeping going on in her head and she was damn sure it wasn't the only thought going through his either.

Was this what she wanted? After ten years of monogamous matrimonial sex, was she ready to move onto another man whom she'd only just met?

Eric skimmed his hand up her back again and she gazed into his wanting eyes. She didn't know much about him. He was a bit standoffish and perhaps a little crabby. And look at him. His face was a mess because he'd gotten into a fight. All signs pointed to her needing to get off his lap and let him out the front door.

But she couldn't do that. There was so much more here. Was this just letting go of her past? Would he be a fleeting moment in her life? No. She didn't actually believe that. Eric Walker was something more—something she wanted to still discover.

Eric's hands moved to her arms. "You're shaking. Susan, we don't have to do this. I can go home. I wouldn't be walking out. I don't want to pressure…"

"I want this," she said and meant it. "I do."

The smile now lit in his eyes. "I'll take care of you."

Nervously, Susan stood, and taking his hand, she pulled him to his feet. A million words filled her head, but none of them would string into the perfect sentence to explain how she felt. It would be better if she simply walked him up to her bedroom, shut the door, and let them figure out what they were feeling without the use of any of those words. Words were suddenly overrated. All Susan wanted to do was feel.

His fingers intertwined with hers as she led him up the stairs. With each step, she took a quick breath and willed her rapid heart to slow down, but it was no use.

Only moonlight glowed under Bethany's door a she tiptoed by to her room. When she pushed open the door her own room was filled with brilliant light from the window.

It cast a silver shimmer over the room and she heard the door close and lock behind her.

Susan turned to see Eric leaned up against the door. His bruises and cuts were darker in the shadows.

"You're beautiful in the moonlight," he said, his voice in a low, sensual growl.

"Thank you." She watched him grip the doorknob with his hands behind his back. "Aren't you going to come in?"

She watched as the white of his smile gleamed in the dark. "I'm afraid that if I let go of this door I'll want to touch you. I know you said you'd sleep in my arms, but…"

Susan controlled her breathing and calmed her mind. Then she walked too him and rested her hands on his chest. With slow, deliberate movements, she began to unsnap his shirt. When it hung open, she pushed it back. He moved from the door and his shirt slid off his arms and down to the floor.

"I guess you shouldn't worry too much about it. I'm thinking maybe we should work on making ourselves tired," she said as she slid her hands over his firm chest."

She felt the rise of his breath as it caught in his lungs. "Are you sure that's what you want?"

Susan nodded, perhaps a little to eagerly. "Yes."

Without another word, Eric hoisted her to his hips. Her legs wrapped around him and his mouth took possession of hers.

Every part of her heated in response to him as he carried her to the bed and gently laid her down. "If you change your mind…"

She reached behind his neck and inched her face to his. "I won't," she promised as she pulled him back atop of her and let the course of the night lead them into passion, pleasure as they took their time undressing each other and learning every curve and every muscle of the other.

Eric pleased her with kisses in places she had never thought to be sensual. And when he took her under him and their bodies came together, Susan knew the night had become more than comfort for each of them. They had tumbled into bed and into something so much bigger.

Chapter Seventeen

Eric watched her in the moonlight. Silently, Susan slept in his arms, just as he'd asked her to do.

Sleep eluded him. There was too much to think about to sleep, but she'd eased his worry and for that he was grateful. She didn't even know what she'd done for him by agreeing to just let him in the house last night. Actually making love to her hadn't even been in his plans when he'd driven to her house, but he was grateful for it.

He needed someone who could just make the pain go away for a while. Any woman could have done that—caused a distraction. Susan, on the other hand, seemed invested in him.

They hadn't said one word to each other from the moment she took his hand and led him to her bedroom. It had become pure emotion that had fueled them and guided them.

The pain, which riddled his body, had faded with her kisses—her touches. Even thinking about it had his breath coming quicker. She'd guided him—not the other way around. Susan had initiated their lovemaking, which only made him want her even more. It went far past sexual—he was feeling things for her he'd never felt for any other woman.

She stirred and nuzzled her head closer to his chest. He fought to not wake her and take her again. He needed to feel that connection that making love to her had brought him.

It wasn't fair to her. None of this was fair to her. The urge to tell her his deepest feelings was suppressed by the darkness that seemed to loom over him.

He had nothing.

His business was a loss. It was only a matter of time before he lost his home. There was family drama where he was concerned and why would any woman want to take that on? No, something told him this was a fleeting moment of passion—though that wasn't what he wanted.

Eric pressed a kiss to the top of her head, which woke her. With her eyes still closed she smiled. "Why are you awake?" she whispered.

"Just can't sleep."

"You should be exhausted," she said on a small laugh.

She was precious he thought, as he brushed a strand of hair from her forehead.

"Go back to sleep," he said softly.

Susan slowly opened her eyes. They were still dark and filled with need, he thought. She pressed her hands to his chest and rolled him onto his back. A moment later she was straddling him. Her hair curtained her face, but as his eyes closed by the very pleasure of feeling her again, it didn't matter. He had her face memorized.

His hands came to her hips as she rocked atop of him. The words he was thinking teetered on the tip of his tongue as she worked him over the edge and he only allowed quiet whimpers to escape his throat. A few minutes later Susan collapsed against him, her breath ragged, her skin moist.

"I'm enjoying having you right here," she said breathlessly.

"I didn't come over tonight, for this reason," he said to assure her.

"Oh, but I'm so glad you did."

Eric had rested, briefly. As the sun barely crested the horizon, he found himself restless.

He wiggled out of the bed without disturbing her, pulled on his pants, and quietly walked down to the kitchen.

Coffee. He needed coffee before he could even think about making the long drive back to his place. He still had responsibilities, even if they didn't include Whiskey River or any of the other horses.

The very thought caught in his chest and he had to suck in a breath to fill his lungs. What would he do without his horse and his business? He'd never given up before, but he was sure thinking about doing that now.

The kitchen light turned on and Eric spun to see his cousin leaned up against the doorjamb. Her long hair was pulled back and she was sporting running shoes and matching attire.

"I thought I'd heard your voice last night," she said grinning. But her face then went serious. "What the hell happened to your face?"

"Nothing."

"Bull!" She moved in toward him. "Did you get kicked too? Dane was a mess."

"It would have been better to have been kicked by a horse. This was kin caused."

"One of your brothers?" He shook his head and she inched in closer. "One of mine?"

"A cousin I had the pleasure of meeting yesterday when I accused our grandfather of poisoning our horses and cattle."

Bethany reached for him. "Eric, I didn't know."

He shook his head. "Your dad really did a job on this family," he said before realizing how horrible it sounded. "I'm sorry. I shouldn't…"

"It's okay. I'm not him, Eric. I'll never hurt you or your family."

"I know that." He looked at her again. "Are you going running?"

"Every morning."

"Can you find me coffee before you head out?"

She crossed her arms in front of her and grinned. "Tell me why you're here first."

"Do I really need to?"

"I really like her. You're not just using her for sex are you? I mean, I know it's not my business, but..."

"I'd never do that to anyone," he said firmly. "After the day I had yesterday I couldn't think of anywhere else I wanted to be. I needed her. Not just sexually."

"Are you in love with her?"

Eric cleared his throat. "Let's talk about where the coffee is."

She nodded, but the grin said she understood him better than he probably understood himself.

As Bethany gathered the items for his coffee, he inventoried what he was feeling. Yes, he was very sure he did indeed love Susan. But until he knew what he could offer her he'd keep that to himself. He still wasn't sure she'd want to stick around when she learned of all the troubles he'd bring to the relationship.

Susan woke with a start and sat up in bed. She pulled the sheet up over her naked body and looked around the empty bedroom. She was alone.

Quickly she picked up her cell phone and looked at the time. It was only six-fifteen. Had he run out that quickly?

She took a deep breath. He had obligations on his land. She'd surely be disappointed if she thought he'd stick around all day. Just because they'd made love she couldn't expect...

She heard heavy footsteps in the hallway and a moment later he pushed open the bedroom door with his elbow and carried in two cups of coffee.

He only wore his jeans and she thought perhaps she'd never seen a sexier specimen in her life.

"I thought maybe you had second thoughts and left," she admitted as he handed her a cup. "Thank you."

"I'm usually up much earlier. I couldn't sleep. Bethany helped me get the coffee started." He sat down next to her and studied her.

"Bethany," she said on a sigh. "What did she have to say?"

"Nothing much. She wanted to make sure I wasn't just using you for sex."

The very thought caught her off guard. "She said that?"

He nodded before taking a careful sip of his coffee. "She really likes you and doesn't want me hurting you."

"That's nice."

Eric lifted his hand to her cheek. "I really like you too. I have no plans on hurting you. Last night was really nice. I didn't come here to sleep with you."

"You said that."

"I feel as though I need to make it very clear."

She was fine with that. She seemed to need to hear it now that she was the only one naked on the bed. "I don't expect you to drive into town all the time. You need to know that. I won't be calling and texting you all the time wondering where you are."

"That's disappointing."

Susan's mouth dropped open. "Eric, I'm not some bothersome little girl. I really like what we have going. But we're adults trying to build lives. I just don't want you to think I'm going to be…"

He pressed his finger to her lips. "I don't have any expectations except that I want to get to know you much better. And damn, I really want to have some more nights like we had last night. Perhaps on better terms," he added. "Don't discredit me yet. I'm very interested in creating something here."

Susan sucked in a breath and forced herself to sip the coffee in her hand to keep from tearing up.

"I assume you have to head home."

Eric nodded. "I do. I want to see you later. Are you free tonight?"

"I actually am."

"Good. Will you come out and stay with me?"

The smile tugged at her lips and came straight from her heart. "I would love to."

Eric let out a loud breath. "Good. I'll try not to get beat up before you get there." He laughed as he stood and picked up his shirt from the floor, but Susan felt that uncertainty weigh heavy in her gut.

"Eric, you don't think someone will hurt you again, do you?"

"We have a lot going on right now. I don't know what to expect," he said as he pulled on his shirt. "But trust me, I'll protect what's mine. My family. My house." He leveled his eyes on her. "You. I'd never let anything happen to you."

"Are you in some kind of danger?" The words shook as she said them. What had she gotten involved with—who had she gotten involved with?

Eric sat down on the bed. "No. I don't think so. I promise to fill you in on everything tonight. I don't want you to worry. None of my family's problems have anything to do with us."

He pressed a gentle kiss to her lips before he stood.

"I'll see you tonight. Whenever you get the chance, come on out."

Susan nodded and watched as he walked out of her bedroom. A few moments later she heard the front door open and close and then the unmistakable grumble of his truck.

She set her cup next to his on the nightstand and fell back onto the bed.

There was something going on that was deeper than a family's grief over a lost grandfather. She squeezed her eyes shut. The last man she'd fallen in love with belittled her every move and that stemmed from the family he was born into. Was it worth getting involved with another man who had family issues?

It was then she remembered the dinner she was invited to on Sunday. Perhaps that would give her a clear picture of Eric's family. Maybe then she'd understand what she'd fallen into.

Susan pressed her hands to her bare stomach to calm the butterflies that had her so jumpy. She couldn't help but hope she was just being paranoid because very deep inside of her she wanted Eric to be that perfect match she'd always known was out there for her.

Chapter Eighteen

A day without his horse hurt more than Eric could have imagined. But another night with Susan wrapped in his arms had been just what the doctor had ordered.

She'd brought him a gift when she'd arrived with a tin pan of spaghetti and meatballs, just for him.

Now on his mantel was the picture she'd taken that morning in the barn, of him and Whiskey River. It was priceless, Eric thought in the early morning light of the quiet Saturday morning. She'd captured them interacting just as they always did, but the depth even had nearly brought him to tears.

In the past two days, he'd tried to remind himself he was just a horse. But he'd been more than that. They'd been a team and now a part of him was missing.

Susan moved in behind him and wrapped her arms around him. "I'm going to have to learn to wake up earlier," she said softly with her cheek pressed to his back.

"It's nice to wake with you next to me," Eric said turning and gathering her in his arms. "Looks like it's going to be foggy today."

"It'll be a good day to snuggle up to a fire then."

"I have to go check on the cattle."

She nodded. "I know your work is never done. I'll make breakfast for you and be here when you get back."

Eric kissed the top of her head. "I'd like that."

A half hour later, Eric was driving the fields in his truck and missing Whiskey River more than he had the morning before. He drove the fence line and noted that the fence they'd fixed earlier that week was still holding. It seemed strange that one simple fence was the border between the

Morgans and the Walkers. And that made him think of his mother.

Of course, she'd been on his mind a lot. The older he became, the more faint a memory she'd become, until he'd met Lydia on the front step of the Morgan house. In her face, he could see his mother again. Lydia had her eyes, the pout of her lips, and the same build in body as he remembered as a child. Why didn't that comfort him?

Eric stopped the truck and put it into park. He closed his eyes and thought about her voice. He almost couldn't hear it anymore. The words *Eric darling* still resonated in his mind in her voice, but those were the only words. A tear slid down his cheek and he quickly wiped it clear. He missed her terribly.

"Why is all of this happening?" he asked aloud as if he were asking her. He opened his eyes. "What do I do?"

Suddenly the fog seemed to push away as if to let the sun shine down on only him. He breathed in the peace.

For that very moment the thought of losing his home didn't feel so daunting because Susan would still be there—he felt that. His horse, which had been his trusty companion, was a great loss, but Susan was there to comfort him. He hadn't yet grieved his grandfather's death—because of Susan.

There was nothing the Morgans could do that would defeat him. Hurt him emotionally, maybe, but he couldn't help but believe that Susan had somehow been sent to him.

As the sun was again covered by the fog, Eric decided to head back to the house. He figured he'd done what he needed to do for today and for the first time in twenty years he was going to take the rest of the day off.

Susan was grateful for that loud truck of Eric's. She was able to plan his breakfast and have it ready for him as he drove from the barn toward the house.

She hadn't started a fire in years, but she'd managed one in the fireplace in the living room. It took the chill out of the air and certainly made the house homier.

It had been a very long time since she'd learned the preferences of a new man. Her ex-husband was a simple breakfast man. He liked fruit and oatmeal before he rode for twenty miles. Eric, she'd already learned was a little more traditional. He liked eggs and breakfast meats, which she couldn't quite wrap her head around. He'd enjoyed a hearty plate of waffles at the diner the other morning as well.

She chuckled to herself as she slid the eggs from the pan. For having only known the man almost a week, she'd had breakfast with him an awful lot. She never would have imagined that when he came slamming his way into Glenda's kitchen that day, she'd want to always wake in his arms either.

Eric's truck was right in front of the house now as she set the plates on the table and turned back to gather the coffee mugs.

Eric walked through the door carrying the cold on him. He hung up his hat, shrugged out of his coat and hung it up, then toed off his boots leaving them on the mat. This was obviously his process she decided.

"I have a feast laid out for you," she said smiling.

"I'm hungry enough for that. Hopefully, my brothers will keep away today. I'd like to have you to myself. So you can feed me that is."

She laughed as he walked into the kitchen. "If they showed up I'd be obligated to feed them too. It's how I work."

"Don't let them know that. You'll never get away from them."

"Can't be so bad," she said sitting down at the table.

Eric picked up a piece of bacon and bit it as he sat down. "It's not so bad—I guess."

"My sister moved to California for college and stayed there. So I'd give anything for her to just drop in and eat."

"Dane will be the first to move away, further than a few hours away," Eric said as he spooned eggs on his plate.

"Where is he going?"

"Ohio," his voice dropped as he said it. "He's not too excited."

"Why? That's awesome."

Eric shrugged as he took a bite of his eggs. "He's a homeboy. I mean he's still living at home with Dad and Glenda." He washed down the eggs with a sip of coffee. "Okay, to be fair he's living there with the intent to make this move. When his lease was up he moved home."

"It's nice that your parents have the room for him."

"Him and Russell."

"They both live at home?"

"Russ has been in school forever. It makes more sense."

"How old is he?"

"Twenty-eight."

"What kind of school has he been in?"

Eric picked up another piece of bacon and bit it. "He enlisted, did a few years, they put him through college and then he finished up his service. Up until this week, I think his plan was to make the ranch more profitable by expanding it."

"Why does that have to change?"

Eric sat back in his chair and looked at her. "I've more than once been accused of being a closed book."

Susan picked up her coffee mug and shook her head. "Meaning?"

"I don't include the people in my life in the things going on in my life."

"You've had a busy week and even though we've become *very* involved, I wouldn't hold that against you."

Eric studied her. "I want to keep you and continue to be *very* involved."

Susan swallowed hard. "I want that too."

He leaned in and rested his arms on the table. "My family is messed up," he said very matter-of-factly.

"I've met them. I don't think…"

"Not all of them," he interrupted.

Eric reached for her hand. He gave it a squeeze and then ran his thumb over her knuckles.

"My mom died when I was eight. Dad met Glenda and gave me four more brothers. I don't think I appreciated her as much as I should have," he said as if he'd only just realized that.

Eric lifted her hand to his lips and pressed a kiss to it. "My uncle isn't so family oriented. He's obviously married multiple times. He never even married Bethany's mother. He's not very close to any of his children." He sucked in a breath. "And he has a severe gambling problem."

"Is someone getting him some help?"

"It just kinda came to full light the other day at the reading of the will. It seems as if he was in debt over a million dollars."

"A million dollars? Oh, that's a lot of money."

Eric nodded. "Well someone paid it off for him in trade for the acreage I'm living on—including this house."

Susan narrowed her eyes. "He paid off his debt with your land?"

"My grandfather's land. It's written into the will that the land goes back to the original owner, now that my grandfather is gone."

Susan shook her head. "None of that makes sense, really. Isn't there something you all can do about that?"

"We're working on it. There's a lot of strife between my family and the family which will get the land back." Eric sat back in his chair letting go of her hand. "The family in question is my mother's family."

"That's very complicated."

He nodded. "They disowned her when she fell in love with my father. I never laid eyes on my grandfather until the other day. I met my cousins when I got beat up," he said raising his fingers to his blackened eye.

"I wish I could have met her. Anyone who would give up their family for love...well she must have been very certain of that love."

Eric nodded. "I guess so."

"You don't know?"

"I was young when she died. I don't remember their love. She loved me and that was all I cared about then."

Susan picked up her cup of coffee and took a sip only to find that it had gone cold. "Can I warm your coffee?"

Eric looked at his mug and shook his head. Susan stood and walked to the sink to pour out the cold coffee. She filled her mug with hot coffee and sat back down across from Eric.

She lifted the mug to her lips. "So her family wants the land?"

Eric nodded. "They want her back too."

Susan set her mug back on the table. "They want who back?"

"My mother."

She wasn't sure what to think about that. "Where is she?" she asked with her words drawn out as she tried to think it through.

"We have a family plot. My mother is buried there." He kept his gaze steady on her. "The plot is just up over the hill on our original land."

"And now they want her buried on their land?"

"Yes."

Susan reached for his hand now. "You look to lose your land and your mother?"

Eric's eyes narrowed and his lips tightened. "Over my dead body will they take her from me."

Susan certainly didn't like the thought of him putting his life on the line. Though she certainly understood it.

Eric raked his fingers through his hair. "All of this has led us to someone poisoning my horses and my cattle. They cost me my business. You tell me my mother's family isn't involved."

"You know that for sure?"

He shook his head. "No. My father says it's not them. But they sure were defensive when I showed up asking questions."

Susan moved to him and positioned herself on his lap. "If you need a place you can…"

"I won't need a place," he said. "No one is taking my house. No one is taking my mother."

She rested her head on his shoulder. "Thank you."

"For what?"

"Sharing all of this with me."

Eric touched her cheek and then brushed his fingers into her hair. "Your turn, you know."

"My turn for what?"

"Why did you get divorced?"

Susan winced. Yes, it was only fair she supposed. "I was horribly bored."

The surprise in her answer surprised him. That was evident by the flash of shock in his eyes. "Bored?"

"I wanted to go to culinary school. I wanted children. I freaking wanted to drive from one end of town to the other without my husband telling me how bad it was for the world." She took a breath. "I heard the phrases *'you should have, why don't you,* and *I think it would be better if you'* more than I ever would have liked. My obsession with food was wrong."

"Wrong?"

"Yes. Just wrong. I needed to focus on doing good for the environment and the world. I needed a job that brought in decent money. I simply wasn't good enough for anything. I just got bored with being nothing."

Eric brushed his thumb over her cheek. "I don't buy into you being not good enough. I've seen what you're building."

Susan couldn't help but smile. "That's why I'm in Georgia. It was far enough away to not matter what I did. I gladly drive across town and I'm doing what I love."

"You do a good job too."

"He'd never have said that."

"He doesn't have to. I'm saying it." Eric lifted his lips to hers and sealed his words with a kiss that had her clinging to him.

He pushed them back from the table and carried her to the couch, his mouth still firmly pressed to hers. Gently, he laid her on the couch and slid atop of her.

Susan hadn't imagined she'd be happy with a man, ever. She'd written this part of her life away. But Eric had brought back the wanting.

Eric kissed her until her body eased beneath him. The warmth from the fire made the room's new heat grow in intensity. Then, he pulled back and looked down at her with that grin that tugged at only one side of his mouth.

"What the hell does Q stand for?"

Chapter Nineteen

The humor that lit in Susan's eyes had been priceless.
"Q?"
"Your business card. It says Susan Q. Hayes."
She looked up at him and simply grinned. "Is this driving you crazy?"
"I'll just lay here, pinning you down, until you tell me," he said.
Susan puckered her lips as if to keep them tight.
"You're not going to tell me?"
"Didn't you just say you'd lay here if I didn't tell you?"
He let out a groan and lowered his lips to her neck. Having her beneath him was doing him in. In time she'd tell him. She'd probably tell him if he asked again. But his body couldn't be controlled when she toyed with him like she was.
She moaned as she raised her arms to encircle his neck.
As he moved his hands to skim under her shirt and touch her soft, warm skin, he heard the unmistakable sound of a truck driving up to the house.
"My family has the worst timing."
She smiled, her eyes still hazy. "How do you know it's your family?"
"Trust me."
Eric rose and took her hand, pulling her from the couch just as his father burst through the door.
Poised on the tip of his tongue was a colorful comment for the intruder, but when he saw who it was, he swallowed down his comment.
"Dad? What's wrong?" He moved toward the door.
His father looked up at him and then toward Susan. "Sorry. I didn't know you had company." He turned and

looked out the door before turning back to Eric. "I didn't even notice the car."

"I have coffee. We have some breakfast left. Why don't you come join us?"

The look on his father's face said he hadn't made the trek out to his house just to say hello.

"Can we talk?" His father's words were tight and hushed.

Susan smiled sweetly. "I should head out and get some work done."

That wasn't what he'd had in mind, but he certainly wouldn't have wanted to stay if it were *her* father walking in sounding so desperate.

"Give me just a moment, Dad," Eric said following Susan to the kitchen where her car keys sat on the counter. "I'm sorry. You don't have to go."

"He needs you right now. Call me later. If I miss you tonight I'll be out for dinner with your family tomorrow."

Eric grunted knowing this was best. But the positive thing was she was still planning to come back.

He took her hands in his. "This isn't how I planned this."

"I'm flexible. I have a family too. My ex didn't like giving me my space when my family needed me. I'd never do the same to someone else."

"I think I love you," he said quietly.

Her eyes shot open wide and her breath seemed to catch. "I didn't expect that."

"I don't think I did either." He wiped a hand across the back of his neck. "In fact, I don't want you to say anything right now and let's just let that linger there."

She smiled and he took that as a good sign.

Susan touched his cheek with her soft, warm hand. "Call me if you need me."

"Dinner is always at five," he said.

"I'll be there. I'll bring something."

That made him chuckle. "She's never allowed anyone to do that before. But something tells me you'd be allowed."

She lingered a loving gaze on him before she walked past him and toward the door.

"Goodbye, Mr. Walker."

"Oh," his father said as if waking from a trance. "Goodbye…"

"Susan," she said gently offering her name when he stumbled trying to remember. "I met you after your father's funeral."

"Right. I'm sorry. I remember."

She rested her hand on his father's arm. "Take care."

Eric watched as his father's mouth curled slightly and he was sure his father didn't even know he'd fallen for Susan's charm.

They both watched as she pulled on her coat and walked to her car. A few moments later she drove away.

"How about that coffee, Dad?" Eric offered, hoping to break the ice a little. Whatever his father had to say wasn't good. That much was written all over his face.

"Sure."

Eric hadn't actually expected him to accept the offer. His father was a get-down-to-business kind of man.

But Eric would take the slight distraction offered by the time to pour the coffee.

His father took a seat at the table and picked up a piece of bacon from the plate, which had been left there. "I suppose if you get involved with a woman who cooks all the time you eat well."

"I've eaten more full meals this week than I have in a long time. She's a vegetarian though. I suppose I'll have to get used to a few things."

His father took another bite from the strip. "Getting used to things means you're planning on keeping her around?"

Eric swallowed hard as he poured the coffee in two mugs. It was warm enough, for now.

"It seems as if that's what I want to do."

"I'm happy for you. Crappy timing though, huh?"

Eric turned toward the table and set the mugs down before he took his seat. "Who's to say the timing would ever be right?"

His father nodded as he lifted the mug to his lips, sipped, then winced.

Eric sipped his as well. "I guess it got cold." He stood, picked up the mugs and dumped them into the sink.

"They're going to move your mother."

Eric felt the mug slip from his hand and crash into the sink, breaking into big chunks. A ceramic shard bounced from the sink lodging itself into the side of his hand.

"Shit!" He yanked his hand back and pulled the shard from his hand. Blood trickled down his arm and onto the floor.

His father moved quickly, taking the dishtowel from where it hung on the oven door handle.

"Get this wrapped around it."

Eric grit his teeth against the sting.

"Let's look at it. Do you need stitches?" His father reached for him.

Eric pulled his hand back. "I don't need any damn stitches. I'll take care of it."

He held the towel tighter, noticing that the blood was beginning to ooze through the fabric. Blood never bothered Eric, but having it pulse out of his body made his knees feel week. With a swift swipe of his foot, he pulled the kitchen chair out further and sat down.

His father looked down at him, forcing Eric to take a long, deep breath. Before he spoke, he bit down on the inside of his cheek trying to get just a little control over the anger that still boiled in him.

"You're letting her go? You're letting them move her?"

"Eric, there's a lot going on here."

"And I'm the one getting screwed!" If he were sure he wouldn't fall over from the amount of blood soaking into the towel he'd walk out of the room. He didn't need to have this conversation.

"You know this isn't all about you," his father's voice broke. "I loved her. I lost her too."

Eric gasped as his father spat the words toward him.

"They turned her away. They disowned her and pushed her out of their lives. She was your wife. My mother. To them, she was nothing."

Eric watched as the color began to drain from his father's face.

"That was so long ago," his father's voice drifted.

"What does that matter? You can't go back."

"People make mistakes, Eric."

His heart pounded in his chest and his hand throbbed in the towel. He was damn sure he too was going to need stitches, but this conversation just might give him a heart attack first.

"She didn't make a mistake. She fell in love with you, married you, and had me. Where is it written that that is a mistake?"

The color was coming back to his father's face. His cheeks were red and the vein on the side of his temple became pronounced.

"We've had her for forty years. Elias has promised to have her buried in a cemetery in town. Not in their family cemetery and we'd move her from ours."

"This is ridiculous!" He stood and quickly sat back down when the blood rushed from his head. "She's not moving."

"You don't have any say," his father said as he walked out of the kitchen.

Eric stood, fighting off the nausea that was setting in, and followed his father. "You're just going to walk away?"

"I didn't expect you to understand. But I don't need your permission either. So if you want to visit her before they move her, you have three days."

"Three days? When do I need to move out of here? You might as well uproot my whole life while you're at it."

His father's eyes narrowed. "Then maybe you'd better start packing."

"You're giving up? What's done is done? No one is going to fight Elias Morgan for the land that grandpa bought outright? You're not going to fight to keep your wife on your own land? What about the cattle that's dying? What about my business and the horses I lost? I'm not going to just let this lie. Someone is pushing me off my land and out of my house and now I wonder how much you know about it."

"Eric, again, this isn't all about you."

"Like hell it's not."

His father's eyes misted over. "I won't let anyone suffer."

"Except me."

His father shook his head, but said not another word before opening the door and walking out to his truck. When his father had driven away, Eric looked down at the blood soaked towel. The huge gash on the side of his hand wasn't going to heal with just a Band-Aid.

Eric went in search of his truck keys. As manly as he thought he was, and as tough, he knew he needed to get to town and have his hand stitched. The thought of being in town was making him even more nauseous. The last thing he wanted was to be around people.

Susan immediately popped into his mind and he let out a groan as he moved toward the fireplace and carefully worked to extinguish the fire. At this very moment, when having a woman in his life should be top priority, especially after he told her he thought he loved her, he realized he didn't even want to see her. There was no one, except a doctor with a thread and needle that he wanted to see.

Maybe he could tough it out. He'd been hurt enough times in his life this wasn't any different. Hell, he had plenty of scars. But the cut throbbed and reminded him this was different.

Trying to maneuver his left hand around the steering column to turn the key was harder than he thought it would be. Well wasn't that the story of his life? Everything suddenly had become much harder than it needed to be.

Chapter Twenty

Though the day hadn't quite worked out the way Susan had hoped, she was very content sitting in the living room with a cup of tea.

Bethany bounced her head to the music on her iPod as she stretched doing her bedtime routine. Susan felt bad for her. As far as she knew, no one in Bethany's family had reached out to her in the past few days since she'd been there. Susan's mother had called three times in the past few days and so had her sister. Why was it so hard for families to communicate?

Bethany let out a long breath as she unfolded herself from her mat and stood tall stretching her arms over her head.

"When are you going to join me?" she asked as she opened her eyes and took the ear bud out of her ear.

"One of these nights," Susan said sipping her tea.

"Yeah, when you're not shacking up with my cousin."

Susan smiled. "A week ago if you told me I'd be sleeping in the arms of a man I would have laughed at you."

"At least you picked from the right side of the family."

It was unmistakable, the sadness in her voice. "I think you're part of his *side,*" she said. "Aren't we going to dinner at the same house tomorrow?"

"Yes." Bethany rolled up her mat and then folded herself into the oversized chair next to her. "Do you think my father will ever accept me? Or my brothers and sisters?"

Did she think Susan had an actual opinion on this or was she simply asking to ask? "I don't know. I don't understand the dynamics of your father's side of the family. But it does seem that right now they are all a bit out of sorts and perhaps in time everything will work out."

"How can you be so optimistic?"

Susan shrugged. "I don't know. Because my family has overcome everything."

"And your father gambled away other people's livelihood?"

Susan felt the sadness in Bethany's statement sink into her gut. "No."

"I'm not sure what he's done can be fixed and I hope that it doesn't tear you and Eric apart."

Was that a possibility? That heaviness turned from sadness to pure panic. She should have thought about it a little harder before she began sleeping in his bed.

It was a typical pattern wasn't it? A man loses someone close to him and he turns his attention to someone outside of his family to cope? Then his animals die and he needs comfort.

Susan's hands began to shake.

She thought about what he'd said to her. That "L" word had surfaced and now what was she supposed to think about it?

With a glance at the clock on the bookshelf, which had been a gift from her own grandfather, she noticed it was already past ten o'clock. Sure, Eric had showed up on her doorstep even later, but she had been sure he would have at least called after his father left this morning.

That wasn't fair. Wasn't she busy once she'd returned home? She'd been menu planning for her meeting with Lydia. She'd Skyped with her mother and they'd talked about visiting her in Georgia. They'd talked about Eric and her mother was very intrigued in him.

Bethany had gone to the grocery store with her and they'd decided on what to take to dinner at Glenda's tomorrow. Susan was going to make a decadent red velvet cake. Bethany had settled on a bouquet of flowers for the centerpiece.

The man needed his space. That was something that was hard for her to ever understand. Her ex-husband had needed his too. Perhaps that's why she was now so worried about the future of this new relationship. Her ex-husband often chose that solitude over time with her. He'd hike for days. He'd camp with a daypack and sleep under the stars, which was something that didn't thrill her. How often did he take off on his bike and not come back for days?

She'd taken it personally. But it had been personal—to her.

Why would her husband need his space like that? And now why did Eric?

She gripped her trembling hands together. Again, this wasn't fair to Eric to get upset over. She'd fallen into the new relationship just days ago. His grandfather had only passed a week ago and here she was getting too emotional over him.

He needed his space and damn it she was going to give it to him and not get sentimental over it.

Tomorrow she was going to head out to Lydia's and go over the plans she'd been working on. Perhaps she'd walk out with a contract. That would make the evening even sweeter. Then she'd head out to Glenda's for dinner.

He'd appreciate her giving him the space he needed. She could be the woman who didn't need constant attention. She could offer up that condolence when he needed it, the passion when it consumed them, and silence when the situation demanded it.

It was new. She couldn't put her whole heart into it yet— but the truth was she had. In the past four days, she had fallen head over heels in love with Eric Walker. If he walked out of her life, she might actually crack, no matter what she'd just told herself.

He'd call her tomorrow, she told herself as she unfolded herself from the couch.

"Going to bed?" Bethany asked.

"Yes."

"I didn't upset you with what I said did I? About my father tearing you and Eric apart?"

Susan shook her head. She'd nearly forgotten what had set her head into that tailspin.

"No. I have a lot to fit into tomorrow. I need to sleep."

"I'd be happy to drive us out to the Walker's tomorrow, in case you want to stay." She gave her a wink.

"That'll be fine," she said walking out of the room and up the stairs, her stomach still tight from the fear that everything was going downhill.

~*~

Eric's thumb throbbed beneath the gauze wrapped around it. He felt like an idiot with three stitches from a broken dish. Even worse, the nurse had commented on having been the same one who stitched up his little brother. He'd wanted to get in and out of the hospital without conversation. No one needed to talk his ear off and try to be friendly. Eric hadn't been feeling particularly friendly.

He'd driven by Susan's house while he was in town, but her car wasn't there so he drove home in his pathetic mood. Sleep hadn't come easily. A pain pill helped, but not enough.

When he crawled out of bed, he faced the dishes from breakfast the morning before, still sitting on the table and in the sink. This certainly wasn't anything he wanted to deal with. At a moment like this, he'd like to have gone out to Whisky River and taken him out to the fields.

Because he'd already been feeling betrayed and unloved, he drove out to the cemetery to visit his mother. Her presence was there and he could feel her when he'd visit. The one thing he needed most was his mother right now.

The flowers by his grandfather's grave were only beginning to wilt. He wondered how long it would be before the headstone was in place. Now he wished he'd brought his mother some flowers. There had never been a time when he'd come to visit with her when he hadn't brought them to her.

For a long moment, he stood there and just stared at the stone with her name on it. "Why do they think you need to be moved?"

The clouds pushed together and blocked out what sunlight there had been. Figured, he thought. It was a dark time.

"Met a girl," he said as he moved to tuck his hands into his front pockets only to remember that the one throbbed at his side. Instead, he crossed his arms over his chest. "Know it sounds stupid, but I think I love her. Wish you could meet her."

The urge to spend more time with his mother had him lowering to his knees and then to the ground to sit. The soft ground gave beneath him, but it didn't matter. Some days he just needed to be near her.

"They're going to move you and I'm pissed. I'm really pissed," he bit out the words as a cold breeze blew through the cemetery. "I think it should be my choice—no one else's. I don't know what Elias has over Dad, but he's caving. They're killing my horses, my cattle, and pushing me off my land. Now they're moving you. Dad says no one will suffer, but I'm suffering." His voice had risen even alone in the cemetery.

Eric winced at the pain in his hand as much as the pain in his heart. "If this is a sign to start over, I'm not ready."

The thought of Susan moved into his mind and calm took over the pain he'd been wincing from. Maybe it was time to start over.

He let out a long breath.

He always found clarity when he came here. This moment was no different.

But he needed to hear it from Elias. He needed to know why his mother had to be moved. Why was this land so damn important to him that he'd take it back in such a way?

The sun moved from behind the clouds, which had gathered, and a single ray of sunshine seemed to cascade over his mother's name.

"I'll visit you no matter where they put you. Even if they put you on their property—I'll trespass."

He pushed to his feet. Elias Morgan needed to answer some questions and Eric was going to get them face-to-face.

Chapter Twenty-One

The road leading to the Lydia Morgan's house took Susan out a dirt road even longer than the one that led to Eric's. She couldn't help but feel as though she were nearly parallel to the other road.

This one was graded better and she hadn't been tossed around quite as badly. As she crested the last small hill in the road, she noticed the house.

Her breath caught in her lungs as she took in the sight. This was exactly what she thought a huge Georgia estate house would look like. Who was Lydia Morgan?

Susan caught a glimpse of the fascinated smile on her mouth in the mirror. Perhaps she hadn't bid this job quite high enough. She amused herself with the thought.

Pulling into the drive, she pulled through the loop in front of the house and parked.

Before she even stepped out of the car Lydia was opening the front door and walking toward her.

"You found it okay?"

Susan smiled as she stood. "I did. I've been out this way quite a bit, actually."

Lydia only nodded. "Welcome. Come in. My grandfather is just inside and would love to meet you. Then we can discuss the catering."

Susan pulled her bag from the car and shut the door. "This is beautiful."

Lydia smiled. "It is. I've lived out here most of my life. She shrugged her shoulders. Since my father died."

"Oh, I'm sorry."

"My grandfather was very kind to take us in."

"Don't you ever want to live in town?"

Lydia looked around as if to make sure no one was around. "I do. Someday the time might be right. Right now doesn't seem to be that time," she said, smiling sweetly.

Susan knew enough to let that lie for a bit. It did cross her mind that Lydia and Bethany might be kindred souls. After this job maybe she'd set up a coffee date for the three of them. The thought intrigued her.

Lydia opened the front door to the house and led Susan inside. She stopped as she crossed the threshold. The house was as grand inside as it was out. "Wow," she said the word before she even realized it. "Sorry. I don't think I've ever been in a house quite this ornate."

The chandelier that hung in the entry was majestic. The floor was white marble and the wood was a rich cherry. A grand staircase came down both sides of the entry. What a girl wouldn't give to be a bride on those stairs, she thought.

"My grandfather is in his library."

Library. Houses really had those?

As Lydia walked down the hall, a man came toward them. He was tall with a familiar gait to him. He carried his hat in his hand and raked his other hand through his hair. When he lifted his head, Susan caught the gasp before she expelled it. The man had a very striking resemblance to Eric.

"Tyson," Lydia said to get the man's attention. He raised his head and looked at her as if he hadn't seen them. "Everything okay?"

The man, who had obviously been in some kind of fight, winced. "Don't ask. Who's she?"

Lydia narrowed her gaze on him. "This is Susan Hayes, the caterer."

"Right. Nice to meet you."

Lydia shook her head. "My brother Tyson," she offered.

"Nice to meet you, Tyson."

"Yeah." He looked back at Lydia. "Where is Grandpa?"

"In the library. We're headed in there now."

"I'll wait then." He placed his hat back on his head.

Lydia touched his arm. "Something happened."

"Six more cows," he said gruffly and walked out of the house.

Lydia sighed. "Sorry about that."

"Is everything okay?"

She smiled, but Susan could see the tension in it. "Things are a little tense out here right now. No worries. Right this way," she said entering another room.

Susan looked around. This, in fact, was a library. She wasn't sure she'd seen many bookstores with this many books in it.

"Grandpa, Ms. Hayes is here," Lydia said softly to the man seated in the oversized leather chair.

He turned his head and locked his stare on her. She felt her heart stutter as he kept his gaze on her.

He stood and crossed to her. "You're the caterer?"

"I am," she said confidently holding her hand out to shake his. "It's a pleasure to meet you."

"You come highly recommended."

"I appreciate that. I'd love to know who…"

"Lydia, you two head to the office and finish your business. I'll be at the barn."

"Tyson is looking for you," Lydia said softly.

"I thought he might be."

Mr. Morgan left the room and Lydia seemed to deflate. "Follow me."

Susan followed her further into the house to a large office. The walls were lined with bookshelves made of dark cherry, which matched the rest of the house.

"Please, have a seat. I'm sorry for the attitudes of all the men around here today," Lydia said as she shut the thick door. "There is some transitioning going on and a lot of tension." A crease formed between her brows. "I hope that doesn't affect our business dealings. I would hate to have you go."

"I'm fine," Susan said smiling. "Believe it or not a lot of my work is performed in tense situations."

"You did Mr. Walker's funeral, correct?"

"I did."

Lydia nodded. "That's where I got my referral. I didn't tell my grandfather that though. He and George Walker were not what I'd consider friends."

"I see. Well, I work under a veil of confidentiality. I understand. Should we look at the menus I've designed for you?"

~*~

Eric had worked to be calm. Obviously the last time he'd ventured out to the Morgan's house it hadn't gone well. This time he was going to be ready to just speak to the man. No curses. No punches. No yelling—or so he told himself.

He kept the speed of the truck at fifty-five so as not to look like he was coming for a fight. He just wanted answers.

The ornate gate to the house glittered in the sun, which had finally come out and melted away the clouds. Eric clenched his jaw and drove through.

His father had seen to it that they were brought up to respect what they had and to work hard. You didn't flaunt your wealth if you had it and you made sure enough went to charity. It was obvious, by the house before him, that his grandfather hadn't felt the same way.

Eric slowed as he came to the drive that looped in front of the house and he slammed on his breaks when he saw the very familiar car in the drive.

"What in the hell?"

He put the truck in park and jumped out to look at the car parked in front of him. Every ounce of him hoped that there had been some mistake and everyone now had an old Subaru. No luck. There was no doubt at all that this was Susan's car.

Eric snapped up his head and looked around. Where was she and what was she doing here?

"Did you come back here to have your teeth punched in?"

Eric turned to see his cousin coming toward him.

"I came here to speak to my grandfather."

"Why the hell would he want to speak to you after you came accusing him last time? And now you stand accused."

"Accused of what?" Eric's temper didn't hold.

"I lost six cows this morning. Poisoned."

"And you think I had something to do with that?"

Tyson took a step closer to Eric. "Why wouldn't I think that? You want revenge because you think I killed your cattle and your horses. I had nothing to do with that and you're not going to get away with this."

"I didn't do anything. And why is she here?" He pointed to Susan's car.

Tyson glanced at the car and then shifted his eyes to glare at Eric. A hint of a grin curled the corner of his lips.

"What would you care?"

"I asked you a question."

"So you know Susan?"

Eric fisted his one good hand. "Why is she here?"

"Visiting. She's quite stunning, isn't she?"

As hard as he tried, Eric couldn't push down the disdain for this man. "I came for some answers and I want them right now."

"Answers for what? Why your girlfriend is at *my* house?"

That was it. Eric pulled back and took the first swing, but Tyson ducked and landed one right to Eric's cheek.

"Is that all you got? Did your half-wit father teach you to only fight?"

Eric swung again, this time catching Tyson on the jaw.

"That's quite enough." Elias Morgan's voice rang loudly from the front door.

Both men stopped mid-lunge at each other and stepped back.

Eric realized he didn't have to stand there and wait until his grandfather offered punishment. He was much too old to be treated like a child. But something had him standing there wincing from the pain in his cheek and the sting to his knuckles.

Elias kept a steady eye on him. "Why don't we go inside and have a cold glass of tea? I have a feeling you want to talk to me."

Eric looked at Tyson, who was nursing his jaw.

"I have a few questions."

"That's fine, let's go inside." Elias Morgan led the way toward the front door.

"Why is Susan Hayes here?" The question seemed to have a mind of its own and blurted straight from his mouth.

His grandfather turned. "You know Ms. Hayes?"

As if he didn't already know that. "Yes."

"She's a fine woman. She's here on business. She won't bother us."

Bother us? Why would he think such a thing?

The fact that she was in that the house at all, consumed Eric with petty anger. There should be no reason Susan had anything to do with these people. What was she trying to do? What kind of business did she have with them?

His mind simply couldn't shut down the thought that she had no idea who they were or what they'd done to him.

As he followed Elias through the house, he was aware of Tyson turning into another room. Was she in there? What did she have to do with Tyson?

Anger and jealousy seemed to pump as quickly through his veins as blood.

Elias led him into the kitchen. He pulled down two glasses from the cupboard and set them on the counter. "They say it's bad for me, but I take my tea extra sweet. You okay with that?"

"I drink it that way as well."

Elias grinned. "I assume you get that from your mother," he said, opening the refrigerator and taking a pitcher out. He filled the two glasses, replaced the pitcher, and then handed a glass to Eric.

"I don't remember her drinking tea," Eric added and Elias sipped his drink.

"That surprises me. She enjoyed her tea. Let's sit."

Eric wasn't sure he wanted to right now. He wanted to know what Susan was doing and he wanted to know if she was doing it in that room where Tyson had gone. But, remembering that he had a mission here and he had a house and his business on the line, Susan and her visit needed to be pushed to the back of his mind.

"Leave her on our land. You pushed her away and there is no reason you should get her back."

Elias's eyes went wide when forty years of anger was spurted toward him.

"I see you've spoken to your father about this."

"You disowned her. You gave her to us as far as I'm concerned. She's my mother and she should stay with me."

Elias set his glass on the table. "Eric, have you ever made a mistake in your life?"

"Who hasn't?"

"Well, your mother made one—she made a few."

Eric narrowed his stare on his grandfather and clenched his aching jaw. "Is that your opinion?"

"She ran away from home at sixteen. Did you know that?"

Eric's eye twitched from the tears that began to sting. "No."

"Well she did. She ran away and we didn't find her for two years."

Pain began to pierce Eric's thumb, under the bandage, as his hands began to tremble.

Elias pulled out a chair and gestured to Eric. "Sit. Let's get a few things straight."

He waited a beat before he sat down in the offered seat.

Elias sat down next to him and wrapped his hands around his glass of tea.

"She was eighteen when she came back home looking for money. She was pregnant."

Eric shook his head. "She was twenty when I was born."

His grandfather nodded. "There's a reason you and Tyson are equally tempered," he said and an array of gasps came from behind them.

Elias visibly winced as they turned to see Lydia and Tyson standing in the doorway.

Tyson stepped into the kitchen as the men stood from the table. "Do you want to run that by me again?"

"Let's all sit down and discuss this," Elias said with his hands raised as if in surrender.

"I don't need to sit down. Continue explaining."

Eric kept his eyes on the door, but Susan never walked through. She'd had to have seen his truck outside. Wouldn't she want to come in and find out why he was there?

Lydia moved toward her brother and held on to his arm. "Grandpa," she said as if pleading.

Elias picked up his tea and took a sip. He made eye contact with each of them before setting the glass back down.

"Constance was a free spirit. She did what she wanted to do. I never had control over her." Elias rubbed his forehead, between his brows, as if to ward off a headache. "She came home pregnant at eighteen. She stayed until she had the baby and then one night she left."

He looked directly at Eric. "You were three before I knew where she'd gone and she was nearly right under my nose."

Tyson broke from Lydia's grip and moved in closer, now standing right next to Eric—shoulder to shoulder.

"You're missing pieces to this story. What about that baby."

"I'm guessing you have this all figured out."

"Perhaps I need to hear it from you," Tyson growled.

"Constance was your mother. She left you with us and ran again."

Tyson stood, his mouth open, staring at his grandfather. "You're telling me I'm not who I think I am." He paced a small circle. "You let me live here all my life believing that my father and mother were actually mine?"

"Your father and mother had just gotten married. You were his blood and he couldn't bear to see you turned away. They took you in and raised you. You can't tell me your life was in any way misshapen by this."

Tyson ran his fingers through his hair. "This is about the craziest thing I've ever heard."

"Me too," Eric chimed in. "My mother never would have left a child. She was loving and caring."

Elias evened his stare on him. "You were eight when she died. What do you really remember about her?"

Eric actually flinched. Hadn't he thought, just the other day, that he hardly remembered her at all? Glenda had been his mother for much longer and the memories of his mother had faded away.

Elias nodded his head. "That's what I thought."

"Eric, I didn't turn your mother away. I loved her very much. I loved both of my children. She stayed away for whatever reason. Your father was gracious and cordial to her, but…"

He didn't have to finish the sentence. He was sure he knew the next phrase would be that his father never loved her—or at least the way Eric had always imagined it to be.

Tyson clucked his tongue. "I can't believe you kept this from me. Forty-two years and suddenly…"

"I've tried in the past. I just couldn't do it. I couldn't see the benefit from it."

"Not knowing who the hell I am isn't going to make things any easier on me."

"You're a Morgan. This has no relevance on who you are now. But this is part of the reason I want Constance moved. You deserve to have her near."

Tyson stepped forward until he was nearly head to head with their grandfather. "As if finding out she abandoned me makes me want to celebrate her."

Eric thought he could punch him, again, for talking about her like that. But how could he? They were both absolutely dumbfounded by what their grandfather had told them.

Tyson turned and started out of the kitchen.

"Tyson, wait," Lydia yelled as she ran after him.

Elias shook his head and looked back at Eric. "Do you want to argue my reasons for moving her now?"

Eric looked toward the doorway where Tyson and Lydia had gone out. "You're still taking my land from me. So I have a whole list of reasons to still despise you."

"Fair enough. But the land is a business deal. That has nothing to do with you."

"Like hell it doesn't. My horses were poisoned and so were my cattle."

Eric noted the surprised look on Elias's face. "That's unfortunate."

"Unfortunate? I have nothing. Boarding horses was my business, but now I have no boarders. And why would I? One of my clients lost a beloved animal and that becomes my fault. Now heads of cattle are just dying. That's my family's livelihood."

Eric studied Elias's eyes. Was that worry behind that steely glare?

"Let me move your mother, into town, and I'll see what I can do about the land."

"You want to make deals? Deals with what was mine to begin with?"

"It seems as though you have your uncle to blame for the land crisis. As for your mother, I think perhaps you see another side to her. I'd never deny you access to her."

Eric's chest actually hurt at the thought of giving in to Elias Morgan. "If I let her go, what can you do about the land?"

"I can at least promise that you can stay there—forever."

Eric considered his offer. It was the least a man could do for keeping secrets from his grandchildren for over forty years.

"Okay, but if I don't like where you're putting her I won't let her go."

Elias nodded, but Eric was sure she'd disappear in the middle of the night again if he didn't agree.

"As for your cattle. We need to get to the bottom of who's responsible. Tyson informed me we'd lost a few heads as well."

"He seems to think I had something to do with that," Eric added.

"If I recall you said the same to him."

Funny how a change of heart could happen so quickly.

"I assure you I had nothing to do with your loss," Eric said firmly.

"And I assure you we had nothing to do with yours."

Fair enough, he thought.

"Susan Hayes," Eric brought her up in subject again. "Why was she here?"

Elias picked up his tea again and sipped. "Why would that concern you? What dealings do you have with Ms. Hayes?"

"That's my business."

The old man's lips curved into a crooked smile. "Well, then I can assume her being here is my business."

They'd made some progress today, but Eric still didn't like the man. He'd find out what Susan was doing there. The very thought angered him nearly as much as realizing he needed to find his long lost brother and make amends. After all, he couldn't have anyone having ill will toward his mother—no matter what she'd done in her past.

Chapter Twenty-Two

The contract was in her pocket! Susan drove down the bumpy road toward home with an enormous grin on her face. The only problem she was going to have was finding someone to serve, since they'd specifically asked for Bethany not to work the dinner.

A million questions had filled her head as to why, but she'd already promised that she wouldn't mention the dinner to anyone—and she supposed that included Bethany.

She looked at the clock on her dash. She had time to throw together another dish for dinner before heading out. Nothing fancy. Maybe just a caprese salad. After all, when she was happy she loved to create.

Bethany was in the kitchen when she arrived, arranging the flower bouquet into a vase. "I found this at a yard sale and couldn't pass it up for a quarter. That doesn't make it a cheap gift does it? I mean in sentiment."

"I think it looks beautiful. You have a real gift."

Bethany's smile faded. "My mother worked for a short time in a flower shop. She taught me a few things."

"My mother taught me to cook. Those are some amazing gifts they passed on to us. Maybe you could work that talent into our catering. Centerpieces and things like that."

The smile returned to Bethany's face. "I'd like that."

"I'm going to go take a shower and then plate a caprese salad."

"You're taking more food?"

"I can't help myself. I'm happy and I cook when I'm happy. I'm nervous and I cook when I'm nervous."

"Why are you nervous? You've met all these people."

"But I wasn't sleeping with Glenda's son then."

That had Bethany bust out in laughter. "I thought I was nervous, but you're right. You should be more nervous."

~*~

Tyson had left the Morgan's and Eric had no idea where to find him. One minute he'd found out he had a cousin he'd never met and now to find out that man was his brother was a little too much to take in. What the hell else could happen in the day that would trump that?

Eric was emotionally spent. The mother he loved and had thought he'd known was now a complete stranger. Who was Tyson's father and why had she been with him? And how had she ended up with his father? Having lived with Glenda his entire life, he couldn't imagine his father choosing his mother—if she was of the character that Elias had made her out to be.

Eric didn't want to believe that either. The woman he remembered—or at least seemed to have concocted in his mind—was a saint. He'd keep her that way. It gave him comfort.

A headache began to form behind his eyes. His cheek hurt from the punch Tyson had landed there, for the second time in a week, and his thumb throbbed. He needed to get the bandage off. He needed a stiff drink, some Motrin, and about ten minutes alone to figure out how he was going to approach Susan about being at the Morgan's house.

Anger still pumped through his veins when he thought of Elias Morgan's grin when he said, *"Well, then I can assume her being here is my business."*

She had no business with those people. He didn't want her to have anything to do with Tyson and especially Elias. She was his and he wasn't going to share her too, he thought as he pulled up in front of his house and slammed on the brakes.

The thought seemed to be sticking in his head too strong. Perhaps that was the ploy. Wasn't it convenient that Susan arrived in his life when his grandfather died and Elias began his descent on the Walkers?

His mouth went dry.

She'd been there the morning before Whiskey River died. She'd been at the barn before he got there.

His palms were wet and his breath came in pants.

What was Susan doing with the Morgan's? Was she part of the plan to destroy him? How convenient to have been there when his grandfather died and to be there as each part of his life unfolded.

Eric ripped the bandage off his thumb and cursed as he brushed the stitches.

How could he have been so stupid? Oh, and he'd put Bethany right in the middle of things too. Just how much information were they trying to get?

Eric pushed open the door on his truck and jumped down. He kicked the earth at his feet and looked up at the house he loved so much. Why the hell should he stay there now? Didn't it seem as if every single person in his life was against him—including his mother?

The sound of tires kicking up dirt behind him had him turning around. A brand new blue pickup came racing toward him.

Eric quickly moved in front of his truck as the other truck skidded to a stop beside him. It shouldn't have surprised him when Tyson hurried out of his truck and right for him.

Obviously they were going to beat the crap out of each other again, so Eric had his one good fist ready to go.

"You didn't know about all that?" Tyson said with venom in his voice as he stared toward Eric with a hurried walk.

Eric simply stared at the man who's fury was red hot on his cheeks. "About what? My mother?"

"Our mother," Tyson said with a wince. "If that is, in fact, true."

"Did it seem as if I knew about it? Jesus, I didn't even know you existed until the other day when you began punching me."

"I think you came at me."

Had he actually smiled and had Eric returned it? He let down his defensive stance—slightly.

"I didn't know shit. None of this makes sense. Why wouldn't someone have told us that if it were true? Why now? Why when we're grown men?"

Tyson narrowed his eyes. "Look at us. I'd think we were brothers if I didn't know better." He ran his hands over his head. "And when I called my mother she broke into hysterics and couldn't even speak to me," he admitted. "She hung up on me. Actually hung up."

"I guess we don't understand our families as well as we thought we did."

Tyson nodded. "Never did feel like I belonged. Maybe this is why."

Eric felt the throb in his thumb and tried to bend the stiffness from it. "Want a drink?"

Tyson looked at his watch. "Yeah. Maybe we can decide who's killing our cattle. I'm going to take a leap and assume, in a *brotherly* trust, we're not doing that to each other."

"You can take that leap. I didn't kill your animals."

"I didn't kill yours either," Tyson said as they walked up the front steps and into the house. "My grandpa," he let out a groan. "Our grandpa is up to something. I'm beginning to think it has something to do with your land and the issue with our animals."

Eric walked to the kitchen, opened the cupboard, and took out a bottle of Jack and two shot glasses. "Then we need to find out what and stop it. And so help me if I can keep him from moving my mother I'll still do it. Visit if you want, and he can too, she still belongs here."

He poured the whiskey into the glasses and handed one to Tyson.

Tyson threw the drink back and swallowed hard. "I don't blame you for wanting to keep her. I'd want the same."

Eric lifted his glass and swallowed down the liquid, which burned as it slid down his throat. "I don't suppose he even cared that she was gone."

"You'd be wrong. He talked about her all the time. He celebrates her birthday every year. This year would have been her sixtieth."

"I know that." He didn't quite know what to do with Tyson's knowledge of it, however.

It still hurt to think that if Elias Morgan loved and missed his daughter so much he'd have wanted to know his grandson.

Tyson set his glass on the counter. "I'm going to head to town and find a place to stay. It's time to find a place away from him to live. I thought I'd been there all my life to take over what belonged to me."

"It does. Just as part of this belongs to me."

"Just doesn't feel right at this moment."

Eric nodded. He certainly understood that.

"What was Susan doing there?" The urge to ask had taken over.

Tyler shrugged. "I don't know. Honestly, she has something going on with my grandfather and my sister."

His answer wasn't satisfying Eric's curiosity as to what she was involved with. Eric was feeling betrayed, as he knew Tyson was.

"Hey, I'm sorry for punching you," Eric said quietly.

"Me too. Years of built up frustration."

That did, in fact, sum it up.

"Let me know if you learn anything."

"I'll do that."

Tyson let himself out the door and Eric listened as he drove away. If they weren't responsible for killing each other's herds and horses who was then?

No one suffers.

He thought of his father's words. Didn't it seem like everyone was suffering, including the Morgans?

There was more, he knew. Why were his father and uncle at the Morgan's the other day? Why was Susan?

He looked at his watch. It was almost time for dinner. Maybe it was time to see what they were all plotting. How convenient to have his father and his *lover* all in the same room.

Chapter Twenty-Three

Susan couldn't remember the last time she was this nervous. Her fingers were cold and her hands shook. Bethany was rattling on a story to her left, but she wasn't hearing any of it. She was thinking of facing Eric's father after he'd come to the house yesterday morning and had to have known she'd slept with his son.

Would they all know? Did it matter?

She was quite sure she'd fallen in love with Eric and he'd let that slip from his lips too. Surely they would be skeptical of her. Who wouldn't be?

"Don't you think so?" Bethany asked as she turned down the road that would lead them to the Walker's house.

"I'm sorry. Think what?"

"That I should do that topless magazine spread?"

Susan snapped her attention to Bethany with a gasp. "No! And what are you talking about?"

Bethany laughed. "I knew you weren't listening to me. I didn't actually say anything about a topless magazine spread. I said that I'm nervous about being around my family since I don't really know them."

Susan relaxed against the seat. "Oh. I'm nervous too."

"I can tell. There are finger marks in the tinfoil on that dish."

Susan looked down and realized she did have the dish in a death grip.

"What are they going to think of me?" she asked.

"They already know you."

"As the caterer. They have a lot going on in their lives right now. So does Eric. I haven't even talked to him. So what if he's changed his mind? What if they thought I was a great caterer but I'm lousy daughter-in-law material?"

"Daughter-in-law?"

"Just figuratively speaking," she emphasized with her finger in the air. "But I wouldn't mind it."

"You're in love with him," Bethany said grinning as they pulled up in front of the house. "You can say no, but I wouldn't believe you."

"I think I do."

"He loves you too."

"He told you that?"

"I saw it in his eyes when he showed up at your house that first time with me. Only a man who loves a woman is so moved by her art." She winked as she parked the car, turned off the engine, and climbed out.

Susan contemplated Bethany's words for a moment. It was going to be a wonderful night, she decided as she climbed from the car.

Another car drove up and parked behind them. A man, one she'd seen at the funeral and the reading of the will, parked and stepped out of the car.

"Hey, Bethany," the man said.

"Gerald. How are you?" She could hear Bethany's voice shake, but that didn't stop the man from walking toward her and putting an arm around her shoulders.

"I'm having dinner at Mom's and I didn't have to cook. Things are good," he joked and looked toward Susan. "Hi."

"Hi," Susan managed as she juggled the two items in her hands.

"Let me help." Gerald took the dessert tray. "You're the caterer, right?"

"Susan," she said.

"Right. And you're dating my brother?"

Susan kept her smile intact as she swallowed hard. "I am."

"My mom mentioned it. She's pretty excited about it."
He walked toward the house and the women followed.

Susan's nerves began to settle. Maybe she wouldn't have
to try too hard to impress.

The house bustled with noise when they entered.
Warmth spread to Susan's chest. This was something she
missed, living so far away from her parents and her sister.

Glenda was in the kitchen, an apron wrapped around her
waist. She'd dressed for dinner. Suddenly Susan felt as
though she hadn't taken the invitation serious enough.

"Gerald." Glenda smiled wide when her son walked into
the room. She kissed him on the cheek and took the plate
from him. "I see you've met our guest?"

Gerald turned and looked at her. "Yeah. He's a lucky
guy," she heard him whisper and her stomach did a flop.

Glenda moved toward her and placed her hands on
Susan's shoulders. She smelled of lavender and vanilla when
she moved in and kissed her on the cheek.

"I'm so glad you came." She looked down at the plate in
her hands. "You didn't have to bring anything."

"I couldn't help myself. I hope I didn't offend you."

"Of course not. The more, the merrier." Glenda turned
toward Bethany and kissed her cheeks as well. "I'm so glad
you were able to come."

"Thank you for the invitation."

"You girls are getting along okay together?"

Bethany gave her an enthusiastic nod, which had her red
curls bouncing. "It's like having a sister." A line formed
between her brows. "A sister I know," she added and
Glenda's face softened.

"I think that's wonderful." Glenda's compassion rang
through her words.

Susan scanned the family that gathered in the kitchen and
dining room.

"Looking for Eric?" Glenda asked and Susan only answered with a smile. "I haven't seen him yet. I'm sure he'll be along shortly."

But he didn't come along shortly. Susan had texted him, discreetly, then called. She was aware that his brothers had called and texted as well.

"I'm sure he has a good reason for being tardy," Glenda said gathering her family around the table. "We'll just start without him."

"I can go up and check on him," Susan said, then remembering she didn't have her car. "If Bethany will lend me her car that is."

"No need," Eric's voice broke the tension of the air and stopped the voices that mumbled around the table. "I'm here."

"Oh, good," Glenda beamed. "Sit. Let's eat."

"How about I just stand and say what I came here to say."

His father stood from the table. "Eric," he said as if it were a scolding. "Your mother said we'd sit and eat."

"Funny, Dad. My mother."

Susan noted the sadness that ripped across Glenda's face.

"Eric, why don't we go into the other room?"

"Why don't we hash this our right here?" Eric said in front of everyone. "Why don't you share with them the news I received today? Let's talk about my mother, should we?"

"Let's go to my office," Everett said, moving from his seat and toward Eric.

"Does everyone know that my mother had another child? That I'm not her only son?"

Glenda gasped and Susan was very sure that no one knew that—except Everett.

"This is what you want to discuss? You want to tarnish your mother's name in front of your family?"

"Why did you marry her, Dad? She certainly didn't seem your type, from what I've learned."

"Stop."

"Why? I met my cousins the other day and then I find out one of them is a brother I didn't even know I had. My own mother abandoned him. So how did you get involved? How is it that she ended up only ten miles from home with you?"

Everett looked at his family. "Things happen, Eric. Not every man is made of steel."

Eric laughed and Susan was quite sure he'd been drinking, by the sway in his body.

She reached for his hand and he jerked away as he scalded her with a look of disdain.

"Why are you here?" he asked and she couldn't form a thought.

"Glenda invited me. Remember?"

"No. I mean how convenient is it that you show up in my life when my grandfather dies? You smoothly move your way into my family. You take in my cousin when you don't even know her and you end up in my bed?"

Susan felt the piercing shock of his words, but it was Glenda's sob that caused her to look away from him.

His father moved to him and took his arm. "That's enough. Why don't you go home until you're sober enough…"

"I am sober," he said very firmly. "This is anger pulsing through me. Not alcohol." He looked back down at Susan. "Why were you at the Morgan's house? What do you and Elias and Lydia have going on?"

Susan bit down on her bottom lip. "How did you know I was…"

"I was parked right behind you when you left today. Are you really going to tell me you didn't know I was there?"

"I didn't."

"You're a liar."

Glenda stood from her seat and slapped her hands on the table. "Susan is my guest, Eric. You're not going to talk to her like that."

"She's a traitor. She has something to do with all of this…whatever it is with Elias. The transferring of the land. The moving of my mother. The poisoning of my horse."

Now Susan stood up. "Excuse me! I have nothing to do with any of that. I would never hurt an animal, especially one that meant so much to the man I love."

"You're easy to say that when I'm accusing you. Not when I said it."

"You told me not to."

"Why were you there?" He stepped closer and she pushed her shoulders back. She took a breath to tell him, and the swallowed it down. She had a contract of confidentiality and she couldn't break that or she'd lose the job—the job that would pay off her education.

"None of your business."

"It is when you're out to destroy me."

There was no controlling herself now. She raised her hand and smacked his cheek so hard her wrist instantly ached. "Go to hell, Eric Walker."

"I think I'm already there," he said as he turned and walked out of the house.

Chapter Twenty-Four

As soon as they all heard his tires peel out of the driveway all four of his brothers were up and out of the door. No doubt following the ass back to his place.

Susan sat, her hands in her lap as they shook. She could hear her own breath as it moved in and out heavily.

"Everett, do something," Glenda said.

"I think he's about to get a visit from four somethings. I don't think we've had this many black eyes and stitches at one dinner table in all the years we had five boys."

"You can't let them beat him up," she defended him.

"I can. I will. They'll also heal him better than any doctor. What he found out today is quite a blow to a kid who idolized his mother for so long."

"He's not a kid. He's a man and that is much more dangerous."

Susan lifted her head. "I should go. I will go. I'm so sorry I hit your son. I'm so sorry for…"

Glenda reached her hand to Susan's shoulder. "You're not going anywhere."

"Oh, oh, yes I am," she stammered. "Not only do I think it's time for me to leave your home, but I think it's time for me to go back to mine. Back to Colorado. I can't do this. I can't do temper like this again."

The breath now came in pants and Bethany moved in closer to her. "Honey, what happened with your ex?"

"One time. Just one time," she cried. "He hit me one time and I left. Why stay?"

"Good for you," Everett said, his arms crossed over his chest as if this sort of drama happened every night at dinner. "No woman should ever be disrespected by a man."

"Eric seems to think that's what I did."

Everett shook his head. "I don't believe it. Tell me, what were you doing at Elias's house?"

Susan swallowed hard. "Sir, I can't disclose that."

Everett nodded slowly. "Did you poison his horse?"

"No! Oh, God no. I'd never do something like that. He loved that horse. I took a picture of them. You can see how much the horse meant to him. I didn't do that. I wouldn't do that."

"I believe you."

Susan rested back in her seat as the two women still held on to her. "Sir, my business is very important to me. When clients don't want someone to know about something I have to uphold that."

He nodded again. "Just tell me you have nothing to do with this land swapping or animal killing and I'll believe you."

"I swear."

Everett stood. "Do you love my son?"

The tears turned on and spilled down Susan's cheeks. "I do. I did," she whimpered. "I don't understand any of this. I'd never—ever—hurt him, sir."

He shifted his glance to his wife. "I'll go stop them from killing each other. Susan, I suggest you consider what you have with Elias Morgan very carefully. If you want Eric in your life, you can't have Elias."

He strode out of the room on a huff, pulled his keys from the peg by the door in the kitchen, and disappeared.

"I don't know who Elias is to Eric. I don't understand this."

Glenda handed her a napkin to wipe her eyes. "Elias is his grandfather. His mother's father."

"Oh." She shook her head. "I didn't know."

Glenda smiled. "Of course you didn't dear."

~*~

The first son-of-a-bitch that came through that front door was going to have a boot up their ass and a fist in their mouth, Eric decided when he saw the cloud of dust traveling toward his house.

He didn't need a confrontation with his brothers. They had no idea what he was going through. His entire family had betrayed him on both sides and now the woman he loved had too. He was fed up.

Russell's truck pulled up first with him and Dane inside. Gerald and Ben were in the next truck that pulled up. What could they possibly have to say?

He waited with his fists ready for the first brother to walk in the door, but no one came. What in the hell were they doing? It wasn't as if he hadn't seen them.

Eric moved toward the door, but still no one came it.

Swiftly, he pulled it open. No one was on the porch.

He stepped out and looked around the side of the house. The only evidence that his brothers were there were their trucks parked outside. He moved back to the front door. Perhaps they headed up to the barn. But as he walked into the house he found them. There they stood, all four of them, shoulder to shoulder with their arms crossed in front of their chests.

"Going somewhere?" Ben asked.

"Get out!"

Dane shook his head. "Sit down."

"Kiss my ass," Eric said as he took a step toward his brothers and in unison they moved a step toward him—stopping him.

Russell motioned toward the couch with his head. "Sit. You ain't going anywhere."

"I don't have to go. You do. This is my house."

Ben clucked his tongue. "Seems to me Elias Morgan owns it."

Eric bolted toward Ben first, but only found himself on his ass in front of the wall made of brothers.

Gerald held out a hand to help him up. "You upset Mom. No one goes for that."

Eric let go of Gerald's hand as soon as he was solid on his feet. "Your mom. Not mine."

"Just as much yours as mine. Don't play that desperate card with us. She fixed your wounds, fed your stomach, and comforted you when you needed it. She washed your clothes and cheered you on at every damn basketball game you ever had. So get off your high horse and sit down," Gerald said through gritted teeth.

Fine. He'd appease them. Eric walked around the sofa and sat down. Each of his brothers then filed in and took a seat around the room.

Dane clasped his hands together and leaned his arms on his thighs. "What is this about your mom having more kids?"

"Tyson Morgan," Eric said with a shake of his head. "She ran away when she was sixteen. Came back when she was eighteen and pregnant. Had him, left him with Elias, and ran off. She didn't get far though. Somehow she ended up with dad and here I am."

"Dad must have fallen in love and…"

"I don't think that's really how the story goes."

Dane sat back in his chair. "I'm sorry, man."

Eric ran his hands over his hair. "What do you do with this when you're forty? How do you accept this?"

There was silence for a moment.

"What about Tyson? What did he say? Did he know?" Ben asked.

"No. His whole world has been rocked. Elias said he wanted to move her into town so we could all visit her. That leads me to believe he was going to tell Tyson at some point."

Russell ran his hand over the growth of whiskers on his chin. "Damn. I can't imagine how I'd feel."

"That's not all. Someone is killing off their cattle too."

Ben's forehead creased. "The Morgans' cattle?"

Eric nodded.

"That says they didn't kill ours."

"I don't think they did."

Gerald stood and paced the room. "Then who? Who else wants this land?"

Eric shook his head. "I don't know, but I'm thinking there is more than one deal going on and Byron's weaknesses were used against us."

"Do you think Tyson knows anything?"

"No. But I'm thinking together we can find out."

Dane let out a long breath. "What about Susan? Do you think she knows what's going on?"

Eric tossed his head back against the couch and covered his face with his hands. "No. I actually don't think she knows."

Gerald stood at the edge of the sofa next to Eric. "You were an absolute ass to her. You deserved the smack she laid on you."

He couldn't deny that. He did deserve that.

Russell scratched his head. "If you don't think she's involved you need to apologize."

"God, now you sound like Glenda." That received a few chuckles. "But you're right."

"Maybe she's just catering for them. What else could she be doing?"

Again, Russell was right and Eric was getting tired of his little brother having all the common sense.

"She's working with Lydia, Tyson said. Maybe she's having a surprise tea party or something."

Gerald smiled. "We certainly aren't getting an invitation to that."

Eric stood. "Okay, get out now. I have to drive to town and grovel."

Gerald slapped him on the shoulder. "I'm going back to Mom's. Did you see that dessert Susan brought? I'm not letting that go to waste."

They all moved to the door and filed out. As the others walked to the trucks, Dane turned around. "Come back and apologize to Mom."

"I will."

He watched his brothers drive away as he leaned against the doorjamb. He wondered which woman would be harder to apologize to. The one he'd neglected most of his life over pride or the one he neglected only a day after telling her he loved her.

Eric watched as the dust kicked up again and soon his father's truck pulled up in front of the house. What had they all thought he would do to come in shifts?

His father parked and climbed from the truck. "You don't look any worse. I figured they'd have hog tied you and I'd have to come cut you out of it."

Eric snickered. "I'm surprised they didn't. I think they were pretty mad."

"Everyone had a right to be."

How could he possibly deny that? "I'm sorry."

"You'll tell that to your mother. To Glenda," his father added as if suddenly he wouldn't have called her Mom.

"I will. I owe her and Susan both an apology."

"Good. No matter what happens romantically between you and Susan, you can't leave it like that. I don't think she knew who Elias was."

"I don't get it. I parked right behind her when I went there. How could she not have seen my truck?"

His father looked outside at the old truck, which had been on that land driving through fields for nearly twenty years. "I've never been on a piece of land that didn't have some beat up piece of crap pickup like that one. Trust me, it doesn't stand out as much as you think it does."

"What do you think she was doing out there? It doesn't line up right."

"I think she was hired for a job. She won't tell anyone, but I have no doubt that she's telling the truth."

Eric pinched the bridge of his nose. "Just when I find the perfect woman I mess it all up."

"I'll let you blame this on Byron too," his father joked. "Without the mess he's put us in, life would certainly be boring."

Eric narrowed his gaze on his father. "They're losing cattle too. I think this is bigger than Byron. I think Elias is into something too. Someone wants all of us off this land and they're pushing us out." The realization of that hit him too. "I'll bet that's why he's so eager to move Mom."

His father winced at that. "I guess it's time to embrace family, Eric. You need Elias and he needs you."

The words had Eric's heart racing. He hated to admit it, but he knew his father was right. It was going to take more than his Walker pride to get them out of this.

Chapter Twenty-Five

The suitcase on Susan's bed overflowed with clothes she'd pulled from her drawers and her closet.

Bethany stood in the doorway with a cup of tea. "Drink this and calm down."

"Tea isn't going to make me feel better and neither is bending over with my butt in the air in some ridiculous yoga pose. I'm leaving. I have to get out of here."

"Just tell them what you were doing at the Morgan's and they'll be over it."

Susan pushed down on the top of the suitcase as if it would magically close—but to no avail. Instead of zipping the case, she tossed it open again and began pulling things out and throwing them on the bed.

"I have a confidentiality contract they wanted signed. Who the hell makes a caterer sign that?" she asked with a bra dangling from each hand. "It's food!"

Bethany stepped in and set the tea on the dresser before moving to her and taking the bras out of her hands. "You need to relax. Sit down and breathe," she said easing her to the bed. "Just drink the tea."

Bethany picked the cup up from the dresser and handed it to her. "Sip."

Susan willed her breathing to slow as she lifted the cup to her lips. "He hates me. I didn't do anything, but he hates me."

"I think that's the problem," Bethany said as she sat down on the bed next to her. "I don't think he hates you at all.

"I didn't hurt his horse."

"You wouldn't."

"I don't really know the Morgans. Elias called then said Lydia would be in touch. We met her at the book club and then I drove out there today. I didn't know he was there. I…" she didn't want to disclose more than that. But her head had been in the clouds. She didn't see his truck.

They both raised their heads when they heard knocking.

Bethany stood. "I'll get rid of whoever it is. When I get back up here, we're going to put your room back together and we *are* doing yoga. You can't say no. You need to."

She disappeared and Susan sipped the tea. It was kinda nice to have someone fuss over her, though it did make her miss her sister.

Susan looked around the room. She had completely destroyed her dresser and closet. Covering her mouth with a hand, she let out a little sob. Nothing was worth this. A week ago she had a perfect life. There was no reason to throw it all away over a man and his family.

"Your housekeeping skills seem to have slipped."

Susan's attention snapped to the door where Eric stood, his hat in his hands, and his head bowed.

She jolted up off the bed. "What are you doing here? Go. You just need to go."

He didn't move. His large frame encompassed nearly the entire doorway. If she tried to run past him, he'd stop her with a simple movement.

"I'm not here to fight with you."

"Good. You look as if you've been in enough fights this week and you didn't win any of them."

Eric stepped into the room, closed the door behind him, and set his hat on the dresser. Susan quickly moved to set the cup down, just in case she needed both of her hands.

"I was wrong to accuse you like that," he said, still standing by the now closed door with his head hung low.

"Damn right you were. Where do you get off thinking I'd do something like that? You know, you were in my bed too. I didn't come crawling to you in the middle of the night."

He pursed his lips. "You're right."

"And how dare you say those things in front of your parents. They must think I'm some kind of slut thanks to you."

A smile formed on his lips. "I apologized to Glenda first. She doesn't think anything of the sort. In fact, she thinks that if I come back from apologizing to you with my manhood still intact then I should marry you."

Susan gasped loud enough Eric lifted his head. "First of all I wouldn't poison a horse and I wouldn't dismember you either."

"I didn't assume you would." He wrinkled up his nose. "Actually, I accused you of the latter and I can't apologize enough. I just don't know what to think of all this."

She wanted to hate him. She wanted to throw that teacup at his head and make him bleed. That was the wrong thing to want when she also wanted to just scoop him up and hold him.

"Eric, you're under a lot of stress right now. I can't even pretend to understand it. And when you get it all sorted out then maybe…"

"No," he moved to her quickly and gathered her hands in his. "Don't dismiss me."

"You did that when you walked into your parents' house accusing me."

"Susan, I need you. I love you."

"Now who is easy with the words?"

"I'm not kidding. I've never felt this way before."

"You're emotional. Come back tomorrow when…"

Her words were cut short when his mouth came to hers. She wanted to push back, but he still held her hands in his. Or maybe she wasn't trying hard enough. Or maybe she loved him too much to try and break free.

Susan felt herself sink into the kiss as he released her hands and pulled her in close.

There was no use wanting to fight him. She loved him and she couldn't be sure it wouldn't be the biggest mistake of her life.

Eric's lips moved from hers and traveled down her neck. Her insides melted into goo, forcing her to lift her arms around his neck just to keep standing.

"I'll say I'm sorry for the rest of my life if you'll just forgive me," he whispered in her ear.

"I want to hate you."

He pressed his forehead to hers. "You want to, but you don't?"

"I love you, you ass. You hurt me worse than my ex hitting me, but…"

His hands came to her arms and he pushed back to look down at her. "He hit you?"

"Once. Just once. I'm not one to put up with crap like that. Not from him. Not from you," her voice was solid as she delivered her ultimatum.

"I'd never hit you."

"I believe you. Though looking at you, I shouldn't." She lifted his hand and examined the stitches on his finger. "What happened to you?"

The corner of his mouth curled up. "I thought Dane looked so fierce with stitches I thought I'd get a set."

Susan narrowed her gaze.

"Fine. A bowl from breakfast broke and sliced it open. Not a glorious story."

"You didn't come by and tell me."

"I was mad. And I did drive by. You weren't home."

"Would you have stopped?"

Eric shrugged. "I don't know."

Susan fell against him, resting her head on his chest as he pulled her close. "It's too late to say let's start slow."

She felt the rumble in his chest as he chuckled. "You're right."

"Besides, it sounds like your step-mother has us married."

A low hum resonated now. "Mother. I think it's far past time I just consider her my mother."

Susan stepped back and looked up into his dark eyes. "That's quite a comment."

"In this past week the losses and gains seem to be keeping me in check." He ran his hand over her hair. "I need to know why you were at Elias's house."

"I can't tell you. Not because I don't want to. I can't legally tell you."

Eric nodded. "I'm going to assume Lydia is throwing a surprise tea party. I'm going to just go with that to settle my nerves."

She smiled up at him. "That would be good."

"You can't trust him," he said.

"Maybe not. But I really like her and I don't think she's part of anything going on with you."

"Don't get hurt, Susan."

"I already have been."

"Not anymore. I promise."

There was no logic behind the promise or her belief in it, but she did believe. Love made a woman do crazy things. This might have been the craziest.

~*~

Somehow Eric had talked his cousin out of a fury she'd worked up for him. He didn't figure it would be warranted as a compliment to tell her she had her father's anger, so he kept that to himself.

He also figured Susan had heard every word that had been sworn to him while she was upstairs putting her bedroom back together.

They'd both had the right to let him have it. His own temper had cost him a few things over his life, but he wasn't ready to lose Susan over it.

He'd talked her into staying the night with him. They were going to call Lydia and see if she'd put them in touch with Tyson. It was time to find out what was going on and who was doing it. Tyson had led him to believe they were a team now working with each other and not against. If it got him another black eye, it was worth the chance.

Susan called Lydia as they drove out to his house. "Eric said he'd talked to him earlier. We were just hoping, maybe, he'd come talk to us again." She nodded her head and wrote down a phone number in a small book she'd pulled out of her purse. "I really appreciate it. Oh, really? I'd enjoy that. Thanks," she said just before she hung up.

"What was that about?"

"She hasn't seen him. But here's his phone number and…"

"No, the last part of the conversation?"

Susan smiled wide. "She invited me to her book club."

"To cater again?"

"No, to join them."

The smile she wore became infectious and reminded him of the bruise Tyson gave him on the cheek. It was worth it. He reached across the cab of the truck and took her hand.

"Whatever happens from here on out, I promise to talk it out with you first."

She pushed up her sunglasses and narrowed her gaze at him. "I'd appreciate that."

"I meant it when I said I loved you."

"And I meant it in return."

"We're headed in the right direction I guess."

"Looks like it."

Twenty minutes later they pulled up in front of Eric's house and parked next to Tyson's truck. Parked on the other side of it was another truck with a pink camo crown on the back window.

Eric turned off the engine and they both stepped out as Tyson and Lydia walked around the front of his truck.

"I guess sisters get things done," Eric tipped his hat to Lydia.

"It sounded urgent enough I hunted him down. Thought I'd come out too. Maybe I can help you guys find out who's messing with everything," Lydia offered.

"I was out here visiting your mom. *Our* mom." Tyson scratched his head. "My mom told me everything once she calmed down."

"I know it's not easy for you."

"I can see why grandpa wants to move her though. I mean maybe we can get her a new headstone. Your cemetery plots are worn down."

Eric tucked his hands in his pockets to keep from wanting to use them. "That cemetery is very well taken care of."

"Her stone is in three pieces and a few others have been knocked over. It looks like no one has been up there in years."

That wasn't sitting well with him. Eric shook his head as he grit his teeth. "I was up there two days ago and everything was just right."

"Then they're getting closer. Whoever it is we're looking for. They're moving in to run us off. They're hitting us where it hurts."

"Ain't going to happen.

"Damn, straight," Tyson agreed.

Chapter Twenty-Six

Tyson had been right. The cemetery had been hit and Eric felt violently ill. His mother's headstone had been the worst hit.

"They know this is important," Eric said as he picked up a piece of the stone. "I don't think your grandfather is behind this. I think something else is going on."

"He wouldn't condone this," Lydia said. "He's a ruthless businessman, but he's not...malicious."

A week ago Eric would have argued that, but today, standing over his mother's grave with his *brother*, he just didn't believe it anymore.

"Elias has to talk to us. Why did he want this land? And if he's not set to destroy it who is?"

Lydia tapped her foot and tightened her lips. "I shouldn't do this, but..." She looked at Susan then back at Eric. "He's having a party on your mother's birthday to celebrate her sixtieth birthday."

Eric exchanged glances with Susan. It was obvious she only knew her part and not what it was for.

"He always celebrates her birthday, privately," she told Eric. "But this year it's bigger. It's a formal dinner party with people who didn't know your mother. People who didn't know our father," she said.

"Why?"

She shrugged. "I don't know. He asked me to work with Susan and set it up."

Eric looked at Susan whose eyes had gone wide. "Is that all?"

She looked at Lydia and still said nothing.

Lydia rested her hand on Susan's arm. "We asked her to sign a confidentiality statement and she did. I can see we made the right choice in caterers. She isn't even talking now. But that is what she was doing at the house." She looked at Susan. "I won't tell him that the agreement was broken in any way."

"I need to cancel the contract. I can't do this now. Not when it's a conflict of interest like this. I love Eric. I can't hurt him by going through with it."

Lydia nodded in understanding.

Tyson held up a finger. "Wait. You're planning the party," he said to Lydia. "Susan is already embedded. I have a funny feeling that the guest list includes maybe business associates that I don't know. Maybe it includes someone who is messing with our land."

"You're thinking he should have his party and we should gather information," Eric offered.

"Exactly. Lydia and I can work on getting the guest list and figuring out who everyone is. Susan will be working the room during their lunch. We can certainly keep tabs on what's going on."

Eric turned to Susan. "What about Bethany? She's serving?"

Susan looked to Lydia, who gave her a nod. "I was asked to not use her as a server."

"My grandfather's request," Lydia answered.

"Because she's Byron's daughter," Eric said smoothly as he fit the connection together. "I'll bet my uncle is on that guest list."

"Do you think he's involved?" Susan asked.

"No, I really don't. I don't think he's smart enough or savvy enough. I think he's being played. And I think Elias is being played too."

"I'll head home and see if I can get my hands on that guest list. Grandpa is in his eighties. He often misplaces things," she said smiling.

"I'll go with you. Maybe if I get more of this story about my parents, I will know something as well." He visibly shuttered. "And if I come back calmly maybe he'll tell me what's going on."

They both walked back to Tyson's truck and then Lydia turned back to them. "Eric, I'm really sorry about your mother's headstone. I'm sure this was a lovely place and will be again."

Eric graciously smiled. "Thank you. It will be."

As they drove away, Eric knelt down next to his mother's broken headstone. "I can't believe someone would do this to you. You'll have a new one. A better one," he promised.

"Why don't I leave you alone for a little bit," Susan offered. "I'll walk back to your place. You spend some time with her."

Eric shook his head. "No." He stood. "She would have liked you, I think. I remember her being no nonsense. You're like that."

"Thank you. I'm sure I would have liked her too."

Eric took her hand. "Glenda likes you. I think your charm and my sad single life got you that job."

"I'd like to think I got that job on my own credits."

Eric laughed as he lifted her hand to his lips. "You did. She chose well, for both a caterer and a girlfriend."

"You said she has us married off."

"I think she does. Maybe we'll have to talk about that soon."

"I'm in no hurry," Susan quickly said. "I'm not against it. I'm just in no hurry."

He had to accept that, but as far as he was concerned, she'd stuck by him this week. He'd marry her tomorrow if he could. But he'd wait until she was ready. It didn't look as though either of them were going anywhere.

It felt right to sleep in Eric's arms again and Susan was grateful. However, as she laid there, Eric breathing heavily with his chest against her back, she wondered what he would be like when there wasn't so much drama.

There was no reason for her not to think he'd be as calm as he was the day she'd met him. Taking life at his own pace and not answering to anyone but himself.

She closed her eyes. She remembered falling in love with her ex-husband. She was young and easily persuaded. The whole world revolved around him and she'd have done anything to marry him as soon as she could—and she had.

In the back of her mind would always be the question of when it began to go so wrong. Just the thought of him now made her skin go cold.

Their relationship had turned one day. No explanations. Suddenly everything she did or thought was wrong. He spent more time away from her. She knew it wasn't another woman, it was his life. A man like him needed the outdoors more than he needed a woman in their cozy house. However, he'd returned more lean and tanned from any of his adventures, but his mood would be foul. She had finally decided it was because he didn't want to come home to her. The night his fist hit her jaw was the last night she ever saw him.

What would stop Eric from becoming a beast?

He was beaten and bruised because his temper had gotten in the way. Would it happen again?

She just wouldn't rush into anything else with him. Of course she was sleeping in his bed, again, after only a week of knowing him. But she just couldn't help it. She was absolutely in love with him.

Eric snuggled in closer and she let herself relax against him. She let herself drift away to the sound of his breathing until she heard the unmistakable sound of footsteps as they moved past the bedroom window.

She sat up with a start and that woke Eric.

"What's wrong?"

"Someone's outside," she said.

He moved quickly to his feet and pulled on his pants. Susan scrambled for her clothes and stopped when she heard the unmistakable sound of her car starting.

"They're stealing my car!"

Eric pulled his shotgun out from under the bed and headed out of the house with Susan following close behind, pulling on her clothes.

Susan's car sped away down the road. Eric swung open the door on his truck and then slammed it again. "They freaking sliced my tires!"

He kicked the flat rubber.

"I'll call the police," Susan hurried back into the house as Eric walked the perimeter.

Ten minutes later Eric walked in, shotgun still in his hand.

Susan buttoned up her shirt. "Police are on their way."

"I've had enough of this. What the hell do they want? This is just freaking land!" He set his gun on the couch and ran his hands over his hair.

She wished she understood the situation more. How could someone kill off animals and destroy property? Why would someone want to drive them away?

It was three in the morning, but they certainly weren't going back to bed. Susan decided to make a pot of coffee and have it ready when the police arrived. As it brewed, she went to the bathroom and tied up her hair, then texted Bethany to let her know what was going on. It worried her that if they were messing with Eric's life they'd begin to focus on her as well. She didn't want to mention that to him, but it was in her head.

The one problem with living so far out of town, it took longer for the police to arrive. It had been nearly forty-five minutes since she'd called before a police car pulled up.

Eric opened the door as the man walked up the front steps.

"Hey, Douglas. How'd you get this crappy shift?" Eric asked as the man took his hat off and stepped through the front door.

"Luck of the draw I guess. So what's going on?"

"Come in and have some coffee. We have a long list."

"We?" Douglas asked as Susan walked around the wall from the kitchen. "Oh, look at that. You have a woman here."

"Don't act so surprised," Eric said as he shut the door. "This is Susan Hayes."

"Ma'am," Douglas said with a nod. "It's nice to meet you."

"Likewise," she said. "Can I offer you a cup of coffee?"

"I'd like that."

The men followed her into the kitchen.

"I was sorry to hear about your grandfather," Douglas said as he sat down at the table with Eric. "He was a good man."

"He was."

Susan set the coffee carafe on the table and retrieved three cups. "Do you need milk?"

Douglas shook his head. "Black is fine."

She nodded and sat down next to Eric.

"So you two have known each other awhile?" she asked as she poured the coffee.

Douglas picked up his cup and took a sip. "Yeah. I grew up with Dane. Eric was like everyone's big brother."

"That makes me sound old."

"I said you were like everyone's brother, not their father. But okay. You acted old enough," he said on a chuckle. "So, down to business. Your car was stolen?"

"Yes. Someone was outside. I heard them. Then they drove off in my car and sliced the tires on Eric's truck."

Douglas pulled his cell phone from his pocket and set it on the table. "Do you mind if I record this? That way I have all the facts."

"No problem."

"Great, would you repeat that?"

Susan did as he asked.

"Any reason someone would be out here this far?"

Eric clasped his hands together and let out a breath. "Since my grandfather's death we've had a lot of things going on out here."

"Such as?"

"Stuff," Eric snapped out.

"Someone poisoned his cows and horses," Susan quickly added.

"You didn't report that?"

Eric snapped his teeth together. "Thought I knew who was responsible."

"And who did you think it was?"

"Not important," Eric said as leaned back in his chair.

Douglas ran his tongue over his teeth. "It's not important. Someone is poisoning your animals, stealing your cars, and slicing your tires and this isn't important?"

Susan took a quick breath before blurting out, "And vandalizing the cemetery."

She noticed the quick flash of irritation in Eric's eyes.

Douglas raised his brows. "Vandalized your cemetery?"

Eric didn't answer right away. Susan could see the vein pulse at his temple and his fingers tense against his thighs.

"Yes."

Douglas cracked his thumbs. "You haven't changed, huh? Eric Walker is always bigger than the world. He can handle anything on his own?"

She watched as Eric's eyes narrowed and the glare intensified.

"Sometimes, Walker, I think you make this crap up to look tough."

The vein on the side of Eric's neck thickened as his jaw tightened.

"This is why you pay taxes, Walker. The police are here to protect you and keep your family and crap safe. How are we supposed to do that when you don't report things?"

"I can handle this."

"Really? At this point, you can't even drive away from your house. This is pretty serious stuff."

Eric pushed back from the table and Susan worried that he'd begin to hit the police officer in front of them, just as he'd obviously done when he'd confronted Tyson in the past week.

He paced the kitchen and just as he turned to take a breath to speak the front door flew open.

"Susan?" Bethany's voice rang through the house and a moment later she raced into the kitchen, panting. "Thank God you're here."

Susan stood and moved to her. "I told you I was here. I texted you."

"You said your car had been stolen and Eric's tires cut, but your car is parked outside our house." She sucked in a breath and looked at Douglas. "Oh, hi."

He gave her a nod. "Bethany Waterbury?"

"Yes," she said on an obviously annoyed sigh.

Douglas stood and handed her a business card from his pocket. "I've seen all of your movies. You're pretty gifted."

"Thanks," she said, as she looked down at his card. "Douglas Brant?"

"Yes, ma'am."

"You gave me a ticket the last time I was here."

"I remember."

"You remember that? It was at least four years ago."

Susan wondered if Douglas even realized he was grinning at Bethany.

"I was still dishing out tickets back then. You were parked over the line and in a fire lane. You argued with me for at least thirty minutes."

Bethany crossed her arms in front of her. "And now you're drinking coffee in my cousin's kitchen at four in the morning?"

"Believe it or not, this is a promotion." He shifted his glance to Eric. "Cousin?"

"Byron's youngest daughter."

Douglas's mouth formed an "O" as he looked at Bethany.

"Oh, great," she growled. "People know Byron Walker and simply roll their eyes when they know I'm his daughter."

"I didn't roll my eyes," Douglas said as he narrowed his gaze. "You're Violet Waterbury's daughter?"

"Yes."

"You're the spitting image of her."

"I know."

Douglas gave her a nod. "You said her car was at home?"

"I live with Susan. She texted me to tell me her car had been stolen. But it's parked outside the house."

Susan placed her hands on her abdomen. The adrenaline of the evening had landed like a lead ball in the pit of her stomach.

She noticed Eric's quick move to her side as he stepped toward Douglas. "I don't know who the hell is messing with us, but this says they're too close. I don't want them near the girls."

Douglas stood. "Someone is trying to scare you."

"It's working."

"Why don't you go to your family's house tonight? Susan, I need your address so I can go by your house." He turned toward Bethany. "Did you see anything? Hear anything?"

"No. I did my yoga and went to bed. Next thing I knew she texted me and told me her car was stolen and Eric's tires cut. I decided to come out. When I left, her car was there."

"I'll call you," Douglas said putting on his hat and walking toward the door. "Anything else happens you call me directly."

Eric nodded. "We will."

"I mean it," Douglas reiterated before he walked out the door.

They watched as Douglas drove away, his headlights illuminating the dark road.

Eric shut the front door and turned toward them. "I don't like this. Someone's going to get hurt."

"I don't understand what they want," Bethany held her hand over her mouth. "My father lost the land to the Morgans. Why are they trying to push you off now?"

"I firmly believe the Morgans aren't part of this. There's more to it. Someone wants all this land. They're not going to get it. They'll have to kill me first."

That knot in Susan's stomach tightened. She certainly didn't like the sound of that.

"Should we call your parents and tell them we're coming to their house to stay? They should know what's going on."

Eric tightened his lips. "I'll call them and tell them what's going on. I'll have Russ set me up with some new tires, but I'm not going to start staying at their house. No one is running me off."

She could admire that about him. His Walker pride ran deep, but she was scared. She certainly didn't want to go back to her house and she didn't want Bethany to either. It looked like the three of them were going to be roommates for a little while. At least until they truly knew what was going on.

Later when they were alone and getting ready for bed, she approached the subject of Douglas Brant.

"You and Douglas have some history together, don't you?"

"Why do you say that?"

She pulled back the covers and climbed into the bed. "He seemed a bit anxious around you."

"Like he said, I'm an older brother."

"There's something else. The bit about you having to take care of things and making stuff up. That got you angry."

"He's just a punk who happens to be a cop now."

That made some sense. "That bothers you?"

Eric climbed into bed and fell back onto his pillow, his hands behind his head. "Do we need to talk about this?"

"I'm just curious about it."

"I saved his ass once by lying for him. Who knows, had he gotten in trouble maybe he'd not be a cop now. But as it is, I lied so he wouldn't get in trouble. I sometimes think he forgets the reason I made stuff up."

She was certainly intrigued now. "What did he do?"

Eric turned on his side to face her. "I hate talking about things in the past."

"I'm in your bed after knowing you only a week. I think it's okay to tell me everything. I want to know who I'm sleeping next to."

"I haven't scared you off yet?"

"You're about to tell me how you covered for a friend. That's admirable."

His lips puckered as if he thought she was wrong. "He borrowed my truck for an intimate night with some girl. They got drunk and he crashed it out by the lake. Then he left it there with all the beer cans left in it. When the cops came looking for the owner they came looking for me."

"Eric, you covered for him? That's not okay."

"No one was hurt. My truck was totaled. He was screwing around with some older woman. I don't know why I covered for him. I guess I had a lot less to lose and a family that would bail me out and still love me. He wasn't that guy. He didn't have that kind of home.

"You said you'd crashed the truck?"

He shrugged. "That's what friends do."

"Not his."

"It was a long time ago. We need his help now and I'm willing to let him have his power trip. We all make mistakes."

Susan snuggled in closer to him. How could she not love a man who took care of everyone?

Chapter Twenty-Seven

There had been some tension when Russell brought Eric's new tires out and Tyson pulled up behind him. Russell would be gracious, but they'd all disliked the Morgans for so long it was hard to accept it all so quickly without looking over your shoulder. Eric could respect that.

"They slashed the tires on Lydia's car too," Tyson said as he approached them. "I just got hers changed out. What time did they hit you?"

"About three," Eric said. "They stole Susan's car only to drive it to her house and leave it."

Tyson bit down on his bottom lip. "They have a lot of information then. They know who she is and where she lives."

"She lives here now," he said. "She and Bethany. I'm not chancing anyone getting to them."

Russell grunted as he tightened the nut on the tire, which Eric assumed was on purpose.

Tyson grinned. It must have been very obvious.

"Where are they now?"

Eric ran his hand over the back of his neck. "She had classes. We argued about her going, but she won. Bethany was going to hang out there. They promised not to go to the house unless they had a police escort."

"I have some friends on the force I could call," Tyson offered.

"Douglas Brant has their numbers. He's going to check in with them."

Tyson nodded. "Good guy. They're in good hands."

"I'm done." Russell stood and brushed the dirt from his pants.

"Thanks. Have you met Tyson?"

There was an unmistakable flash of irritation in Russell's eyes. But he nodded. "Nice to meet you."

"Likewise," Tyson said. Neither of them extended hands to shake.

They were both in a strange position, Eric thought. These were his brothers and yet they were total strangers, even in blood.

Russell threw the tire iron in the back of his truck. "That fence in the east quad is in need of repair. I'm heading over. You coming?"

"I'll be right behind you."

Without another word, Russell climbed into his truck and drove off.

"He doesn't like me much," Tyson said kicking the dirt with his boot.

"It's going to take some getting used to. Morgan isn't a name we've been known to embrace."

"Walker at our house wasn't too nicely met either," he said with a crooked grin. "Lydia got a hold of the guest list."

"Anyone we know?"

Tyson rubbed the stubble on his cheek. "Your uncle is there, just as you'd assumed."

"Figures."

"Your dad is too."

Eric snapped his head up. "My father?"

"It's on the list."

Eric tightened his jaw. "Who else?"

"Dwight Peterson."

He thought on the name. "I don't know him."

"Are you familiar with Peterson Oil?"

"Of course."

"Looks like they are coming to dinner. He and his son, who is about our age."

"We're not going to find out we have more brothers are we?" Eric joked, but there was some realistic worry in the joke.

Tyson must have thought so too, but he laughed. "I don't think so. The grandson's name is Shooter."

"You're kidding me, right?"

"Afraid I'm not. But there's no reason not to assume that this land stuff has something to do with them."

"If it's a legit deal, why destroy our properties?"

"I don't know. That's what concerns me. Who else is involved aside from Dwight and Shooter?"

"That's the whole list?"

"It's all she got."

"I'll ask Douglas about it. We have a few days before the dinner. Maybe we can find out more."

~*~

Susan's mind certainly wasn't on her class. Luckily it was a business class and not one that focused on using fire.

Her mind had been spinning since she'd seen her car drive away.

Why was someone messing with her? She wasn't a Walker and she didn't have anything to do with the land that Byron had lost.

The thought had crossed her mind, more than she'd have liked, that it was too dangerous to be involved with Eric. Now would be the prime opportunity to cut her ties and run.

But her heart wasn't in that. She loved him and that too was equally as confusing.

As soon as her class let out she gathered her things and found Bethany on a bench outside with Douglas Brant.

Her purse was on her lap and gripped like an old lady afraid some man might steal her coffee candies. Douglas looked equally as uncomfortable.

They both stood the moment she neared them.

"Thought you were never going to get out of there," Bethany huffed as she swung her purse over her shoulder.

"Officer Brant, why are you here?"

"It's Douglas or Doug. You don't have to be formal with me. But I was asked to watch out for you both. I figured you'd need to stop by the house and collect a few things before heading back out."

Susan smiled, trying to diffuse the tension that surrounded the two of them. "That's very kind. I think that would be very nice."

Bethany glared at her through narrowed lids.

"C'mon," he said. "I think she'd like to get out of here. She's not a big fan of mine."

"I still don't see why you ticketed me or why you find it necessary to remember it," Bethany said as she hurried ahead of them and toward her car in the lot.

Douglas laughed as he settled in next to Susan and walked at her pace. "She wants to hate me. I just don't think she really does."

Susan wasn't sure about that. Watching her swing open the car door and throw her purse inside said differently.

"Thank you for looking after us. I'm sure we'll be okay."

"No taking chances. Besides, the last thing I need is Eric Walker coming after me."

"He's not violent."

Douglas clucked his tongue. "I didn't say he was."

Then why had he clucked his tongue? There was more to that story too.

Bethany was strumming her fingers on the steering wheel when they approached the car. She kept the windows up and her gaze forward.

Douglas chuckled. "I get under her skin. I'll follow you ladies to your house."

"Thank you." Susan said as she pulled open the car door and slid inside.

She watched as Douglas walked back to his car.

"Why do you hate him?" she asked as Bethany revved the engine and shifted into drive. "He's a nice guy."

"I didn't deserve that ticket."

Susan couldn't help but laugh. "That was four years ago. You can't still hold that against him, can you?"

"I most certainly can. It's the only ticket I've ever gotten."

"Really? I've had like six. Seven, I forgot about the parking ticket on Pearl Street."

Bethany turned the corner quickly, forcing Susan to grab hold of the door to keep in her seat.

"You don't understand," Bethany gripped the wheel. "I have been able to talk myself out of every ticket anyone ever tried to give me. But not his. He was nice and sweet and damn it, he still gave me the ticket."

"So? You were in the wrong."

"By four inches."

"It's the law."

Bethany huffed as she took the next turn as hard as she'd taken the last.

"I want to know what's wrong with him. I'm a sexy, young woman. He wasn't married. He wasn't involved."

"How do you know that?"

"It's part of the charm I have."

Susan let out a low hum as they pulled up in front of the house.

Bethany pulled up right behind Susan's car which was parked on the street as if Susan had come home and parked it there herself.

"I told you it was here," Bethany said as she put the car in park and turned off the engine. "I never heard it drive up and I never heard anyone in the house."

"It all seems strange to me."

"Maybe they just don't like Subarus," Bethany joked as they climbed from the car.

"Who wouldn't want a Subaru? It'll last forever."

Douglas pulled up right behind them, parked, and climbed from his cruiser. "This is your car?"

"This is it," Susan said. "Right where I would have parked it had I driven it home."

Douglas walked up alongside of it. "They jimmied it to start it. Dash is kind of a mess."

"Great."

"I'll see if I can lift anything from it. Did you have anything inside that would be missing?"

Susan gave it some thought. "No. I keep it empty to transport my containers in. So I don't think anything would have been in there."

Douglas looked toward the house and then at Bethany. "Which way did you leave the house early this morning?"

"Through the back door."

"I'm going to walk around the house. I don't want the two of you going in without me. Stay right here," he ordered as he started around the side of the house and through to the back yard.

"He's a pain in the ass. Do we really need him?"

Susan tried to conceal the smile she knew was forming on her lips by puckering them together. "I think you like him."

"Bite your tongue."

"Why else would he be under your skin like this?"

"I'm not interested. I just want all of this to be over. It's quite humiliating knowing my father started all of this. If he didn't have his problems Eric wouldn't be having all these issues. We wouldn't have to leave our house and wait for some cop to let us into it. I can't believe I'm related to Byron Walker," she said with a wince.

Susan thought perhaps that was some of the truth, but she was still going to hold on to the thought that Bethany liked Douglas Brant more than she was letting on.

However, she didn't even know what to say about what her father had done to everyone. It was true. Had he not gambled away the land, perhaps none of this would have happened.

Douglas came around the side of the house. "Do you have your key?"

"Of course," Susan said as she fished it from her purse.

"I'm going to go in through the front door. Do not follow me," he said very curtly as he took the key from her hand. "No sign of forced entry."

Bethany cocked her head to the side and blew a strand of red hair from her eyes. "If there is no sign of forced entry, we can just go in, right?"

"I said no sign of forced entry. I have every reason to believe your residence was compromised." He bore his stare into Bethany. "In fact, I'd venture to guess they waited for you to leave. So if you don't think you're in danger, perhaps you'll change your mind in a few moments. Don't follow me in," he restated as he turned and walked up to the house.

"They were in my house," Susan's voice quivered as she said it. "They were in my car and in my house. Who the hell is doing this?"

"Maybe it's one of my brothers or even my dad."

Susan shook her head. "I don't think so. Your dad might have gotten the Walkers involved in this, but I certainly don't think he's the one doing all of this."

"How would I know? I don't really know them at all."

"Well, as soon as this is over, I think that needs to change. You need to get to know your brothers and sisters. I'd assume they're hanging their heads in shame too."

Bethany's shoulders dropped as if she'd been deflated. "I didn't think about that."

Susan wrapped her arm around Bethany's shoulders and pulled her close as Douglas walked out of the front door.

"It's clear, but I'm going to need you to come look at it. I'm going to call for backup."

"Backup? Why?"

"I assume whoever stole your car let themselves into your house once Bethany left this morning. I'll need you to tell me if anything is missing. I'd never assume your housekeeping skills are this bad."

Susan felt the blood drain from her head and now Bethany was holding her up.

Slowly they walked toward the house.

She didn't even have to enter to see the destruction. Pictures were off the wall. Her office had been nearly turned inside-out. "My computer is missing."

Douglas took his phone out of his pocket to make a note. "Look around and make a list."

Susan nodded slowly as she scanned the cute house she'd been so proud of. Now she felt violated.

"Will you please call Eric?"

Douglas nodded and backed out of the room to make the call.

"Why would they do this?"

Bethany, with her hands firmly on Susan's shoulders, followed her into the room. "If this really has anything to do with the land then maybe they think you have some documentation."

"I met the Walkers a week ago. This is ridiculous."

"Maybe they don't know that. They just know you and Eric are very involved. If I were a stranger, I'd assume you knew everything there was to know about him."

"I know so little."

Bethany gave Susan's arms a little squeeze. "I'm related and I know just as little." She released Susan. "Maybe they think I know something. Maybe this has nothing to do with you at all. After all, I'm Byron's bastard daughter."

"Don't say that."

"It's true. I'm not going to mix my words. But if he's involved they'd assume I knew something."

Bethany turned and ran out of the room and up the stairs.

Susan followed and Douglas after her.

Bethany ran to her room and stood there, frozen. Not one thing had been touched. She looked at Susan. "Nothing has been moved."

"Most of the damage is up and down the stairs to the pictures," Douglas said. "The office. And some of the cabinets in the kitchen."

Susan turned to see her photos hanging as if they'd been run into as someone walked down the stairs, but one was missing. She walked out of the room and looked down. She hadn't noticed it as she'd run after Bethany, but the generational photo of wedding bands was broken and on the ground. As she picked it up, a shard of glass stabbed her finger. She quickly dropped the frame again causing it to crash with a horrific noise.

"Are you okay?" Douglas moved to her quickly and took her hand. "Tell me where to find the Band-Aids and I'll get you one. I don't think you'll need stitches."

"In my bathroom. In the medicine cabinet."

Susan held her throbbing, bleeding finger and looked down at the picture, which held such sentiment.

Douglas returned a moment later with the Band-Aid and wrapped it around the cut.

"You're good to go. Have you seen anything else missing?"

Susan shook her head. "So far just the computer."

"What did you have on it?"

"My business information. Proposals. Bookkeeping. Menus." She winced.

"I want you to look around a little more. Just make sure."

Susan nodded and headed back downstairs to check things out.

Chapter Twenty-Eight

Tyson had talked his way into driving with Eric into town. He wasn't sure why it mattered, but he'd agreed. Russell's curses were still ringing in Eric's ear from when he'd called him. But this had to be dealt with. He wasn't going to have anything happen to Susan or Bethany.

Douglas was leaned up against his cruiser with another officer parked behind him, when Eric pulled up.

Officer Smyth lifted the brim of his hat with his index finger and gave Eric that smirk of a grin he'd learned to despise since high school.

Eric put his truck into park and killed the engine.

"Smyth," Tyson said the name on a low growl.

"You know him?"

"Biggest pain in the ass officer in Macon," he said.

Eric let out a low chuckle. "Yeah. I'm no troublemaker, but you wouldn't know it if you talked to him. He's issued me three tickets in the past year. I've gotten out of them, but he has it out for me. Has ever since high school."

"He's hit me six times this year," Tyson said as he opened his door. "Tried to run me in for a DUI a month ago after having seen me at the bar. I'd had one beer. It didn't hold up. He's sweet on Lydia too and that doesn't sit well with me."

"Wonder what he's up to now?" Eric said as he opened his door and stepped out of the truck.

"Hey, guys." Douglas smiled as they walked toward them. "Susan wanted me to call you."

"How bad did they hit her house?" Tyson asked, his hands tucked in his pockets, just as Eric's were and he knew it was to keep them still.

"Tore it up a bit, but only took her computer with her business information on it. She's packing up a few things and so is Bethany. We've taken statements and pictures. As soon as they want to they can begin to clean up."

Eric turned toward Officer Smyth. "You just happen by?"

Smyth moved his tongue over his teeth. "Saw that this involved the two of you and thought it was worth checking out. What do you have going on with Miss Hayes?"

"We're seeing each other," Eric said very matter-of-factly.

"Nice and tidy, huh?"

Eric kept his hands tucked into his pockets. "Tidy?"

"All the vandalism up at your places and now here. Makes it look like the families and their friends are getting hit. I've never known the Morgans and the Walkers to be real friendly."

Tyson stiffened. "Some things change."

"I'll bet," Smyth smiled and turned to Douglas. "I'll head back. Keep me informed."

A moment later he drove away and both men let out the breath they'd been holding.

Douglas gave Smyth a wave and then turned back to Eric. "Not a fan of that man, but he's thorough."

"Makes crap up is what he does," Tyson added and turned to head up to the house.

"Heard the Morgan's house got hit last night too. Lydia's tires?"

Eric nodded. "That's what he said."

"Any idea what's going on? This isn't normal activity around here."

"A few days ago Tyson and I threw some punches assuming we were doing it to each other. But that isn't the case. My uncle lost some of our land in a poker game. It's supposed to revert back to the Morgans. That's all legal, even if I hate the thought of it. But the destruction on both properties doesn't make sense."

"So what is with you and Tyson hanging around? I'm with Smyth. The Morgans and the Walkers don't mix."

Eric removed his hat and ran his hand over his hair. He brushed off the rim and set it back on his head. "My mom was a Morgan."

"Oh. Don't think I knew that. So you and Tyson are cousins?"

Eric chuckled. "Thought so. As it pans out, my mother had another son."

"Makes this interesting."

"She left Tyson with Elias Morgan and left. He didn't know."

"Sounds like your world has been turned upside down this week since your grandfather died."

Eric nodded in agreement, though that was certainly an understatement.

"I might have been able to get a jump on all of this had you told me about the animals and the vandalism. The fact that Byron Walker lost the land in a poker game would have helped too. It gives motive."

"Sure it does. It looks like someone on our side would be more apt to doing this than on the Morgan's. They stand to get my home and half our land."

Douglas nodded. "You're right. It does sound peculiar."

"You see why I might be a bit tight lipped."

"I can't help you if I don't have all the facts. Right now I have a case of a stolen car and burglary. It seems a little deeper than that doesn't it?"

"I guess I'd keep your ear to the pavement and let me know if other funny things start happening."

"Smyth is going to be all over this, you know. I think he's already got you pegged for something. Morgan too."

"I'm sure he does. He always has."

Douglas dropped his shoulders. "He's an ass. He's pulled me over three times for failure to stop at a stop sign."

He couldn't help it. Eric grinned at that. "Just keep an eye on this place. I'll have Susan and Bethany with me. I'll let you know if anything else happens."

"You swear it?" I can't do my job if I don't know anything."

"You'll be one of the first to know."

Douglas accepted that with a grunt as he pulled his keys from his pocket. "On a lighter note, why does Bethany dislike me so much?"

"You gave her a ticket."

"She broke the law."

"I guess she holds grudges."

Douglas walked around his car and opened the door. "Do you think she'd go out with me?"

"Your timing sucks."

Douglas gave the roof of the cruiser two solid slaps. "Story of my life," he said as he climbed in and drove away.

Eric took the path to the house slowly. It made him ill to think someone had been in there. Someone had touched her things. He was very afraid that if he found out who had violated Susan's space, and if he did it again, he just might kill him.

Susan walked down the staircase with a suitcase in her hand. "I'm almost done packing."

"We can come by tomorrow and get more things," he offered.

"I'd rather make just one trip. Bethany's just finishing up. Do you have a computer?" she asked.

"I use the one at my parent's house. Why?"

"A lot of my documents were stored on an online server. Regardless of what's going on, I've been hired for a job in three days and I need to plan for it—especially if we're going to use it to get information."

He didn't like the thought of her doing the catering job either, but she was right, they'd have a captive audience.

"It's been a long day. I just want to get home. Is your car drivable?"

Susan shook her head. "No. I'll have to have the dash put back together."

"One of Bethany's brothers can do that. He's an expert. I'll get you anywhere you need to go. I can hang out at my parent's house tonight for a little bit so you can use the computer too."

The smile that crossed her lips warmed him. He admired how she could keep her cool in almost any situation.

"I'd appreciate that. How do you think Glenda would feel about me using her kitchen to prepare for the dinner at the Morgan's?"

"Are you going to let her help?"

"I wouldn't expect her to."

"That's not what I asked. I asked if you were going to let her help. Maybe I should reword that. She's going to want to help you."

A blush formed on her cheeks and it absolutely made his heart flutter. "I'd think that was very sweet. Of course I'd let her help me."

He lifted his hand to her cheek. "She really does like you."

"I'm glad. Because I know she thinks I'm good enough for you."

And that right there was reason enough to make sure Susan Q. Hayes stuck around for the rest of his life.

"What does the Q. stand for?"

She answered with a laugh and turned her attention to Bethany as she pulled her suitcase down the stairs and another box of items.

Eric looked up at her and cringed. "I thought you moved here with just what you had."

"This is it. I won't let it get in your way. I promise."

Eric wrinkled up his nose. Just the thought of two more people in his house was beginning to give him an anxiety attack.

Chapter Twenty-Nine

Glenda must have been waiting for the day Eric brought Susan back to her house.

When he'd called her to tell them they were headed out she'd actually broken down in tears.

"I'm so glad you two mended everything."

As they walked into the house she'd wrapped her arms around Susan so tightly Eric thought she'd nearly squeezed the breath out of her.

"I made some banana bread," she began as she led Susan toward the kitchen. "I'm sure it's not as good as something you would make, but I wanted to try it. I have some water on for tea too. Would you like some?"

"That would be very nice, thank you."

Glenda shifted her look to Bethany. "How about you? Cup of tea? Some banana bread?"

Bethany smiled. "Yes. Thank you."

Eric watched his stepmother continue walking. "What about me?"

"Your father is in his office. Why don't you go see what he's up to?"

Eric let his shoulders drop. He'd been replaced by the two women. This would take some getting used to. He was finding that he enjoyed Glenda's fussing over him. Just being dismissed to the other room, well, maybe he'd have to discuss that with her.

A moment later he heard the three women giggle over something, as if they'd forgotten he were even nearby. That was certainly a sign to dismiss himself to his father's office.

His father had his head resting in his hands, elbows on the desk. This was a sign that he was stressed and Eric didn't see this side of his father very often.

"Hey," he said softly as he entered the office.

His father quickly raised his head and sat up tall in his chair. "Oh, hi. Didn't know you were coming over."

"Susan needed to use the computer."

His father nodded slowly, then gathered the papers on his desk, almost as if he were hiding them from Eric.

"Russ says that you had some excitement, again. Tires slashed?"

"And Susan's car stolen and her house broken into." Eric sat down in front of his father's desk. "They sliced Lydia Morgan's tires too."

His father let out a deflated breath. "That's horrible."

Eric watched his father fidget with the items on his desk. "You knew about Tyson, didn't you?"

His father didn't answer right away. He took the stack of papers he'd piled together, opened a drawer on his desk, and laid them inside. Shutting the drawer, he finally looked up at Eric.

"Yes."

"Why didn't you ever tell me about him?"

"He didn't know the truth. It was an argument I'd had with Elias years ago."

"I don't understand how she could have just left him. Forgotten about him."

His father shook his head. "She never forgot about him. He was two when she had you. She went through a very bad case of postpartum with you. For a time, she was even hospitalized."

"I didn't know that."

"There was no need for you to know." His father wrung his hands together. "Eric, I'm glad that the memories you have of her are wonderful. She had a brilliant side to her despite all the darkness."

"I don't remember the darkness."

"Because I tried to keep you from it," he said. "The only joy she had in life was you and redecorating this house."

That was exactly what Eric remembered.

Everett leaned back in his chair and tucked his hands behind his head. "Elias wanted to raise you too. I wouldn't have that. You were my flesh and blood. He vowed to never speak to us again. He didn't want to know you, I think it hurt too much."

"You let me think she was fine all these years? Does Glenda know all of this?"

His father nodded and he could feel the hole his mother left in his heart expand.

"Eric, don't hate her. She was a confused woman. Her depression paralyzed her. She compensated with medication. It's a real disease."

"Did you love her?"

His father looked him in the eyes and waited a beat. "For a brief time I think I tried. She didn't want to be loved, Eric. If she did, she'd have stayed with Tyson and Elias."

He heard Glenda's laugh from the other room and he closed his eyes. Could he actually feel the swelling of his heart when he realized he'd spited her for so long and she'd loved him unconditionally?

There was no way in hell he was going to cry in front of his father over this. It was a lot to take in. So his mother wasn't who he'd made her to be. There were probably millions of adults who found that to be true in adulthood; why should he be any different?

Glenda was going to get a huge bouquet of roses in the morning from her eldest son. Things were going to be different, he promised himself. He'd make things right with Tyson too. They'd done okay up to this point, but they certainly could be better to each other.

He'd taken the conversation into a different direction than he'd anticipated. They'd been talking about tires and stolen cars. Eric still needed those answers too.

Eric leaned in on the desk with his elbows. "What's going on with the Morgans?" He changed the subject back to the destruction going on. "Bryon loses the property over his gambling losses and now someone is out to destroy the land? Animals are dead. The cemetery is vandalized. Cars are targeted. Not just ours but the Morgans' too. What's going on?"

Worry creased his father's eyes. "I don't know. Elias invited me over for dinner this week to discuss plans, but that was all before this started to happen. I don't understand it. And I'm very afraid someone is going to get hurt."

"Not if I can help it." Eric scooted the chair closer to the desk. "Breaking confidentiality, Susan is catering that dinner. She's serving."

"That's nice," he said with a genuine smile.

"I don't like it, but we'll be able to gather information. Lydia was able to get hold of some of the guest list and Dwight Peterson and his grandson Shooter are on it."

Another nod from his father told him he knew who they were. "Oil."

"You think that's what this is about?"

"Yes. But it doesn't make sense to destroy the property over it. Especially if the deal is to sell him oil rights."

"Is that what's going on? He's selling the oil rights?"

His father looked down and bit his lip.

"You already know all of this," Eric drew out slowly.

"Some things need to be done in silence so that my brother doesn't get a hold of the information. Can you imagine what would happen then?"

"So he loses the land and now there's oil there? We lose everything?"

"Not if we let Morgan move your mother. He'll cut us in."

Eric sat back in his chair. "That's what this is all about? She's a bargaining chip?"

"It's all I had."

"So you're saving us?"

"Yes."

He didn't like it. He didn't like it one bit. "So who's messing with us? And why, if it's the Morgans, are they sabotaging their own property? To make it look like we're not the only ones?"

"I don't know what all of that's about. Eric, I think there's more going on here than you know about."

"Then tell me."

"That's all I know. Listen, we have to get this deal with Peterson to make this work. To keep up the lifestyle we're accustomed to and to support this family. If someone keeps messing with the land then we're all going to be out looking for work."

Eric stood. "They're getting too close for comfort. And so help me if they touch Susan or Bethany, or even Lydia, I'll go after them. I swear it."

His father stood. "Don't do anything stupid."

"I'm not the one messing with a Walker."

~*~

Thanks to Glenda, Susan had retrieved her menus and somehow picked up a sous chef. She smiled when she thought about the opportunity to bond with Glenda. It made her relationship with Eric that much stronger, she thought.

She watched him pace around the bed as he readied himself to climb into it. Something was on his mind. He'd been in a hurry to leave his parents' house. He'd been curt with Bethany about her staying in the house and letting him know where she was at all times of the day.

"Are you okay?" she finally asked.

"No. No, I'm not okay. My father knows that Elias is selling off the oil rights." He raked his hands through his hair. "To get a cut he offered to move my mother."

Susan climbed out of bed and stood, watching him. "So then if this is a done deal, why is someone destroying the properties?"

"I don't know. I don't understand any of this. But you're going to keep an eye on things at the dinner. Tyson and Lydia will be there. Bethany and I will be nearby. Douglas can be involved too, he already is."

"So now we're all C.I.A.?"

That caused him to chuckle. "Yeah, I guess we are."

"Well, I never thought my culinary career would take me in this direction."

His stance eased as he walked toward her and gathered her in his arms. "You're the kind of woman that always stands by her man, aren't you?"

"Of course."

"I believe in your dreams, Susan. I want to see great things happen for you."

"They will. Everything takes time."

His smile was wide now and she pulled back to look at him. "What are you thinking?"

"Just of the future," he said as he placed his hands on her waist and walked her back toward the bed. Easily, he laid her backward onto the mattress and eased himself down next to her. "Will you be here for the future?"

"If it's my decision, then yes, I will be."

"Then that's what I'm thinking," he said before he moved atop of her and took control of her mouth with the heat and need of his.

~*~

The sun rose, the smell of coffee filled the house, and the laughter of women woke Eric. It had been the first peaceful night's sleep he'd had in a week.

He could hear the mooing of cattle. No cars had driven away in the night. No phones had rung either.

There had just been peace.

Eric took his time pulling on his clothes before he stumbled his way to the kitchen to Susan and Bethany. They both had their hair high on their heads in some kind of knot where hairs poked out. Their skin was glistened in sweat and their cheeks full of color.

"What have you gals been up to?" he asked as he pushed through to get a mug of coffee and take the first sip before anyone answered.

"I finally got her to do a full yoga workout," Bethany beamed as she said it. "She needs to do more to keep her flexibility."

He only grumbled in answer.

Susan leaned up against the counter. His favorite mug from a truck stop in Texas was wrapped between her hands.

"So how is this all going to work? I have class. I have a meeting with Lydia, in town, at a coffee shop," she added as if there were no compromises. "I can still hear cattle, so I know you have a job to do. How do we go on with our lives?"

He took another sip of his coffee, burning his tongue in the process. He turned his gaze to his cousin. "What are you doing today?"

"As she's my boss I guess I do what she needs me to do."

"I'm going to call your brother Jake and have him look at Susan's car. If anyone can fix it, it's him."

He watched as her face contorted into a controlled grin. "Fine."

"Why don't you drive her to class? When I know Jake is at the house, and only then, you can head over there." He looked back at Susan. "What time are you meeting Lydia?"

"Three."

"You'll pick her up from class," he instructed Bethany. "Both of you go to the meeting. We already know all about it. I'm not going to worry about any confidentiality crap. Then straight home."

"Yes, Dad," Susan smirked behind her cup.

"I don't care if they wreck my cars," he started his rant that burned through him. "I'm extremely pissed that they took my horse from me, my cattle, and ruined my business. But I would die if anything happened to either of you."

Her eyes softened as she moved closer to him. "That's why I love you." She pressed her lips to his and then quickly backed away, rubbing them. "You need a shave."

He needed a long hot shower too, to wash away the guilt he was feeling over not escorting them all over town.

But the truth was, he couldn't hover over them forever. There was going to need to be a line drawn in the sand where they didn't feel suffocated. It was hard, but he knew he needed to respect that or he'd be no better than her ex-husband.

Chapter Thirty

It felt good walking into class knowing that Eric wasn't nearby and Bethany could spend some time with her brother. She wasn't too sure how Bethany felt about it, but it would be good for her.

A part of her was actually giddy to have coffee with Lydia too. She couldn't wait to get her and Bethany together. She knew there would be an instant connection. It had been nice to make a new friend, who could have known she'd be related to the man she loved?

When class was over, Susan sat out front and waited for Bethany to pick her up. She thought they'd been very specific on the time, but maybe Bethany was just caught up in spending time with her brother.

She'd wait fifteen minutes before she began calling around and panicking.

Just before she was ready to make her call, her own car pulled up. She recognized the man driving as one of the men from the funeral, but Bethany wasn't with him.

He climbed from the car and perched over the top with his arms rested on the roof.

"Susan?"

"Yes," she stood, but kept her distance.

"Thought I recognized you. I got your car fixed."

"You're Jake?"

"That's me."

She decided it was safe enough to move toward the car. Eric wouldn't have asked him to fix her car if didn't trust him.

"Where is Bethany?"

Jake rolled his eyes. "Douglas came by when we were out front of the house. I think he's sweet on her, but it seems to just piss her off. So she was going to run by the mall and buy something—anything."

Susan pursed her lips. She didn't like that. "She's alone?"

Jake shook his head. "Our sister Pearl stopped by when she heard I'd be there. I think they're going to have a bonding moment. Which is good since Dad never really included Bethany in anything."

Susan felt enlightened. She hoped they did hit it off. Bethany deserved her family.

"Anyway, she asked me to come for you. I figured if I drove up in my truck you wouldn't know who I was. So I'll need a ride back to your place."

"Okay." She walked toward the driver's side and looked in as he stepped aside. "They did a job on it, huh?"

"Yeah."

"I ordered you a new piece so we could make it look new again. But for now it'll hold up."

"And this is what you do?"

"When I'm not racing."

"You race cars?"

The grin on his face was childlike. "I do. Maybe you'll come see me some day."

She nodded and climbed into the car.

As much as she'd wanted to, Susan didn't go into the house when she dropped Jake off at his truck. It scared her now. Would she feel safe there again, she wondered.

Bethany had called and said she and Pearl were headed to the coffee shop. She wasn't sure that was going to go over too well with Lydia, but she'd feel it out.

When Susan arrived, all three of them were already seated at a table with drinks. The laughter had ensued and now Susan was feeling out of place.

"Oh, hey! Come over!" Bethany stood and waved her in. "Susan, this is my sister Pearl."

The girl whom she'd met briefly at the funeral stood and shook her hand. "So you're Eric's girl, huh? I didn't see that coming at the funeral."

"I didn't either," she admitted.

"Is he still as moody as he always was? I won't lie. He scares me a little."

That certainly wasn't comforting. "I suppose everyone has a set of moods."

Susan took the vacant seat between Lydia and Bethany.

Lydia covered Susan's hand with hers. "Can you believe how small the world it is? Pearl and I grew up together."

"You were friends?"

Both women laughed. "No. Not really. I think our interests were much different back then."

Pearl picked up her fancy coffee and held it to her lips. "I was a trouble maker and Lydia was a good girl."

Susan looked at Pearl in her pretty pink pastel nail polish, perfectly curled hair, and her designer outfit. There was no way this girl wasn't on the honor roll.

"You don't look like a trouble maker."

Pearl laughed. "I took after my dad alright. He's an ass and I'm not, but yeah, rules didn't apply to me back then," she said as if she regretted that.

"What do you do now?"

"I own a bridal shop." She smiled wide as she took a sip from her cup. "Bethany says maybe I'll be seeing you soon. You and Eric are pretty serious."

"Oh, well, I'm in no hurry."

Pearl nodded. "Sure. But you and I should talk. I'll bet we could do some great networking with our businesses. I refer people to photographers and caterers all the time. I hear you do both."

"Photography is only a hobby."

Pearl dabbed her lips with her napkin. "You never know." She looked at her watch. "I have to go, girls. I have a fitting in twenty-minutes. The bride is a full-size girl who has been dieting for three months. She's convinced the dress will need to be taken in about six inches." She shook her head. "I saw her at Baskin Robbins last night and I'm thinking different alterations are needed."

She kissed Bethany on the cheek before she left and Bethany's soft smile warmed Susan's heart. Perhaps the best thing in the world was to have had her car broken into.

When Pearl had left, Lydia pulled a file from her bag and laid it on the table. "This is what he wants to serve. The list includes both Everett and Byron Walker, Dwight Peterson, and Shooter Magee. What a stupid name," she added her commentary. "Tyson and I. And of course, my grandfather."

"I thought this was going to be a much bigger event," Susan said as she looked over the papers.

"I thought that too, with it being Constance's birthday and all."

Susan realized it might have been the first time she'd actually heard Eric's mother's name said. What a beautiful name.

"Eric says his father told him that the reason Dwight Peterson is going to be there is because he's buying the oil rights of the land."

"I think that's right. They did some preliminary tests on both properties, with Byron's permission," she added and Susan assumed so they wouldn't accuse her of trespassing. "They think if they put wells out there it'll net quite a bit."

"So why mess with the land at all? It seems as though your grandfather was willing to share the wealth as long as

Everett Walker moved his daughter's grave. It seems cut and dry. Why all the drama?"

"I wish I knew." Lydia looked around the coffee house and moved in over the table. "Someone was lurking around our house last night. It set off the motion lights and one sensor. Grandpa didn't hear a thing, but Tyson and I did. He couldn't see anyone though. But we knew they were there."

Susan's arm broke out in goose bumps. "I don't like that."

"I don't either."

When the door to the coffee shop opened again, Officer Smyth walked through and quickly took off his sunglasses. Susan wasn't sure he'd known Lydia was there, but he'd b-lined right to the table and locked his eyes on her.

"Lydia, what are you doing in town?"

"Looks like I'm having coffee."

"Not keeping very good company, huh?"

Susan felt the heat rise in her cheeks. Really?

"What can I do for , officer?" Lydia kept a calm about her that Susan wasn't going to be able to do for much longer.

"Dinner?"

"Not in a million years."

Smyth puckered his lips. "Too bad. I'm thinking you'll change your mind soon enough."

"Haven't in all these years."

He ran his tongue over his teeth. "I guess I'll leave you ladies be." He narrowed his eyes on Lydia. "We'll bump into each other again soon."

As he walked away, and out of the coffee shop, Susan watched as Lydia's shoulders dropped.

"I hate him," Lydia hissed.

"I don't blame you. Feelings for him are mutual on my end."

"Mine too," Bethany added. "Who treats women like that?"

"He does," Lydia picked up the folder. "Been divorced three times. Each wife claims domestic violence, he weasels his way out of it and keeps his job on the force."

"Maybe someone will run him over when he tries to give them a ticket," Bethany added, causing all three of them to break out into laughter.

"Can't believe no one has tried that." Lydia put the folder in her bag. "So what is our plan? I assume that during dinner we will try to get Peterson and Magee to confess to messing with our property. I mean maybe they're trying to force us off of it so they can buy the land and then they don't have to pay out on it."

"That's low. But then what?" Susan asked.

"You could just keep a cell phone on. You know Eric and I could monitor it. Just like they do on TV."

Lydia considered Bethany's thought. "We could do that. Tyson always has his phone next to him at dinner. If he put it on the table with the display down, no one would think a thing about it."

"Okay, that's what we'll do," Susan agreed. "Eric and Bethany can hole up at his house. They'll be close enough if anything happens.

Again, Susan thought, this wasn't where she'd thought her career was going to take her.

~*~

Eric had come out of his seat when she told him the plan.

"This is stupid. I say we just come in there and confront them. What if they're dangerous and find out you're spying with a cell phone?"

"You think it'll be any more dangerous than them sneaking around the house at night? Lydia said there was someone out there last night. I say we do this and get it over with. We can't live like this, Eric. You don't deserve to lose anything else over this."

He continued to pace, but he didn't argue.

Bethany kicked her legs up onto the coffee table. "Seriously though, no matter how messed up all of this is, it brought our family together."

Eric simply narrowed his glare at her.

She put her feet down and sat forward. "You met your grandfather. You met your cousin and the truth about your mother and Tyson came out. And I don't care what you think. I've seen you together. You like him."

Susan watched his jaw tighten.

"Russell, Gerald, Ben, and Dane have been here for you whenever you needed them. You've even opened up and accepted Glenda after all these years."

Susan smiled thinking about how he'd decided she should be called Mom now.

"And, Eric, you made the phone call that put me in touch with Jake, who put me in touch with Pearl. She kissed me goodbye today." She beamed. "None of this would have happened if my father hadn't royally screwed everyone over," she finished on a laugh.

"We could have just had a barbecue."

Bethany shrugged. "This has more adventure to it."

Chapter Thirty-One

The next two days were filled with planning, shopping, and preparing. Bethany and Glenda were more valuable than Susan could have ever thought.

Eric still didn't like the idea of her alone in the house with family he really didn't know and investors, or whatever they were, that he didn't know at all. She understood his hesitation.

Then there was the debate that what if Dwight Peterson and Shooter didn't have anything to do with what had been going on? What if they were just killing time and the real person was still out there? They'd killed animals. They'd stolen cars and broken into houses. They continued to lurk around the Morgan house. There was a lot of uncertainty.

Glenda covered the last dish with tin foil and held it out to Susan to pack. "This was so much fun. Not having any girls, I never had anyone to cook with like this."

"My mother taught me to cook. I cherish time in the kitchen with other women."

"Maybe we could do it again someday," she said with wide eyes and a bright smile.

"Anytime. I may have to do it a few more times before I can go back to my house. I still have jobs coming up."

"Oh, honey, you could use my kitchen any time. Even when you move back to your house." She picked up a towel and brushed off the counter. "Are you going back to your house?"

"I wouldn't see why not."

"I thought maybe you and Eric might be planning something."

Susan packed the dish into the box. "We've talked about it a little. But we just met."

"I married his father after having known him a month," she said grinning wide with her eyes beaming in delight. "He backed into my car. Made a mess of it. But the minute he got out of the car—it was love at first sight for me." She rested her hand on her chest. "Eric was eight. I'm not sure he ever liked me much. I'm not sure he does even now," her words shook. "He was a handful, but he loved his brothers and his father. I couldn't ask for more."

Susan was sure she could see Glenda's eyes moisten. She moved to her and pulled her in to hug her. "He thinks of you as his mother. He's a bit stubborn to admit it to anyone else, but he does."

"Do you really think so?" Glenda asked as she wiped her eyes. "He sent me roses the other day. Did you know that?"

"I didn't. But would you believe me if I told you he said so, to me? That he thinks of you as his mother."

"I would believe it. Oh, that makes my heart so full."

Susan looked up at the clock over the microwave. "I have to go."

"Is Eric or Bethany going with you?"

"No. It'll just be me tonight." She said hoping she hadn't let on to her what was going on. It was very obvious that she didn't know anything about the dinner or where Susan was going.

"Maybe someday if Bethany is busy I could help you serve at one of your events."

Susan felt the warmth spread through her body. "I'd really like that."

After loading up her car, she waved goodbye to Glenda and started down the road toward Eric's. She would change there and then head toward the Morgan's.

Half way to Eric's another car came toward her. It was a police cruiser and it slowed, so she did the same.

Douglas rolled down his window. "Heading to Eric's?"

"For a moment before I head to work."

He nodded slowly. "I'm just checking up on the area. Seems as though things have been quiet."

"They have."

Douglas looked around as if he were observing the area. "I was thinking about asking Bethany out this weekend. She's something, isn't she?"

"She is."

"Lydia never would go out with me."

"I didn't realize you knew Lydia."

"Sure. Small town feel around here, ya know? Her temper is as short as her hair."

"I haven't seen that side of her." Susan looked at the clock on her dash. "I have to go. I'll see you around. Good luck on your date proposal," she offered, but having seen Bethany's reaction to him she wasn't sure he'd win her over. But then again, anything was possible.

Douglas gave her a wave and headed on. Susan continued toward Eric's.

Bethany, Tyson, and Eric sat at his kitchen table. Between them were news articles they'd printed from the Internet as well as drawings Tyson had obtained from his grandfather on where they'd put the wells.

"If this is legit, this land is worth a lot," Tyson said as Susan walked through the house to the kitchen. "Hey," Tyson said with a smile. "Are you ready?"

Susan nodded as Eric stood. He wrapped an arm around her waist and planted a warm kiss on her lips. "I still don't like this."

"It'll be okay. Did you already talk to Douglas about this?"

"Not about tonight, why?"

"I just ran into him between here and your parents' house. He was just checking on things."

"Good. That means he's close if we need him."

Susan turned to Bethany. "He wants to ask you out."

Bethany's shoulders dropped and she visibly deflated. "He gave me a freaking ticket."

"Four years ago."

"Still. I'm mad over that."

She couldn't help it, but Susan laughed. "I have to change, then head over."

Tyson stood. "I have to get there too. He wants us to dress for dinner. I swear that man..." he stopped. "Oh, well. The things we do for our family, huh?"

Susan watched Eric's eyes soften. He understood family more than he'd ever have let on under that crusty exterior.

~*~

Susan headed toward the Morgans' to set up their dinner.

The dining room had already been set and a beaming Lydia stood next to the ornate table and looked it over with a very keen eye.

"I think everything is where it's supposed to be," she said, her fists firmly planted on her hips.

"It's a beautiful table."

"My mother is a stickler for this kind of thing. Tyson could have set it and it would look equally as perfect."

"I'd like to see that too," Susan said on a laugh.

Lydia turned to her. "What can I help you with? I'm as ready as I'm going to get," she said with a whisk of her hands down the sides of her dress.

"I just need to get the pans in the oven to keep them warm and begin plating everything that will go out. I'd love some help if you're offering. I'm missing my assistant tonight."

"Sorry about that," Lydia said softly as they walked into the kitchen.

"I understand. Don't worry about it." Susan pulled on her apron and handed another one to Lydia. "When I left the house Bethany and Eric had a command center set up on the kitchen table," she said in a hushed tone.

"Part of me hopes we nab them. Another part hopes they are just genuine and nice."

"Douglas Brant was already out this way. I think he suspects something. We've planned to call him if we find out anything."

Lydia wrinkled up her nose. "There's another one of those losers on the force that has been hitting on me for years. What is it with this town hiring cops that do that?"

"He said you'd turned him down for a date. He's sweet on Bethany now."

"Who wouldn't be? She's hot, but she's better to stay away."

"Why? What's wrong with him?"

Lydia shrugged. "He's just got a bad vibe to him. Not as bad as Smyth's, but bad."

Susan thought about Eric's story and how he covered for him. Maybe it would be better for everyone involved to find someone else to check into Dwight Peterson and Shooter Magee.

Tyson walked through the kitchen before their guests arrived. "This smells great."

"It's one of my favorite menus. Certainly a more upscale catering meal."

"I think Eric's a lucky guy. I admire you for what you've built."

She was completely unprepared for the compliment, but she smiled graciously. "Thank you."

"I hope someday I'll find a gal who will stick by my side when the world around me falls apart."

There were tears stinging her throat and she didn't know what to do with that.

Tyson must have known that too when he leaned in and kissed her cheek. "I'll take care of you in his absence. No one is going to get hurt tonight in any way."

He pulled his phone out of his pocket just as the doorbell rang. He pushed a button and held it to his ear. "Eric? It's show time. I'm going to put my phone in my shirt pocket mic up. If you can't hear me call Susan and let her know." He nodded. "I'll tell her."

Tyson slid his phone into his pocket and turned back toward Susan. "He says he loves you and he'll kick my ass if anything happens to you."

"I love him too," she said leaning toward Tyson's pocket. He gave her a wink and headed out of the kitchen.

Susan placed her hand on her chest. Her pulse had quickened with the nerves that bolted around in her stomach.

She took in a long soothing breath. She had a job to do and she was going to do it well. On the counter next to her the birthday cake Elias Morgan had requested for his daughter. It was all too personal now and there could be no mistakes.

Now she waited for Lydia to let them know it was time to serve dinner.

Chapter Thirty- Two

Eric had found an old Bluetooth earpiece he'd used for his phone a few times when he was out with the cattle birthing calves. He'd muted his phone and placed the earpiece in his ear.

He could hear the rustling of Tyson's shirt, but he could hear the conversations well enough.

The one thing he'd learned in the fifteen minutes that Shooter Magee was in the Morgans' house was that he was an asshole.

From the way the man replied when introduced to the crude whistle he gave when Lydia walked into the room, Eric was sure this was the guy messing up his life.

"Why don't you call Douglas and tell him to head over this way. I don't like this guy. He gives me bad vibes," Eric said and Bethany nodded.

He continued to listen as she called. The moment Susan walked into the room a chill zipped up Eric's spine.

"You're keeping the hotties locked up in this place ain't ya?" Shooter said and his grandfather shushed him.

Eric didn't hear Susan's voice, but he was sure she was gritting her teeth at the comment.

The talk was boring. Elias and Dwight Peterson bantered about oil. His father made a few good comments about the placement of the wells, if they were to drill them. Byron's voice, however, was never heard. Eric wasn't even sure he'd shown up.

Susan had served up the first plate and Shooter had made some comment about how nasty lettuce was. Still, he never heard Susan's voice, she was simply doing her job, he thought.

It hadn't been but five minutes when he heard a car pull up in front of his house. A moment later Douglas walked in.

"What, were you close by?" Eric snapped covering the earpiece.

"Maybe I was." He scanned a look over Bethany and she turned to look the other way. "So what's going on?"

"Peterson and Magee are at the Morgans'. Tyson has his phone on so I can listen."

"That doesn't sound legal to me. Does it to you?"

"It sounds like I'm being safe," Eric said as he heard the doorbell at the Morgans'. He held a hand up so he could hear clearer.

~*~

Susan carried the last of the salad plates to the kitchen as the doorbell rang. She wondered if it were Byron Walker, as he'd yet to show for dinner, but no one seemed to mind.

With the main course plated she carried three of the plates out to the dining room. Tyson must have gone to open the door, because his seat was vacant.

Susan set the first plate in front of Lydia—ladies first. Then she served Dwight Peterson. He was a distinguished looking gentleman, whom she assumed might be nearing sixty. He had a mind for business by the way he spoke of his. As she set down his plate, he thanked her with a generous smile.

Shooter Magee, on the other hand, was nothing like his grandfather. Susan would have assumed Dwight Peterson picked Shooter up from a bar and brought him to dinner. He reeked of alcohol. Wearing a pair of dark jeans and a leather jacket, he certainly didn't fit in.

It was obvious he hadn't shaved in at least a week and it had probably been a year or more since he'd had a haircut.

The man gave her the creeps. If they found out he'd been the one to steal her car, she was going to sell it. Just the thought of him being in it gave her chills.

As she turned to set Shooter's plate down, he patted her butt causing her to reel back, nearly spilling his plate in his lap.

Just as she took a breath to let the S.O.B. have it, Tyson stepped through the door with Smyth in tow.

"I suggest you never touch her again," Smyth said in a low growl.

Susan stepped back from the table and found that Lydia too had risen to move.

Shooter leaned back in his chair and crossed his arms over his chest. "Nice to see you, Officer Smyth. Didn't know you were coming to dinner."

Smyth walked into the room fully. "I'm guessing you know exactly why I'm here."

Dwight Peterson squeezed his eyes shut and pinched the bridge of his nose. "What have you done now?" he asked.

Shooter merely grinned at Smyth.

"I'll tell you what he did. He approached an under-aged woman to solicit sex while in our fine city. That's after he parked in a fire lane and exited his car with an open container."

Dwight looked up. "Why didn't you arrest him then?"

"He was under suspicion of another charge, we just needed him to lead us right to that."

Shooter scratched the scruff of a beard that traveled down his neck. "I didn't realize you were such a detective."

"It seems Shooter was the man who set up the card game in which Byron Walker lost."

Elias cleared his throat and held up his hands. "I paid his gambling debt. Mr. Walker owes no one."

"Didn't say he did," Smyth said. "Illegal gambling operation set up by Mr. Magee. That's one offense. The other is the game was rigged. Mr. Walker shouldn't have lost."

Shooter snorted a laugh. "You can't prove that."

"You should be careful what you say to a wired under-aged woman when you're soliciting her. Sometimes the sting hurts," Smyth said as he moved in and yanked Shooter to his feet.

Shooter grunted as Smyth slapped handcuffs on him and another officer walked through the front door.

Tyson moved toward them. "What about our properties? The poisoned animals? The slashed tires? The stolen cars? The lurking about, setting off the alarms?"

Shooter shook his head. "I have no idea what the hell you're talking about. I really don't even give a crap who you are, let alone what you have. The old man drug me along, trying to change my image," he said as Smyth began to lead him from the room.

Tyson stopped Smyth from leading him out of the dining room. "Wait. You had nothing to do with all of that? But the oil rights? The land merger?"

Dwight Peterson rose. "I never told him about any of that. I didn't trust him with the information."

Everett Walker stood from his seat and walked toward Susan and Lydia. "I think it's about time for us to leave," he whispered. "Call Eric and tell him you'll be heading home."

Susan nodded then she and Lydia retreated to the kitchen.

~*~

Eric ripped the earpiece from his ear and threw it onto the table. "Damn it!" He picked up his phone and unmuted it.

"What happened?" Bethany asked.

"They just arrested Shooter Magee."

"For what he did to you?"

"No. What he did to your father. He rigged the card game your father lost. He had nothing to do with the rest of it."

Eric put his phone to his ear and listened to Tyson's phone, still hidden in his pocket. "Tyson? Tyson?" he repeated. When there was no answer, he lowered the phone, but didn't yet turn it off. He'd been recording the call just in case they'd needed the evidence. He didn't see any reason to stop the recording until Shooter Magee had been driven away.

Douglas stood with his back against the refrigerator. His arms were folded over his chest and his ankles were crossed. He hadn't taken his eyes off of Bethany since he'd walked through the door.

"You look so much like your mother," he said as if he hadn't been paying any attention to what Eric and Bethany had been talking about.

Bethany turned her attention to Douglas. "You knew my mother?"

A grin formed on his mouth. "Oh, I knew her. I knew her very well."

Eric wasn't sure where this conversation was headed, but he didn't like it. "Doug, why don't you head home? Doesn't seem as though we got any information we were looking for."

Doug didn't react or seem as though he'd even heard him.

"You have her hair. Her color eyes. Even that same dimple in your cheek."

Bethany pushed from the table.

"I don't know how you knew my…"

Douglas moved closer to Bethany. "I knew your mother on levels no one else knew her."

"Doug, that's enough. It's time for you to…"

Douglas withdrew his gun and pointed it at Eric. "Shut your mouth. I'm so sick of listening to you. I've listened to you my whole life and you've never had anything to say."

"Please put the gun down," Bethany pleaded. "I'm not my mother."

"She left Georgia when you were two. Your father turned her away and she left."

"He didn't want us."

"I wanted her. Don't you understand? I loved her."

Eric felt the pressure build behind his eyes. "That's the older woman you were having the affair with?"

Doug cocked the gun. "I told you to shut up. You have no idea what we had. Your uncle was an idiot who neglected her. She was such a woman and she loved me."

Eric heard Bethany sob. "This isn't true. My mother wouldn't do that."

Douglas moved closer to her, forcing Bethany to step back until she was pressed up against the wall. "We could have it all again, Violet." He lifted his hand to her cheek. "We could love like that again."

"I'm not Violet," Bethany's voice shook under her tears. "Violet is dead."

Douglas's face contorted in near pain. "Don't say that ever again," he growled as he wrapped his hand around Bethany's throat.

"Get your hands off of her," Eric charged toward him just as Douglas pulled the trigger of the gun.

Chapter Thirty-Three

Tyson pulled his phone from his pocket. "I'll let Eric know what's going on," he said as he lifted the phone to his ear.

Susan watched as his forehead creased.

"Tyson, what's wrong?"

"Is Douglas at Eric's?"

"He was in the area," she said with a shrug.

Smyth handed Shooter over to the other deputy who walked him out to a car. "Did you say Brant is with Walker?"

Tyson nodded, the phone still pressed to his ear. "They're arguing." He continued to listen and then his eyes opened wide and his face went white. "Someone just fired a gun."

Susan's breath caught in her lungs and she felt her head begin to spin. Slowly her world was going black and she couldn't force herself to breathe until a set of hands gripped her shoulders. The air that had been trapped inside of her gave and she took a breath.

"Get in my car," Everett Walker said firmly.

Susan nodded and hurried toward the car just as everyone else did the same.

Tyson had been the first to speed away from the house followed by Smyth. The other officer drove away in the other direction with Magee.

Everett Walker followed behind with Susan and Lydia both sobbing.

He reached for Susan's hand and gave it a squeeze. "He's going to be okay. This is Eric. He's always prepared."

~*~

Eric rolled on the kitchen floor. This pain was worse than any other pain he'd ever had in his life.

Blood soaked his shirt from where the bullet had penetrated his arm.

He sucked in breath after ragged breath trying to get a grip on what had happened, but he'd hit his head when he fell and he thought perhaps he'd blacked out for a moment. But how many moments?

Eric coughed and his lungs burned.

Where was Bethany? Where was Douglas?

He coughed again.

The house was filled with smoke. He couldn't pinpoint the source. He tried to crawl out, but with one arm the task seemed nearly impossible.

"Eric! Eric!" The voice broke through the smoke. "Where the hell are you son?"

It was Byron.

Eric coughed again and a moment later someone reached out for him.

"Let's get you out of here. The back of the house is engulfed."

"Beth…"

"We have to get to her. Brant has her. C'mon."

Byron pulled him to his feet and led him through the front door.

~*~

"Oh, God!" Susan's voice quaked as they crested the top of the hill and she saw the small house engulfed in flames.

Tyson's truck sped up passing another truck going the opposite direction.

"That's Byron's truck," Everett said.

Lydia gripped the seats as if she were getting a good look. "Eric is with him."

Everett nodded and Smyth must have noticed too as he followed Byron and didn't go up to the house.

Everett followed Smyth, but stopped as two more trucks sped toward Eric's.

He slowed and rolled down his window as Russell stopped. "Eric's not in the house, but it's engulfed. Don't go inside."

"We'll try to get a handle on it."

"Get to Tyson before he goes in looking for Eric. I'm following Byron."

"What's going on?"

"I don't know yet," Everett said as he took off down the dirt road following his brother's truck.

~*~

Eric held tight to his arm as his uncle sped down the road.

"Where the hell are you going?" Eric asked through clenched teeth.

"I assume he's headed to the lake. Son-of-a bitch!" He slapped his hands on the steering wheel.

"He was calling her Violet."

"He's lost his ever loving mind," Byron said as he turned the corner at full speed causing the tires to slide on the gravel.

Holding on increased the pain in Eric's arm.

"What happened between him and Violet?"

"They had something going on. It had been going on since he was in high school. Right before Bethany was born."

Byron sped over the bouncy gravel and Eric winced at the pain it caused. He wasn't sure how much longer he could hold out.

Byron wiped his hand over his forehead. "She was a failing model and a horrible actress. She felt as though she were too old. I guess having affairs with seventeen-year-old boys made her feel younger."

The thought made Eric sick.

"I met her when she was thirty-five. I fell in love hard."

Eric seemed to remember that. He didn't remember Violet very well at all, but he'd remembered his uncle falling for the red head.

"She broke it off with Brant. She got pregnant and that set off her depression again. Now she was fat to boot. After Bethany was born ,she started up her thing with Brant again and he became obsessive about her."

"She left then?"

Byron shook his head. "She broke it off with him. We were going to work it out. Get married. But she got scared. Not of marriage, but of Brant."

"That's when she moved to California?"

Byron nodded as he skidded into the entrance of the park where Douglas had once wrecked Eric's truck. The thought of Douglas having had Violet Waterbury in his truck when he'd crashed it made Eric even madder, which only made the pain throbbing in his arm worse.

"This is why I didn't want Bethany out here. I didn't want her this close to the psychopath. She's the spitting image of her mother."

Douglas's car was parked by the lake and shaded by a small grove of trees.

Eric felt the vile feeling rise up in his throat.

Byron skidded his truck to a stop and slammed it into park. He quickly jumped out and pulled the shotgun from his backseat.

Eric managed his way out of the truck as Byron started toward the car.

A patrol car skidded to a stop behind Byron's truck just as the unmistakable sound of sobbing was heard from behind them.

"She's over there." He nodded his head in the direction of the sound.

"Bethany! Bethany," Byron shouted.

"Here, Dad. I'm here."

Smyth pulled out his flashlight and illuminated the area.

Bethany sat with her back against a tree. Blood stained her face and her torn shirt. Her red mane hung around her shoulders and she held a gun in her hands.

Byron knelt down in front of her. "Are you okay? Baby, did he hurt you?"

Her eyes were wide and glossed over. She nodded and that made Eric even sicker.

"I shot him," she said on a quick breath and then dropped the gun on the ground.

Smyth slowly walked toward the car parked in the grove of trees.

Eric could hear Douglas now as he cried, cursed, and moaned. Smyth had stopped and Eric wasn't so sure he hadn't heard him chuckle.

A moment later he called for backup and ambulances.

Eric felt the need to sit on the ground next to Bethany. His legs were growing weaker by the second.

"He shot you," she sobbed looking at his arm. "You fell. You hit your head."

"I'm okay."

She shook her head and the curls bounced. "I thought you were going to die. He set the bed on fire and dragged me out to the car." Her teeth chattered and Byron slipped off his jacket and wrapped it around her. "He thought I was my mother."

"I know, baby," Byron said softly as he pulled her into his arms.

Smyth walked back toward them with what looked like a smirk planted on his face.

"Your girl can certainly take care of herself," he said.

Byron kissed the top of her head. "What happened?"

"She managed to shoot him in the ass with his own gun and cuff him face down in the backseat." Smyth knelt down next to her. "I have an ambulance coming for you so they can look you over. Did he do anything to you?"

"He hit me," she stuttered. "He pulled my hair and ripped my shirt."

Smyth nodded. "Did he do anything else?"

Bethany shook her head. "I told him I was Violet, my mother, and he set the gun down. That's when I took it and shot him."

Smyth rested his hand on her shoulder. "Smart girl." He turned toward Eric. "I have an ambulance coming for you too," he said and Eric nodded before he leaned back against the tree.

Another truck sped through the entrance of the park. It was his father's.

He winced from the high beams that shined toward him and from beyond them he could see her...Susan.

"Oh, God! Look at you," Susan cried as she fell to his side. "You're shot! We have to get you to a hospital."

Smyth touched her arm in a very calm manner. "I called one for him. It's on the way."

"Your house."

"I know." The pain seemed to fade as she knelt there beside him. Her hands came to his face and tears streamed down her cheeks.

"I was worried. Oh, God, you're okay."

"I'm okay. The house can be rebuilt."

She nodded. "Right." She lifted her head and her eyes went wide. "Bethany," she sobbed as she crawled toward her.

"I'm okay. I'm—okay," she said again.

"Who did this? Why?"

"Douglas. He's messed up," she said.

"No wonder you didn't want to go out with him."

Bethany actually laughed. "I'll tell you about it later."

Byron walked toward Everett, who stood at Eric's side. "I was afraid he'd get to her if she came," he said. "That's why I didn't tell her about Dad's funeral. I didn't want her here for her own safety."

"I take it Douglas was the young man Violet had the affair with."

Byron nodded. "I ran into him a few weeks ago. It was like he snapped when he saw me. Suddenly it was twenty years ago to him. When I told him Violet had died, that's when he began destroying everything."

"He's the one that killed my horse?" Eric asked.

"I'm sure that's what you're going to find out when Smyth is done with him. I lived in your house back then, remember?"

"Yeah."

"He's a messed up, young man."

Bethany stood from her seat against the tree and moved to her father. "You kept from me to keep me safe?"

"I'm a lousy father. I was a lousy husband too, but I don't wish bad things on my children. You're stunning, Bethany. You're the spitting image of your mother. I was afraid that he'd come after you if he saw you in person and he did."

She placed her hands over her face. "This is all my fault."

Eric came to his feet as quickly as he could with his arm dangling to his side. Susan helped him and he wrapped his arm around her shoulders for support.

"You can't blame yourself for this. Douglas has always been a mess. I covered his ass for years and I didn't even know who he was messing around with. I'm sorry it came out like this. I guess we both got a dose of reality this week when it came to mothers."

Byron rubbed his hand over the back of his neck and looked at his brother. "We can pick 'em, can't we?"

"Despite the mother, we make some terrific kids."

Bethany smiled through her tears.

The sirens of the ambulances and extra police cars pierced the night. Soon Eric was on a gurney with people poking and prodding at him. The only constant was that Susan was still by his side, holding his hand all the way to the hospital.

The bullet was lodged in his arm, but when he woke from surgery, she was still sitting there, asleep with her head rested on his pillow from where she sat in the chair.

What a messed up few weeks, he thought as he kissed the top of her head softly.

As soon as they released him, he was going to make everything right for her. He loved her and he was never going to let her go.

Chapter Thirty-Four

With his arm secure in a sling, Eric stood with his other arm wrapped around Susan's shoulders as they looked at the burned shell that had been his house. A crew was there to tear the rest of it down. Nothing had been salvageable.

He was glad that Bethany had taken the advice from the psychologist at the police department to talk to a counselor. After Douglas admitted to having been the person that had been destroying the property of the Walkers and the Morgans, she'd been bombarded with guilt that had made her physically sick.

Tyson's truck was visible up at the barn. A horse trailer was attached. He'd managed to get three new horses for Eric to board. Thanks to his brother, he was back in business. Russell had agreed to work the horses until Eric was back to full strength.

Pride swelled in his chest. Family was a good thing to have on your side, he thought.

Susan's shoulders shifted under his arm and he looked down at her. Tears streaked her cheeks as she watched the house come down.

"What's wrong? Why are you crying?"

She looked up at him with those sad, dark eyes. "Why aren't you crying? This is your home!"

Eric turned her toward him. "My home is wherever you are." He cupped her cheek with his free hand. "Right now my home is in town where you're letting me stay. But we'll rebuild this."

"And then your home will be here."

"With you."

"Eric, I'm not in any hurry."

"I am. Life is too short not to grab on with both hands. I don't want to live without you and if that means I live in town, well then that's what I'll do. But this is a fresh start," he said as he brushed his thumb over her lips. "I'll build you a kitchen of your dreams."

She was trying hard to control her smile, but it seemed to slip through and that warmed his heart.

"What kind of kitchen?"

"You get to design it."

"Really?"

"Really. But the stipulation is, you have to live here to use it."

She stepped closer to him and rested her hands on his chest. "I could live here."

"You'll need to change your name too."

She raised her brows. "You don't like my name?"

"Your catering company will need to be called Susan Walker catering."

"Oh," she let out a long breath.

"I like the sound of it, don't you?"

For a moment, he was sure she was going to argue it, but he wasn't going to let her win. He knew what he wanted and Eric Walker always got what he wanted.

"I think it has a very nice ring to it," she said, her eyes wide and a beaming smile on her lips.

"You'll marry me?"

"I'll marry you."

He quickly sealed her answer with a warm kiss that he felt surge from the tip of his head all the way to his toes. She was going to be his wife. Never in a million years would he have guessed that he'd meet the woman of his dreams at his grandfather's funeral.

"We have one more thing to settle."

"What's that?" She rested her cheek against his chest.

"What the hell does Q stand for?"

Susan pulled back and smiled. "Quick."

"Quick? That's not a name."

"I used to tell people it was the dog's name."

"It's not?"

She shook her head. "Something you should know about my parents. They're hippies, still are."

He knew his mouth had fallen open and nothing came out in response.

She raised her arms around his neck. "My mother went into labor three weeks early and I was born in the bathtub within an hour. Quick."

"That's where you got the name?"

Susan nodded. "Would it humor you to know my sister's middle name is Molasses?"

He couldn't help but laugh. "She took longer than an hour to be born?"

"Forty-eight hours longer and she was a week late."

Eric looked at her with the rose in her cheeks, her long hair cascading over her shoulders, and the thought of her Subaru and her Birkenstocks suddenly flashed into his head.

"You're a vegetarian that drives a Subaru. How come I didn't see the hippy parent thing coming?"

"I'm quick and you're not?"

"That's funny." He pulled her in. "Susan Quick Walker. It has a ring to it."

They turned and started back for his truck.

"Are you open to non-traditional baby names?" She jabbed him with her elbow. "I have a list of some really great names."

"Are you going to move into my house, use the kitchen, and take my last name?"

"I am."

"Then we can discuss that. The pride is in the Walker."

He smiled as he opened the door for her and she climbed into his beat-up red truck. Yes, pride was having a family that stuck together even when things were not the way everyone thought they should be.

We hope you enjoyed the first installment of
THE WALKERS

Here is a sneak peek into the second book in the series
STARGAZING

Please visit us at www.5princebooks.com for updated
release information on this and other books in the series.

Chapter One ~ STARGAZING

Hands in front of her chest, palms pressed together, Bethany inhaled as she pressed her foot to her inner thigh. Her body wobbled on one leg as she closed her eyes in an attempt to achieve her balance.

The Georgia sun glittered through the trees and the spring air filled her lungs on the patio outside of her bedroom.

She held the pose for five full breaths, letting the peace of the morning wash over her.

Letting her foot slide to the floor, she lifted her hands over her head, sucked in a deep cleansing breath and folded in half. Her spine gave a few pops as it lengthened.

The problem with this pose was she could see her toes were in desperate need of a pedicure. The next exhale was a sigh.

Bethany Waterbury stood, reached for her lemon infused water, and her towel. She wiped the sweat from her brow and sipped her water. In six , she had an audition for a commercial. This would be her first audition in nearly a year. Deep inside she didn't know what was worse, having done the horror movies she'd made in L.A. or wanting a grocery store commercial so bad she could taste it.

There was a tapping on her bedroom door.

"Come in," she shouted as the door opened and her roommate Susan walked in, a cup of coffee in her hand.

"It's beautiful out here today," she said as she joined her on the porch.

"It is. Still can't believe you gave me this room and didn't take it for yourself."

Susan shrugged and sipped her coffee. "As soon as the house is built I'll have my own porch off my master suite," she said with a smile.

Bethany knew the day was coming. Susan would be moving in with her fiancé, who happened to be Bethany's cousin Eric.

Two months ago a psychopath, who had once had an affair with Bethany's mother, had shot Eric and burned his house to the ground. Weeks earlier he'd killed off his animals and caused destruction to Eric's property as well as his grandfather's. It seemed as though Douglas was obsessed with Eric's cousin Lydia as well.

She sipped her water again. Guilt still plagued her when she thought about it. Had she just stayed in California, where the magic of Hollywood had long given up on her, none of this would have happened to Eric.

It was her fault. She was the spitting image of her late mother. Just having seen her had set the man into some psychotic episode.

He'd been locked up and she'd been in counseling. When she'd come to Georgia, this wasn't what she thought she'd be doing. The point in moving was to bond with her father.

Okay, she'd done that—a little bit.

He was a mess of a man, just as her mother had been a mess of a woman. Perhaps that was the common factor that had them together for the short time in which she was conceived.

"You look like you have a lot on your mind," Susan said as she walked out onto the patio. Her new diamond ring sparkled in the sunlight.

"I was just thinking about everything. My counselor says I can't blame myself for Eric's loss, but it's hard not to."

"He doesn't blame you. No one does."

"Just me."

Susan moved closer to her. "This is really bothering you."

"How can it not? I'm lucky that when Douglas shot Eric it didn't kill him. Or that he didn't die in the fire."

Susan knelt down in front of her and rested her hand on Bethany's knee. "Eric is fine. The house is framed. The stalls are full of horses and you are safe. Honey, you have to be able to move on."

She nodded. This wasn't anything that she hadn't been told already.

Susan stood and held out her hand to Bethany to stand. "What are your plans today?"

"I have an audition."

Susan's eyes grew wide. "Really? That's wonderful."

"We'll see."

"And you're going with me to Pearl's bridal shop this afternoon, right?"

Bethany had forgotten she'd promised to go wedding dress shopping with Susan. At least her sister owned the store. It was another step in getting to know her family— spending time bridal shopping would do that.

"I'll be there. Pearl is expecting us."

Susan sipped her coffee. "You're still able to work tomorrow, right? Lydia has us set to cater the book club dinner. They have Kent Black coming."

"Kent Black?"

"The writer." She held out her hand to gesture. "Haven't you read him? Oh, he's genius."

Bethany narrowed her gaze on her. "He writes science-fiction doesn't he?" she asked and Susan nodded. "Why would I read that? Why do you?"

Susan laughed. "I'm thinking you must be the only person who hasn't read it. It's been a New York Times bestseller for months. They're looking to make a movie of it.

Hey, maybe you can put in a good word to him and he can suggest they cast you as Dessilla."

"Dessilla? Sounds like a role I was designed for." She blew a hair from her forehead. "I'm done with horror movies."

"No, she's a beautiful alien."

Bethany groaned. "I don't think I want to be an alien either. I'd better get ready. And yes, I'll be available for the book club."

"Good."

"How did she get him to come to the book club anyway?"

"I think she's more connected than we think," Susan winked. "I'll talk to you later. Good luck on your audition."

"Don't say that. It's bad luck."

"Right. Are you supposed to break a leg for TV too?"

"It'll do," she joked as Susan walked back out of the bedroom.

~*~

Coffee houses once were a source of inspiration. They had a vibe and a feel to them. Now, Kent thought, they were more like a bar.

The same people walked in and out of the door every day. They ordered the same addictive concoction and either carried it out or sat for hours and chatted with others.

He missed the days where he could pull up to a table and no one bothered him for hours. Since he was traveling, it was one of his only options. Sure, he could hole up in his hotel room, but that wasn't very inspirational either.

Even though he'd rather be alone, he needed to surround himself with people for inspiration—he just wished they weren't so noisy.

The door opened again. It had become habit to look up and study the person. This one had him sitting up, removing his fingers from the keyboard of his laptop, and following her with his eyes.

Long red curls bounced over her shoulders, which were bare in a sundress with yellow flowers. She was lean and toned and absolutely radiant.

She walked to the end of the line and Kent turned in his chair to follow her with his gaze.

Smiling at the boy behind the counter, Kent noted that the young man flushed at her simple gesture. That said something.

She continued on to pay for her drink. He heard the woman ringing up her order offer a pastry to which the redhead waved off with her hand and a laugh. Obviously she'd avoid that, he knew just by looking at her. Her drink was probably low-fat blah too.

When she turned the beauty of her hit Kent right in the chest. He'd never seen such a beautiful specimen.

She was scanning the room looking for an open seat. Wasn't it his very lucky day? The only free chair was at his table.

He stood, bravely—as bravely as any man who locked himself in his house and wrote about aliens could possibly be.

Quickly he wiped the crumbs from the front of his shirt and put on a grand smile, just as the redhead waved at a man across the room and headed toward him.

Kent slithered down into his chair and ducked behind his computer screen. He was used to that. Why should today be any different?

He took a Harry Potter movie pen from his Star Wars Celebration bag and jotted a note on the napkin on the table.

Redhead, glorious redhead in a yellow flowered sundress.

She'd live on forever, he decided, on the pages of his books as the princess he'd needed to write who lived in the far away galaxy of Vela Centauri.

Meet the Author

Bestselling Author Bernadette Marie is known for building families readers want to be part of. Her series *The Keller Family* has graced bestseller charts since its release in 2011, along with her other series and single title books. The married mother of five sons promises *Happily Ever After always*...and says she can write it, because she lives it.

When not writing, Bernadette Marie is shuffling her sons to their many events—mostly hockey—and enjoying the beautiful views of the Colorado Rocky Mountains from her front step. She is also an accomplished martial artist with a second degree black belt in Tang Soo Do.

A chronic entrepreneur, Bernadette Marie opened her own publishing house in 2011, *5 Prince Publishing*, so that she could publish the books she liked to write and help make the dreams of other aspiring authors come true too. Bernadette Marie is also the CEO of *Illumination Author Events*.

Books from 5 Prince Publishing
www.5princebooks.com

A Secret to Keep *Railyn Stone*
The Doom of Undal *Katrina Sisowath*
Fatal Obsession *Christina OW*
The Escape Clause *Bernadette Marie*
Reasons to Stay *Lisa J. Hobman*
Permanent Spring Showers *Scott D. Southard*
Wings *Pete Abela*
Reason to Leave *Lisa J. Hobman*
Love Finds its Way *Wilhelmina Stolen*
The Paper Masque *Jessica Dall*
The Silver Unicorn *Wayne Orr*
The Merger *Bernadette Marie*
Braving the Darkness *Melynda Price*
The Calling *Jim Hanley*
The Christmas Tree Guy *Railyn Stone*
The Copper Rebellion *Jessica Dall*
Christmas Presence *Lisa J. Hobman*
Lessons From a Two-Year-Old *Pete Abela*
Vivian *Bernadette Marie*
How to Have a Happy Marriage *Lindsay Harper*
A Gift for Chloe *Susan Lohrer*
Penelope *Bernadette Marie*
Bridge of Hope *Lisa J. Hobman*
A Painted Room *Pete Abela*
Amelia *Bernadette Marie*
Lilac Lane *Ann Swann*
Crisis of Serenity *Denise Moncrief*
The Porcelain Child *Jessica Dall*
The Acceptance *Bernadette Marie*